Operation Climate Change

A dystopic novel on the disastrous effects of the West's environmental policies

Stefano Santoni

Operation Climate Change

By Stefano Santoni

First published in Italy in 2023 by Independent Publisher

This is a work of fiction, what else could it be? All names, characters, places and incidents described in this book are indeed fictitious. As is normally noted, and with good reason, any resemblance to actual events or locales or persons, living or dead, is entirely coincidental.

After all, it is well known that the Western Democracies are led by extremely intelligent, high integrity and visionary leaders who could not possibly fall into the Chinese energy transition honey trap maliciously portrayed in this book. Likewise, it is obvious that the Chinese government monopolization of the mining, processing and trading of the key minerals needed by the "renewable" energies, is just a good-hearted effort of theirs to facilitate the energy transition worldwide.

Dedicated to all the oil professionals who are contributing to energize the world in which we live

"No need for new fossil fuel anywhere in the world"

John Kerry
(Special Presidential Envoy for Climate),
2021

"Energy transition worked well, Madam President, until we could put fossil fuel on the table"

Dr. Tearfault
(Energy Transition Geoscience Advisor),
2035

Prologue
2035

Gazing at his image in the mirror, he hardly recognises his features.

He had completely shaved off his otherwise unkempt beard, stopped eating raw garlic, renounced the full-bodied Shiraz that had been fuelling his professional intuitions and dreams for years. In addition, he had lost a lot of weight in the process. These old habits would have been a giveaway that he had been a fossil fuel geologist, a profession banned and vilified following the rise to power of Green parties all over Europe, the US, Canada and Australia.

After fortuitously managing to escape the 'woke' party group that had captured him, Armando had taken refuge in a small vegan hamlet on the northern shore of the Poschiavo lake, in the Grigioni canton of Switzerland, a short distance away from Italy. Like a Nazi hiding in a Jewish ghetto, he felt safe going underground in a vegan community. Armando felt that this would be the last place where 'they' would come to look for a fossil fuel geologist. He managed to pass himself off as a strict vegan, despite being someone who had eaten a lifetime worth of beef during the ten years he had spent exploring for oil in Argentina. He remembered, with an inward smile, a visit to a General Practioner when he was still living in the UK prior to having to find somewhere to hide. Sue, the doctor who had measured his high blood pressure, had asked him if he consumed red meat regularly, something he should have avoided.

"Not really Sue" Armando had explained "I had my share while living in Argentina, lots of juicy *bife de chorizo*, how rib-eye steaks had been called locally. No meat for me anymore."

"You mean that you have become vegetarian?" Sue had asked.

"I meant that the Argentine meat is so good that once you have gotten used to it, it is difficult to eat meat anywhere else. Imagine a man who has lived for many years in a country where all the ladies are like Playboy's playmates. Then he relocates to the real world, and his sex drive is gone, for ever" had explained Armando, with his typical ironic, self-deprecating smile.

But this had been many years ago. Now he had to take care to not reveal anything of his past that could be related to the work he had undertaken for more than 50 years. Times had changed dramatically in the last two decades with the advent of the *cancel culture.* Among other impositions, the search for and production of fossil fuels had been banned, in the EU, the US, Canada and Australia that is. The only country in the western world that had not taken such a rigid and uncompromising attitude toward the oil industry had been the UK where the Socialist government that had succeeded the Conservatives 15-year stint in power, had inherited a nation in complete disarray due to the combined effects of Brexit and the far-right dictatorships of Boris, 44-day Liz and their other crazy friends. Famine was widespread in the UK, with a child death rate not seen since pre-industrial times. Accordingly, the government had much more immediate problems to take care of than pretending to reduce pollution. North Sea oil and gas production had continued, although from fields so mature, they only managed to fulfil a small portion of the nation's needs and even then, only because the economic slump produced by the Conservative government's policies had drastically reduced the need for industrial energy. Scottish coal mines had been rehabilitated however, to supplement the energy balance under the promise that in the near future Scotland could be let free and become an independent country and leading exporter of *coaline*, a liquid fuel obtained by the distillation of coal that was in high demand in China. Since the collapse of the Scottish Whiskey industry, after Brexit had made exporting the precious liquid almost impossible, most of the Whiskey producers had converted their facilities to produce *coaline*. This had become more profitable than Whiskey, the Scottish opium so to speak that. Consequently, aside from its legal use within the UK, was now smuggled to many Asian countries against the international laws put in place by the USA and the EU.

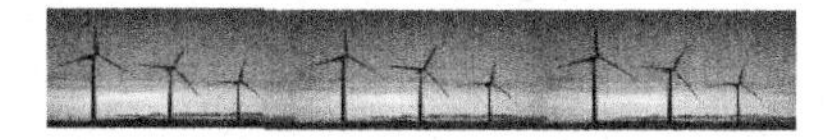

Rounding up the *Fossil Fuel professionals* (FFp) who worked for the national oil companies or those with a significant state equity, had been easy. These were generally individuals who were accustomed to following instructions blindly. However, the hunting down of the FFp's working in the private sector had taken more far more effort and results had been mixed. Initially they had been lured to relocate to so-called *purpose-built facilities* to be 're-trained', that was the *key word* of the programme, to become *Energy Transitionists* (ET). The name had a futuristic allure and many had eventually moved to these residential compounds located in the Xinjiang Province, A vast region of north western China that had at one time been inhabited by the Uyghurs, a vast Muslim population that by 2030 had been almost completely wiped out through forced labour, state-imposed abortions and other oppressive practises sanctioned by the Chinese government.

The *purpose-built facilities,* operated by *Silk Road Friendship Industries* (a 'private' Chinese firm, a cynic might say, as private as any Chinese firm could ever be), had turned out to be the same prison camps used for the Uyghur's, which had been repainted in a bright and cheerful ecological green shade.

When it came to finding and 'retraining' the FFp's who worked for small independent companies, this had proved much harder. These individuals, were by nature inquisitive and highly independent minded. The majority had rejected the idea of relocating to China to be 're-trained'. In a rather unique instance of EU-US-Canada-Australia co-operation, in fact, something unheard off since the time of the first Gulf War triggered by Saddam Hussein's occupation of Kuwait, a special multinational police force called the *Energy Transition Facilitators* (ETF) had been formed. their task was to apprehend and dispose (yes exactly that) of the recalcitrant FFp's. Like a worldwide counterinsurgency war this had initially been very effective and many thousands of independent and non-aligned FFp's had been *neutralised*, this being the legal expression which gave free hand to the ETF units. However, a journalist working for the New York Times and one for the UK Guardian newspaper, who had been embedded with one of the ETF units, had made a complaint that these units used hybrid fuel vehicles and, even worse, conventionally fuelled helicopters. This had made a global joke of the fact, that in the name of ecology, the same individuals that had helped find the energy that was fuelling their vehicles, were being apprehended by them. Eventually, only electric cars were allowed for use. These, with their limited range and uncertain battery life, had dramatically reduced the effectiveness of the ETF's. Even more catastrophically, experimental electric helicopters had been dispatched, many of which had quickly crashed causing hundreds of victims within

the ETF teams. The net result of the above had been that many FFp's had escaped being *neutralised.* Some had tried, with mixed success, to reach the UK across the Channel, often with boats that were not adequate for the journey and had subsequently sunk. With typical British tradition, a memorial had been erected on the Isle of Wight to commemorate the *unknown fossil fuel professionals* that had perished in the sea crossing. Eventually the EU had put into effect a blockade preventing any further escape from the European mainland and many would-be-refugees near the French coast had been apprehended and *neutralised.* The remaining few who had not been apprehended in Europe, the US, Canada or Australia, as was the case with Armando, had tried to hide their past and mingle with the *normal* population.

Chapter 1
Energy Transition
Washington – 2035

Kamelia cannot get the Nespresso machine especially installed for her in the Oval office to work.

She had repeatedly pressed the switch but it was apparent to her that there was an electrical fault. It was 6 am and she was getting ready to start her job protecting the 'western world' from the ever-changing threats and menaces that Russia and China were fabricating at increasing pace. A double-espresso was what she needed, to help her to focus on her priorities. It felt ominous that the Nespresso machine was not working.

‘I am sure it is the result of another cyber-attack by the enemies of democracy’ she thought.

Kamelia belonged to the Democratic party and was the first POTUS of mixed African-Arab-Red Indian heritage. She was Religiously Ambiguous (RA), half Vegan (*Veganish* was the technical term used) and Transgender Fluid (TF) and as such perfectly embodied the non-committal and politically correct times into which the US had evolved following the *Black Lives Matters* (BLM) and *Cancel Culture* (CC) movements of the early 20's. TF was a new gender category which had become fashionable in the late 20's and that allowed individuals to switch their gender according to their mood, often several times in the course of a day. Colored bracelets, specially produced in China by *Silk Road Friendship Industries*, were available for the TF's to make apparent which gender the individual felt to be at any particular time.

The Democratic party had remained in power for 15 years since defeating Trump in 2020. Not necessarily because in the following elections they had the majority of the national vote but because of the split of the Republican party into the 'Trump for God' and 'Republican classics' groups. These had eventually become genuine, independent parties competing at elections with their own presidential candidates against each other and the Democratic party.

Kamelia called up her assistant Jane to fix her morning coffee problem. When Jane arrived, she immediately queried if she was aware of any recent cyber-attack that could have affected the Nespresso machine.

"Nothing so severe Madam President, there is no electricity in the building."

"Are you joking?" Kamelia exclaimed loudly.

"Just the implementation of your executive orders of a week ago, Madam President" calmly explained Jane "to cope with the reduced electricity available across our noble country the White House gets electricity only between 8 am and 2 pm."

"I never intended or considered that the White House could be affected by such orders" Kamelia replied, "what happens if there is an emergency situation and I need to start a nuclear war with Russia or China or both?"

"Actually, Madam President, the Emergency Room has been preserved from the power cut. We have installed an *SRFI energy exchanger*" clarified Jane.

"In that case, please move the Nespresso machine to that secure location. I will get my morning coffee there, making sure to press the right button of course" ordered Kamelia, with her characteristic sarcasm before then asking: "by the way what is the contraption you mentioned?"

"Madam President, it is the most modern and eco-friendly wood burner available on the market and produced by *Silk Road Friendship Industries.* An innovative way to generate electricity, in fact, its shape is something similar to a stove," explained Jane, before reminding Kamelia of the upcoming Energy Transition Meeting:

"Madam President, your schedule shows a 1pm Energy Transition semi-annual meeting."

"I have not forgotten that Jane, although I must confess that if I could I would pass. I don't like to be lectured by that moron John Therry."

"John has worked hard on the Transition changes since Biden took over from Trump" Jane reminded Kamelia.

"That's the point. He is almost 100 years old and senile. Largely useless to drive the Energy Transition group. But, as you know, he is extremely well connected to the *Super-Green-is-our-mission*, our Democratic tea party so to speak, and we need their support to stay in power."

- ***1 pm: semi-annual Energy Transition meeting.***
- ***Attendees:***
- Dr Kamelia Jarris – The *POTUS*
- Mrs Jane Witchwood – Senior Assistant to the *POTUS*
- Mr John Therry – Green Implementation Czar
- Major Yunis – Commander of the Green Jackets Intervention Force
- Dr Snowfall – Climate Change Meteorologist
- Dr Tearfault – Climate Change Geoscientist

After greeting the attendees, Kamelia asked Therry to summarise the major achievements since the initial implementation in 2030, of the *Green Word Agreement.* Following a full week of negotiations in Beijing, that agreement had been signed not only by all the Western World countries, that is to say, the USA, the EU, Canada and Australia but also by Russia, China, India and a number of others from Africa, Latin American and Asia countries. It was a 'solid document', as Therry had characterised it to Kamelia at the time.

Tall but stooped with age, Therry was like an old, wrinkled oak. 92 years old, he talked mostly nonsense, but he had been a hero of the extreme left wing of the Democratic party since his stance on hydrocarbon exploration in the early 20's. He had said then that there was "no need for new fossil fuel anywhere in the world." As such he was immovable, even though hydrocarbon exploration had only ceased in the US, Canada, EU and Australia, not worldwide as promised. In any case he was the political capital on which rested the support of the extreme left to the current president.

Therry put up the slide that summarised the key successes of the *Green World Agreement* in the USA.

USA ENERGY TRANSITION ACHIEVEMENTS SINCE 2030

50% REDUCTION IN GDP = 20% REDUCTION OF ENERGY CONSUMPTION

GREEN ENERGY IMPLEMENTATION = 10% REDUCTION IN CO2 EMISSIONS

VEGAN PLUS SCHEME IMPLEMENTATION = 15% REDUCTION OF OVERWEIGHT CHILDREN

"Madam President" Therry started his presentation only to be immediately stopped by Kamelia waving her wrist bracelet that was now blue.

"Sorry Mr President, I am colour blind" Therry tried to justify his faux-pas before resuming the presentation: "The slide projected on the screen illustrates the key successes of our Energy Transition program that I will briefly review for you."

"I am all ears Therry" Kamelia said.

"As you can see, we have managed to reduce by 20%, actually as of today 21%, the energy consumption of our great country" Therry explained, before continuing "we initially thought this could be achieved through energy efficiency and better working practices, including smart working."

"That's what I thought" intervened Kamelia.

"Unfortunately, we discovered that this was not enough" Therry continued candidly.

"Ah Ah" mumbled Kamelia.

"Yes Mr President" continued Therry "we had to switch the focus onto the *happy degrowth* strategy."

"What is the *happy degrowth?*" queried Kamelia.

"Basically, forcing industry and agriculture to produce less" explained Therry "we discovered that this has been the most effective way to reduce the need for energy."

"I understand the *degrowth* portion" intervened Kamelia "but why *happy?*"

"Only three working days per week. I am told everybody is happy!" explained Therry.

There was a moment of pause to allow Dr Snowfall to take the stage and review the Green Energy Implementation results. In his youth Dr Snowfall had been a supporter of Bernie Sanders and since that time, he had retained a hippie look, with ill-fitting clothes, and long unkempt hair.

"Mr President, it has been a big success. By switching to green energy, that is Photovoltaic and Wind Turbines, we have reduced CO2 emissions in the USA by 10%. We model that this will reduce by 0.01C the average temperature of the planet by 2050 and by 0.02C by 2100" enthusiastically explained Dr Snowfall.

"It sounds strange that the reduction in temperature is so small when compared to the one achieved for CO2 reduction" queried Kamelia.

"Mr President you need to put that in perspective" explained Dr Snowfall "the 10% reduction in CO2 has occurred only in the US. In the EU, with their bureaucracy, they have only achieved a 1% reduction."

"What about China, India and Russia?" asked Kamelia.

"They would have not signed the Beijing agreement unless we gave them a moratorium that extended to 2100, the deadline agreed for them to meet their CO2 reduction targets" explained Dr Snowball, before expanding on his thoughts: "basically they are currently ramping up their CO2 emissions as a result of their increased production to compensate for our *de-growth* strategy but as soon as 2100 is reached they have promised to abruptly stop all their industrial activity and, as illustrated by the slide on the screen, CO2 emissions are projected to reduce immediately to negligible levels."

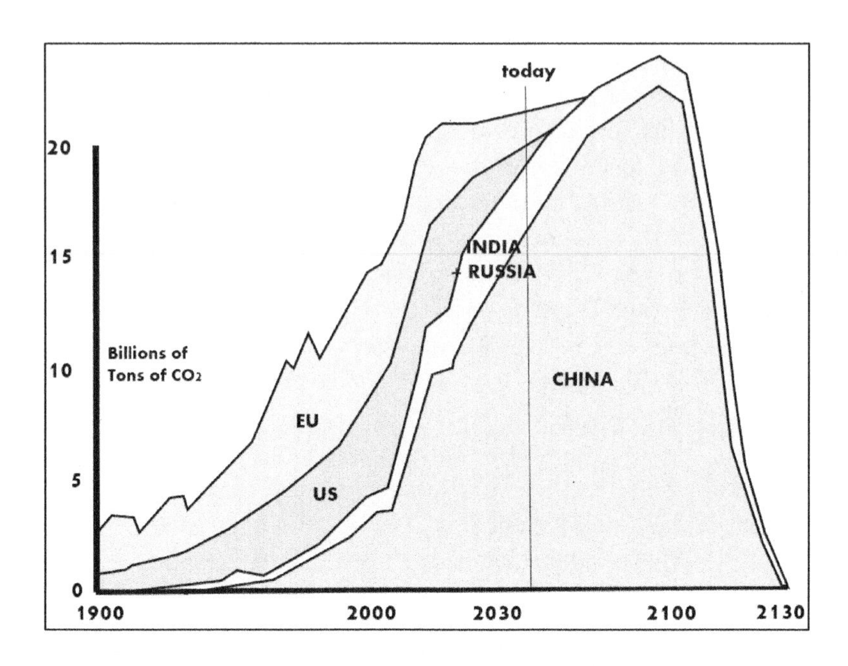

CO2 Emission – Actual data & Forecast

"And how believable are the Chinese? How confident are we that come 2100 they will drop to zero their CO2 emissions" asked Kamelia with a quizzical face.

Dr Snowball understood that Mr President was a little sceptical about this agreement and strategy and so he carefully explained:

"You see Mr President we have moved a long way from the Truman Administration foreign doctrine that consisted of being very aggressive with regimes, like the Chinese or the Russian, that do not adhere to our democratic values. That was recognised as political racism. We have moved to the Obama-Trump-Biden foreign policy doctrine which is by now recognised by many scholars as the most effective way to reach agreements among otherwise conflicting parties."

"Please explain" asked Kamelia.

"In a nutshell, it means that we now sign treaties with enemies, in the full knowledge that they would not honour their side of the agreement. For example, what Obama did with the Iranians. We stopped the sanctions and shortly after they resumed the enrichment of uranium needed for their atomic bomb. Or, talking of Trump, the so-called *Doha peace deal* with the Taliban. He apparently threatened them…" Dr Snowball explained.

"I did not know of the threat…" intervened Kamelia.

Therry felt that he should get into the conversation and explained:

"Mr President, the call between Trump and the Chief of the Taliban negotiators has recently been released. It seems he told them, and I am quoting the transcript, that <*whether you like it or not the US is going to pull all troops out of Afghanistan and leave for you the key to Kabul under the doormat*>."

"However, our application of the Obama-Trump-Biden doctrine for the climate change agreement with the Russians and Chinese has been much more sophisticated" explained Dr Snowfall.

"In which way?" asked Kamelia.

"We set the deadline for them to comply with the CO2 target so far in the future, approximately three generations away from now, that by then nobody will remember the shortcomings of our deal. By then the Chinese would have successfully launched an internet search engine far more potent than Google where history will be re-written. And our leadership team will be off the hook."

"Probably dead as well" joked Kamelia "apart from our John Therry who I am told is getting a new, lithium powered heart."

Everybody laughed, apart from Therry that is.

"And in the meantime, what is happening with Russia and China?" asked Kamelia.

"One needs to distinguish between China and Russia" intervened Therry.

"In which sense?" asked Kamelia.

"China has applied a *nasty growth* policy. Their productivity has increased, more than compensating for our decrease. Their CO_2 emissions have gone up by 30% relative to the level of 2030" explained Therry.

"And Russia?" asked Kamelia.

"They are imploding. Their hydrocarbon production has been cut by 60% because none of the western world countries import fossil fuel anymore, not legally at least. However, they have not implemented any strategy to reduce their CO_2 emissions, so they are more or less as they were in 2030" conceded Therry before concluding triumphally: "but we are on the right path. We have not changed the world targets, only extended the deadline to meet them by 65 years!"

"Going back to the Photovoltaic Panels and Wind Turbines" Kamelia said "I heard there are some issues with importing from China the *rare earths* needed to build new ones and maintain the ones already installed?"

"Trade issues are really the cup of tea of the Trade Department and Foreign Office, Mr President" explained Therry "my job is to focus on the implementation of the Energy Transition only."

"I have just been told by my assistant of this exciting technology that uses the burning of wood to produce electricity" commented Kamelia, "can you give me more info?"

"Most certainly Mr President" replied Therry. "It has been developed by *Silk Road Friendship Industries* (SRFE) and is marketed worldwide by *AmaZing*, the Joint Venture between what was left of Amazon after we started the *happy de-growth* and Mr Lin-Zing, the major stakeholder of SRFE, who, just for your information is also the brother of Xin-Zing, the Supreme Leader of the Democratic Republic of China."

"And how does it work?" queried Kamelia.

"Like a wood fired stove but some of the heat is transformed into electricity. It has been our saviour. Because even with the *happy de-growth* we would have not been able to generate enough energy from the conventional renewable sources to keep us going" explained Therry.

"And where does the wood come from" asked Kamelia, "because I imagine we are talking about a large quantity of wood."

"Mostly from the Amazon, you know, what was once the rain forest of Brazil" explained Therry.

"And we don't have any push back from our Greens?" queried Kamelia with a face showing her amazement.

"You see Mr President; the rain forest is not covered by the *Fossil Fuel Act.* Technically the rain forest is *renewable*, although everybody knows that replanting trees and seeing them grow as tall as the ones that have been cut will take hundreds of years or more" explained Therry with a sardonic smile.

"And what about the ozone layer" asked Kamelia, "we have made a big fuss for decades that preserving the Amazon was key to our worldwide eco-friendly strategy."

"In reality only the ozone layer of Brazil is affected and we make sure that our satellites are switched off when scanning over the Amazon, so that none of our adversaries can see what is happening and acquire a smoking gun, so to speak."

"Really brilliant. This worldwide cooperation between us, the Chinese and the Brazilians. A model for the future development of international relationships" concluded Kamelia.

"And the transition from hydrocarbon fuelled to electric cars" intervened Dr Snowball "has been another great success."

"Coming to the office every morning with my electric *Pontiac* I noted that the traffic is now lighter than ever" commented Kamelia.

"Indeed, a positive collateral effect of switching to electric vehicles is that the total amount of cars circulating has reduced significantly, I understand by at least 50%" explained Dr Snowball.

"That's fantastic!" commented Kamelia before querying: "but why such a dramatic reduction?"

"When the electric vehicle industry started the price of each unit was extremely high" explained Dr Snowball, "but we were expecting the price to decrease with time."

"And?" questioned Kamelia.

"We were absolutely right. The price has decreased from *extremely high* to *very high*, which is as just as good. Few people can afford to buy and maintain electric vehicles. Less vehicles around, less traffic, less need for electricity from the Photovoltaic Panels, Wind Turbines and Wood burning stoves" concluded Dr Snowball with a big smile.

There was a pause for reflection in the meeting. Many loose ends and questions either barely answered or not answered at all. Kamelia could sense that Dr Tearfault disagreed with Dr Snowball and Therry. But he was a very cautious individual who many years before had realised that fossil fuel was going out of fashion and had requested a career move to the Green Energy group within the government. Kamelia realised that he would not come clean in a formal meeting that included his boss. 'I will touch base with him later one to one' Kamelia thought.

"At least our hydrocarbon exploration and production has ceased" said Kamelia, who, as with all individuals in a position of leadership, had been trained to make any disaster sounds good.

"Almost Mr President" said Dr Snowball.

"To take out of commission our pipeline networks, we entered into a Joint Venture with 'Pipelines & Beyond'" Therry explained.

"What company is that?" asked Kamelia with a face that showed her surprise.

"It is a legitimate Nigerian outfit, specialised in sabotaging pipeline and indeed any other oil industry infrastructure" clarified Therry before continuing "they have been very, very effective, particularly in Louisiana where they found a climate very similar to their Benin City."

"Any oil spills?" asked Kamelia.

"A few that we have promptly fixed" explained Therry before continuing "however they have not been able to work in North Dakota and Alaska. Too cold for them in fact."

"How did we fix the oil problem there?" Kamelia asked.

"We sent there our top military engineers. They cemented the pipelines" explained Therry.

"I thought all pipelines were cemented, stabilised to the terrain" questioned Kamelia.

"I meant that our engineers cemented most of the *insides* of the pipelines making them useless" clarified Therry.

"I see. So, no oil and gas production in our country. A great achievement Therry" conceded Kamelia.

"Oil and gas production has virtually halted. I say virtually because in the Rocky Mountains there is still some bootleg oil production but only for local consumption" John Therry explained.

"Why do we tolerate that?" asked Kamelia.

Major Yunis of the *Green Jackets Intervention Force* intervened:

"Mr President, these communities are armed. Seriously armed. You certainly remember that following the *Foreign Disengagement Act* signed in 2026 our troops cannot fight abroad anymore. We had plenty of redundant weapons that have been sold in the free market."

"And so?" Kamelia queried.

"Some, actually a lot of it, has ended up, traded through the dark web, with the remnants of the oil producing community. They now have missile launchers and I have been told also a few tanks."

"Unbelievable!" exclaimed Kamelia

"We lost some of our best *Green Jackets* trying to stop the oil production. In the end we gave up" concluded Major Yunis.

"It is really only in the aviation industry that we have been unable to replace conventional hydrocarbon-based engines with electric engines. None of the latter is effective enough, particularly for the transatlantic flights" explained Therry.

"And how do we manage that challenge?" queried Kamelia.

"We are using the *Strategic Petroleum Reserves*. But we have taxed the plane tickets so heavily that only a few, the super-rich in fact, can afford to fly. Accordingly, also, the number of planes and size of planes have been greatly reduced, minimizing considerably the emission of CO2 by American planes" clarified Therry.

"A few days ago, I was at Dulles International Airport and saw more *Silk Road Airways* planes than American ones" commented Kamelia.

"This is the result of the moratorium. The Chinese are off the hook until 2100" explained Therry.

"And so?" asked Kamelia.

"The short and the long of the story is that the Chinese still freely use jet fuel, without over-taxing it like we do and have taken most of the flight slots that our airlines do not use anymore" concluded Therry.

"Ok" said Kamelia saddened by the news "let's move on now and review the *Vegan Plus* Scheme."

Therry stood up again and explained:

"Another great success Mr President. As highlighted in this slide: 15% of the overweight children of 2030 have now reduced to a 'normal' weight. Changing their eating habits has not been easy but the *happy degrowth* has helped."

"In which way?" asked Kamelia.

"Well Mr President, one of the positive side effects of the *happy degrowth* has been that families can put less food on the table. Particularly expensive items, like meat. The rearing of cattle, chickens and any other animal that in the old times was used to harvest meat is now highly regulated. As you certainly know, among other provisions, meat shops are only allowed to operate in the *Red Meat Districts*, of which there is one per every major town. The shops are obliged to sport thick red curtains that do not allow any sight of the offending merchandise on offer. The access to these districts is rigorously policed. Only people that are on the register of the *meatarians* can get access to these areas."

"Excellent news. On the red meat I mean. But what about the *fake-meat*? I love my egg white omelette with *fake-bacon*, and my southern fried *fake-chicken* let alone the juicy *fake-T-bone-steak* with chips cooked in almond oil" commented Kamelia.

"As you remember *fake-meat* was experimentally produced in the early 2020's by *Memphis Meat*. They collected cells from naturally dead cows, pigs and chickens and brewed them in sterile tanks similar to the ones used in the beer industry. Production is now commercial but very expensive" explained Therry.

"You mean that its market is limited?" queried Kamelia.

"More than that Mr President" explained Therry, "you are keen on this type of product not only because you can afford it but also because you are *Veganish* and therefore more accommodating than the strict *Vegans* or *Vegetarians* that won't touch it anyway because they despise its meaty taste."

"I see, it makes sense, and so, aside from the *Veganish* like myself, who else eats *fake-meat*?" asked Kamelia.

"Basically, its main markets are the rich *meatarians* who either feel guilty but still have their *meaty tooth* so to speak or the ones who do not want to be listed in the *meatarians* register to access the *Red Meat Districts*" clarified Therry.

"I see. And what do you make of the *Black Lives Need Feeding* movement?" asked Kamelia.

"It belongs to the black community fringe that is still able to eat properly…I mean the portion that has not been affected too much by the *happy degrowth*. The rest are so focussed on their search for food that they have no time to protest. Actually, now that you have made me think of it, I realise that I must add this to the positives of *Vegan Plus*. It has virtually stopped all civil unrest."

"I have heard rumours of discontent about limited food supplies among other group of citizens also" commented Kamelia.

"Obviously, organic vegetables and organic fruits are much more expensive than used to be in the pre *happy degrowth* times" explained Therry "the best quality are produced by the hard-line organic farmers that proudly call themselves the *Talibio.*"

"You mean the ones who go around with that t-shirt sporting an image of Mullah Omar chewing a carrot?" queried Kamelia.

"Exactly. Like in the old times the *Radical chic* uniform, so to speak, included the Che Guevara t-shirt. Both *Radicals chic* and *Talibios* had lost the historical memory of the tragedies that their idols have brought to humanity" commented Therry who at his age was ok with long term memory but could often not remember what he had eaten for breakfast.

Then he resumed his presentation on *vegan plus*:

"In the old times only the richest had access to organic produce, the rest of the population would content themselves with normal mass-produced vegetables and fruits. Now the non-organic producers have virtually ceased to exist."

"But how does that affect the children's school meals?" queried Kamelia.

"As part of *Vegan Plus* we initially fed the children a vegetable burger plus two vegetable sides per meal. Then we were unable to produce enough vegetable burgers for that program so we switched to the *no-burger, 2 vegetable*s diet."

"How was that accepted by the children?" asked Kamelia.

"We reduced the size of the plates, so it was more difficult to tell that the total amount of food was less."

"Brilliant!" commented Kamelia.

Kamelia had heard enough for the day, and noticed that it would soon be 2 pm and the White House would run out of electricity for the day. She closed the meeting, remembering however, the need for a private chat in the near future with Dr Tearfault to explore his views of the Energy Transition Program.

Chapter 2
Ten years earlier (December 2025)
The conscience of Armando

The woke party had caught him by surprise. Total surprise. And now he was alone with his conscience, convoluted like a spaghetti junction, or so they said.

He had stopped working several years earlier, well before the ecologist driven madness had resulted in the lynching, both figuratively and for real, of what in the past had been called *oil professionals* and now were derogatively referred to as *fossil fuels people.* For this reason, despite the overall sad situation, he thought himself to be safe.

Armando had retired to live with his wife in the hills of the lake of Garda, in northern Italy. The mild microclimate created by the vast body of water allowed the growth of olive and lemon trees, the northernmost of the world it was claimed by the locals, although the region of Brda in Slovenia had similar claims.

Just before relocating to the lake, they had lived for many years in the Middle East, where the weather tended to be relatively constant, the seasons marked only by small variations in the heat and humidity. But now they enjoyed the marked differences between the hot summers, when they could take refuge from the heat by diving into the swimming pool, and the cold dry days of winter, ideal for an early morning rise to admire the luminosity that the sunrise projected into the clouds dotting the lake's sky. Every day produced a stunning, yet different, combination of visual effects that touched their souls.

Every season brought its delicious fruits and vegetables. The winter blood oranges and honeyed persimmons competed with the sweet textured figs of the summer that they collected (or rather stole) during their long hill walks. And, if the summer had been sunny enough, they would gather from the olive trees of their garden enough olives to obtain ten litres of virgin oil, pressed by a local oil mill.

His professional and family life had been a continuum of changes, challenges and boundless horizons; now that he had stopped working, however, his horizons were always limited by the lake's boundary and this gave him the expectation that his existence would be calm, almost monotonous. This was not something that he was necessarily pleased about. In his heart he knew that men and women of action do not retire, they only regroup for the next adventure.

His friends thought that he was fearless. In reality he was as afraid as anyone, maybe even more than most. But he was even more afraid of the feeling of shame he would have felt if he had not undertaken the risky adventures that his life, his line of work particularly, had presented to him.

With his wife, he had undertaken to do some serious walking, either along the lake shore or in the surrounding hills, exploring the rich nature and discovering the wildlife, with a particular interest in the birds populating the water body. From the friendly mallards always keen to be fed bread or cornflakes, to the seagulls that would scream and dive to rob the mallards of their food without ever touching the ground. But by far the most endearing of the birds was a solitary old white duck, that they named Carlotta, that would wait for them at the same spot every morning and liked to pick her food straight from their hands. Armando often reflected that it may have been true what he had read in a book of an author of whom he did not remember the name, that retired geologists and spies (and evidently their spouses if they had one) spend their time walking and feeding birds.

At the other end of the *social spectrum* of the lake birds were the cormorants, that tended to stay on their own, perched on the many buoys to dry the feathers of their open wings between one dive and the next, aiming to catch the unfortunate fish that came across their path. Their hunting efficiency was so high that from time to time they were culled by the regional government lest no fish would be left in the lake.

The white swans were, however, by far the most beautiful creatures roaming the lake, with their regal posture. During one spring Armando had fed a couple of swans, the pen sitting on five large white eggs, while the cob was on the alert for possible dangers. He was amazed by watching the young swans swimming in the lake, protected by their parents, only a day after their hatching.

They lived in a large villa in a little populated area, as such even the COVID restrictions had not been as harsh as for people living in towns and cities. They only really missed visiting their grown-up children that lived with their own families in the UK, that before COVID, they had visited very often.

In the worst COVID moments, when the lockdown did not allow them to leave home except for buying of food or go to the pharmacy, Armando had envisaged a way to make his spirit wander, if not his body. He would place several books, each one written in a different language, in four of the villa's rooms and spend the day moving from one room to the next. His mind travelled with his books, visiting friends in faraway countries, mentally speaking with them in their own language, smelling aromas that he had memorised from his many travels across the world.

And in the process of analysing himself, more than he had ever previously done, when his work schedule did not allow for that luxury, he had started writing books, memoirs at the beginning. They ended up becoming a trilogy, although not originally planned as such.

Margie had warned him. She was the professional editor of his first book and had explained to Armando that the subjects described in his memoirs would not go down well with the audience of the 2020's. After all, most of the books described his efforts to find oil (a big taboo) that also involved a lot of travelling by plane (another taboo). Books with plenty of large carbon footprints, she had noted with disdain.

They had first met in the gentrified portion of Soho, where para-official brothels and peep show joints had been converted into vegetarian and vegan restaurants and coffee shops, something that Armando had found quite symbolic, yet puzzling: was it *no sex = no meat* or rather *no meat = no sex*?

In any event, Margie, herself a convinced vegan, had suggested they dine at *Mildreds*, one of these vegan upscale venues. He had asked her to order the food for the two of them, because Armando was adventurous but not familiar with vegan food etiquette. Among other dishes they had tasted a *bhatthi ka chick'n kebabs*, that, by the way, was made of pomegranate, carrot and kachumber (whatever that was), jeera yoghurt (another mysterious name) and (finally) a more meaningful pumpkin pickle and a *ranch bbq chick'n*, which as the other course had never seen a chicken but was rather made of chipotle, dill pickles, baby gem lettuce and red onions. Between a mouthful of vegan delice and pumpkin pickle, Margie had explained that he should have written about animals instead, not humans, never mind 'bad guys' working in the oil industry. The best he could expect, if ever a bookshop would agree to stock his memoirs, would be a place out of sight, at the back, where they kept the adult material, away from the innocent eyes of children and *normal* customers. In any case, she was acquainted with the Italian *touch and feel* etiquette having recently divorced an Italian and when they parted company she stamped two noisy kisses on Armando's cheeks, including two perfectly shaped red lip marks that Armando subsequently had a hard time to explain to his jealous wife.

Were these books what had put Armando on the radar screen of the woke parties? He could not say for sure. May be in hindsight even worse has been his fourth book, the theme of which had been a riotous send up of the climate change fanatics. Whatever had been the giveaway, they silently arrived one night, and snatched him in front of his terrified wife. They even arrested her for a while, accused of having harboured a criminal. Evidently common sense was not a strength of the woke parties because: 1- the house was jointly owned and 2- there was no public warrant issued against Armando. Evidently *Logic* and *Renewables* were not compatible subjects, Armando concluded philosophically.
A few hours later his apprehensions rising, he found himself shackled and blind folded inside a dark container in a moving ship. What in the old times had been condemned by the left-

wing politicians as extra-judiciary renditions and that now, evidently, had become acceptable if not fashionable.

After several hours of solitude, he heard a noise and finally someone entered the container. They removed his blind fold and, blinking, he observed two young people. Millennials in their mid-twenties. A boy and a girl, that's how he would think of them during his interrogation. Tall, but with the gaunt face of vegans. Their bodies intensely craving animal proteins, even a small sliver of parmesan cheese would have sufficed, but their minds, like sadistic Nazi prison guards, enjoyed depriving them of that comfort.

They both had cold blue eyes. Heterozygous twins, Armando incongruously thought in that moment of stress. And tried to understand from which country they might come from. Certainly, northern Europe seemed the best bet. When they spoke among themselves it was a language that Armando could not understand. It sounded like a German language to him even though he did not speak German, if that made sense. Eventually he summoned all his courage and asked the many questions that lingered in his mind.

"We are Norwegian" the girl said, "and we are not related, except by our common mission of cleaning the world of scum like yourself."

'Damn' thought Armando, 'not a good start.' Indeed, he had dealt with Norwegians before. When that nation was one of the major producers of hydrocarbon from the North Sea. At that time, they had patronized countries of the third world that were developing their own oil industries. Norwegian experts would swarm into these poor nations, promising funding, but only if Norwegian style regulations, requiring a significant amount of the oil revenues to be set aside for future generations, would be accepted. The governments, however, were mostly run by gangster cliques and dictators. They would obviously agree to whatever the Norwegians requested, and everything went typically fine until production had been established. Shortly after that, the music changed and the dictator in power would cash in the sudden change of fortune of his or her country, fuck the Norwegians so to speak.

"You have been focussed on your addiction, what you called *work*, for all of your entire life. And you put aside the needs of your family. Never helped your children with their school chores…" said the boy.

"I did things with them, drove them to their after-school activities, basketball and athletics…" Armando tried to defend himself.

"Yes, we know, everything has been recorded, we have a full profile of your life. But what you really enjoyed of all your activities was when you left them alone in the playground, sat back on your own and thought of the geological problems you were facing at the time. Your notebooks incriminate you" replied the boy.

"Which notebooks?" asked Armando who had start to lose the thread of the conversation.

"The many notebooks on which, while your children were engaged in their activities, you drew geological cross-sections or created your probability decision tree analysis. Instead of watching them play and enjoy their successes" explained the girl.

"Red, Yellow, Emerald Green your favourite Moleskin's notebook cover colours, always bright. We know everything" explained the boy.

"Each colour a season of my professional life, much like painters do…" Armando tried to justify his choices.

"You are not an artist Armando, you are a self-centred person and a nasty one at that, considering your involvement with the oil industry" the girl shouted.

"Are you the *woke party* or *my demons*, what has this to do with your ecological, politically correct madness?" replied Armando.

"We are *your conscience*" replied the girl with a sad smile. Her frowning indicating that she knew that Armando needed their external support to get to grips with the gravity of what he had done. The implied depravity that had marked his fossil fuel career.

"Some of the things you have done" said the boy with a very sad face "are so awful that we feel uneasy even to talk about them."

"What do you mean?" asked Armando who was taken aback by that statement.

"Your discoveries of oil, for instance" explained the girl.

"Hold on" intervened the boy "we are not here to massage your ego. The opposite. If you had drilled *just* dry holes, wells that had failed to find hydrocarbons, your position would have been much better now."

"You are joking?" replied Armando "the objective of my work was to find oil not to drill dry holes."

"Still, if you had only drilled dry holes the environmental impact of your depravations would have been much smaller" explained the boy before adding "not that we could let you go but...from a legal point of view you would have been in a much better position."

"Legal point of view?" shouted Armando "I have not done anything that was illegal."

"At the time maybe" explained the girl "but not based on the legislation that the EU passed in 2024."

"How on earth could I have acted in, say 1990, based on the legislation of 2024? This does not make any sense. I am now *seriously* convinced that this conversation we are having is *not real*" replied Armando "you are just my *demons*, an invention of my imagination."

"You would like that, Armando" replied the girl "we are real, real like your crimes."

"So, what did I do that was so terrible?" asked Armando.

"We have a long list. But the worst by any scale was the discovery of *El Trapial*" replied the boy, ticking that name on his printed list of Armando's crimes.

"You must be joking? That discovery increased by 20% the oil reserves of Argentina" explained a despairing Armando "how could that be a crime?"

"You pretend not to remember that the gas dissolved in the oil had a high CO2 content" noted the girl.

"Now that you bring it up, I do remember that 40% of the dissolved gas was CO2. That's nature, nobody's fault" admitted Armando.

"But when the field started producing you flared that CO2 into the air…" pointed out the boy.

"We could not flare the gas associated with the oil. You should know that when CO2 is above 30% the gas does not flare" replied Armando who thought, for once, to have a very solid counterargument to the madness of the boy and girl.

"Our education does not go that far. We focus on what is important. We learn through enhanced virtual reality tutorials, you know, through the *metaverse*. The drilling tutorial is over an hour long although it does not deal with CO2 percentages. However, by the completion of the tutorial we are now qualified as notional drilling managers. In fact, we would be entitled to manage the drilling of wells, if wells for oil were drilled anymore" explained the girl.

"Amazing" exclaimed Armando "one hour of *metaverse* tutorial and you are supposed to be able to drill a well??? I would consider that beyond the realms of reality if I had not experienced something similar before. What I mean is, the fast track of incompetents I came across when working in Dubai for Falcon Oil."

"Don't get distracted Armando" continued the boy "what did you do with the CO2 if you were unable to flare it?"

"We quietly dispersed it in the air" admitted Armando.

"Contributing to global warming…" the boy pointed out.

"Maybe" admitted Armando "but what would you have done? Not to produce a field which eventually contributed billions of dollars to the economy of Argentina, creating thousands of jobs and tax revenues to help people?"

"Typical. You try to justify your crime. But this does not work with us" shouted the girl.

"For you guys it is simple. Through its oil industry, which is 100 times or more bigger than the one of Argentina, Norway has built cash reserves in the *Norwegian Sovereign Wealth Fund* that will last for 100's of generations. $1.4 trillion, no exaggeration" shouted back Armando.

"I don't understand how that could justify your crimes in Argentina" calmly noted the boy.

"I mean that it is easy for a rich country to forget how they became rich and then pretend to teach ecological lessons to poorer countries that can only develop using their natural resources, including hydrocarbons. *Statoil*, your national oil company for many decades, has changed its name to *Equinor* to cover its tracks and greenwash itself, but the money you can splash around to chase the *fossil fuel professionals*, to use your derogatory words, comes from the billions of barrels of oil produced in your country in the recent past."

"We have now stopped producing hydrocarbons, we have come clean" the boy tried to explain, knowing that he didn't have a leg to stand on.

"You are like the children of Pablo Escobar. The money in their bank accounts comes from drug trafficking led by their father on an astronomical scale, but they did not do it themselves and so they don't feel guilty" pointed out Armando.

"Who is this Escobar?" asked the girl.

"A famous Colombian drug baron, now seriously dead while his children spend his money worldwide" explained Armando.

"Sorry but our tutorials do not cover this subject" explained the boy before continuing "by the way explain in simple words what do the words *drug* and *Colombia* mean"

Armando was shocked by the ignorance of his interrogators but tried to keep calm and replied:

"*Drugs* are chemical substances that cause a change in a person's physiology or psychology when consumed..."

Armando started explaining, before the boy stopped him short of completing his sentence.

"I am afraid that our tutorials do not cover the words *physiology* and *psychology* either" explained the boy.

"Colombia is a nation of Latin America" Armando hopefully explained.

"*Latin America*?" asked the girl.

"I understand" replied a resigned Armando "not covered by your tutorials."

"Let's go back to the list of your crimes" said the boy.

"Please go ahead" said Armando who was starting to perversely enjoy the process, so Kafkaesque had it become.

"Your Australian project" continued the boy "while you were living in London. How many round trips did you make?"

"I Don't remember" replied Armando "may be 6 or 7 in two years."

"Eight you did" continued the boy "a massive carbon footprint. You are lucky that despite the many discoveries made in the block you captured, the gas price collapsed and Chess had cold feet about developing them."

"I'm not sure I understand the *lucky* part" commented Armando.

"You remember, they sold the block to a local operator. Had they developed the gas your crime would have been even bigger. You understand? The difference between *attempted murder* and *actual murder*" explained the girl.

Eventually there was a pause in the interrogation. They freed his hands and served him a lunch that consisted of an overcooked porridge, a bowl of miso soup and a bitter tea. 'I knew these guys were vegan' thought Armando, finding comfort, not in the crap food but that his guess was on the mark.

"Where you are going next, you will need to keep to a strict and simple vegan diet. So, we thought that it would be useful for you to get acquainted with the relevant dietary regulations" the boy explained to justify the meagre food before handing a vegan food manual to Armando. Although curious about where he would go next Armando decided to keep his powder dry, waiting for the completion of the interrogation.

The boy and the girl spent the rest of the evening pointing out Armando's crimes and ticking them off from their list. *Crimes* that Armando in his naivety would have called *successes*, but that was the state of the nation in 2025. Eventually they summarised the position of Armando.

"We have calculated that the average carbon footprint of your fossil fuel career equates to around 0.9 kg/kWh" said the boy.

"Is that ok?" asked Armando who was not familiar with the unit and ranges of the carbon footprint.

"No, it is not ok Armando" explained the boy "it is the same level as a coal fired power plant."

"Great Scott!" exclaimed Armando before adding "talking of which, do you know that 70% of any of your *clean* wind turbines is made of steel, most of which is produced in China using electricity generated by coal fired power plants, which are known to be the worst emitters of CO2? This is without noting that around 15% of the same *clean* wind turbine is made with fiberglass, resin or plastic that without the oil industry would not be available."

"Armando don't try to change subject" the girl came back angrily.

"When you die, you will need to spend a full geological era in purgatory I am afraid" said the boy.

"You mean that you *Renewable* guys believe in God?" asked Armando with some trepidation.

"Not really. We only believe in Renewable Energies, ours is an Electric God with zero carbon footprint" explained the girl.

Armando had a vision of their Electric God that appeared to him as a cartoon version of the genie from Aladdin. The vision appeared from nowhere, much like the zero-carbon footprint from renewables concept. Both only cartoon characters, unfortunately.

"So even if you are not believers in conventional religions, you know enough to discuss them with your prisoners..." commented Armando.

"It is part of our training" said the boy "four half hour tutorials covering the three monotheistic religions and Hinduism."

"Statistically 95% of the fossil fuel professionals we pursue belong to these religious cults one way or the other. It may be that they are not practising anymore but they come from cultures that were born out of religious beliefs. That's why it is important that we try and understand them. This helps us in profiling the criminals that we are chasing, such as yourself" explained the girl.

"What is going to happen next?" Armando asked eventually.

"You will need to be re-educated" the girl explained with a smile. The first time she had shown any kind of facial expression, as far as Armando could remember.

"In *Xinjiang*" explained the boy "We have a deal with the Chinese. They will take care of your re-education and re-training to convert you into an *Energy Transitioner*."

"I have never ever heard about this *Xinjiang* place" said Armando before completing his sentence in the way the boy and girl would have done: "not covered by my tutorials."

"It is China's resource paradise; you will like it" explained the boy "so rich in natural resources that our Chinese friends need labour to help them extract the maximum value and allow us to use it for re-training the fossil fuel professionals."

"Ah..." exclaimed Armando.

"But before you leave, we need to tattoo a small ***G*** on your right arm" explained the boy calmly.

"A tattoo?" asked Armando.

"You see our Chinese friends are not good with languages, I mean with foreign languages" explained the boy "so to help them in their selection of the fossil fuel professionals we tattoo ***G*** for Geoscientists, ***E*** for Engineers and ***A*** for Administrators."

"Selection?" said Armando "that sounds ominous"

"You should not worry Armando" explained the girl "it is only to help them send you to the right accommodation when you descend from the plane."

When they finally let him out of the container, he enjoyed the breeze and the fresh salty smell coming from the endless water body surrounding the ship. He noted that they had created a small runway on the righthand side of the vessel. It was not an aircraft carrier, but still, small planes could land and take off from the large container ship. They walked him to a small aircraft with only two seats. They then removed his shackles and handed over him to the pilot.

"Please get in Armando" the pilot said, "We will leave shortly."

Armando noticed that the pilot looked like the boy and the girl. 'A third twin?' Armando incongruously thought, before realising that 1- if they were born at the same time from the same mother, the pilot would have been part of a *triplet* rather and 2- the twins were not twins, so whatever resemblance was casual unless.... unless his captors were mass produced through some highly sophisticated industrial process. Armando realised that he was starting to lose his mind, so he decided to engage the pilot to divert his thoughts, while the latter was kept busy taking off from the ship.

"I noticed that the plane has an electric engine" Armando said.

"Indeed" said the pilot.

"Now, I am not sure where we are but I wonder if such a light contraption has the range to reach China" commented Armando with some trepidation in his voice.

"No way. We use Renewables but we are not crazy. We cannot reach the Xinjiang province" calmly confirmed the pilot, showing a sense of humour that baffled and pleased Armando.

"And so…???" asked Armando

"We are currently flying over the Mediterranean, due north. Our objective is Frankfurt. Its airport is one of the five European centres where we gather the fossil fuel people. Every week there is a large plane sent by the Chinese to take them to Xinjiang" explained the pilot.

Armando noticed that the plane was losing altitude. They were only twenty meter above the wavy sea.

"Is that ok?" Armando asked pointing his finger to the waves that almost splashed the plane.

"No, it is not" admitted the pilot, "the thing is that we have so much work going on that I have been fast tracked."

"What does that mean?" asked an increasingly worried Armando.

"Normally, after the three video tutorials covering *taking off*, *flying* and *landing*, I would have been required to do at least two flights with an instructor before flying solo" explained the pilot to Armando "however the workload with you guys is such that many of us fly solo after completing the tutorials, with no supervised practise at all."

"Please explain further?" asked Armando who had really started worrying.

"I comfortably digested the *take-off* tutorial, but the other two were not to my liking" admitted the pilot.

"You mean you just scraped the barrel of the *flying* and *landing* tutorials?" commented Armando who was clever at connecting dots.

"You've got it" said the pilot with a smile.

"Are you some kind of *kamikaze*?" asked Armando, now becoming very upset.

"I have to confess that I do not know what a *kamikaze* is" replied the pilot "in any case the plane was flown to the container ship by a different pilot. So, for me now, this is learning on the job so to speak"

"I understand, the word *kamikaze* has not been covered by your tutorials" wryly commented Armando.

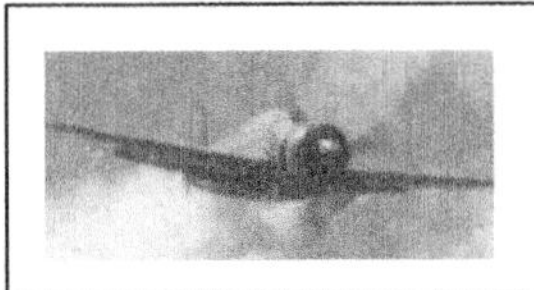  

Had Armando been a religious person he would have started praying. To tell the truth Armando had his own *mystical* moments but normally only related to *food* and *women. The irrefutable proof of the existence of God*, as he would wryly comment, while eating raw red shrimps from Mazzara del Vallo or admiring the lower back, shaped to perfection, of some of his lady friends. But now he was on a plane piloted by an idiot, and his pragmatic side took over. No room for mysticism here. He knew that when the shit hit the fan, and this was a capital SHIT, the best course of action was to divide the actions needed to survive into small sequential segments. He would need to focus on solving each, one at a time. The last one, being the big one, which was safely landing the plane at Frankfurt.

"Let's pull the plane up" he instructed the pilot.

"Sure mate" said the pilot; most Norwegians generally liked to be told what to do, rather than take the initiative on their own.

"Do you have the coordinates of our landing airport?" asked Armando.

"The flight path has been pre-recorded by the previous pilot. It should be enough following its course" explained the pilot.

"Good good" commented Armando, "so the only other thing we should take care off, is to keep the plane flying high enough above ground."

"Well…aside from landing" admitted the pilot "something we will have to do in manual mode."

"Let's get to that bridge first and then we will find a way to cross it" replied Armando trying to keep a positive mind.

They managed to keep the small plane at around 2000 metres height above the ground and at a certain point, they saw in the distance the Italian coastline. They reached land somewhere near Genoa, and about one hour later they were flying over Milan. The pre-programmed flight path then turned them to the north, north east, evidently programmed to navigate the small plane across the alpine valleys through to the plains of Germany. They admired the series of lakes, big and small, that dotted the northern Italian territory and although they were too far away to see the lake of Garda, Armando's heart beat a little faster at the thought of his home. But soon he was focussed back on their safety which at that stage involved reaching Frankfurt airport in one piece and then being able to land the small plane safely.

At this point, the weather began to deteriorate. A strong wind picked up and enveloped the plane making Armando almost throw up. The pilot brought the plane down looking for an altitude with less turbulence. But then, all of a sudden, tragedy struck. They had just entered the air space of Switzerland, the Engadin valley, and skirted along the long narrow valley with increasing difficulty to keep the plane steady in the strong gusts of wind. Then the plane plunged; a blunder of the inexperienced pilot or a mechanical problem? It did not matter in the end, they crash landed in the Poschiavo lake nose first, that is, the nose of the plane first. The impact was violent and the small aircraft broke up into hundreds of pieces.

Armando emerged, injured, from the waters of the lake and gathering himself, recovering quickly from the shock, he looked around for the pilot. The young Norwegian was nowhere to be seen. He dived a few times in the shallow water, trying to find him alive or at least recover his body but without success. Eventually he gave up and slowly swam and crawled toward the shore where he collapsed, the exhaustion of swimming in the cold waters of the lake had finally overwhelmed the adrenaline shot he had felt by surviving the accident.

Armando woke up under a tent, he did not know how many hours or days later. He noticed that his body had been bandaged and that a young lady, covered by a simple wool poncho tied around the waist by a rope, was watching him intensely. She had blue eyes and was gaunt like the Norwegians; for a moment he thought that he had been recaptured. Eventually, though, she spoke in an accented Italian and Armando felt better because it was unlikely that she would have been part of the woke team that had abducted him.

"*Non ti preoccupare. Sei ferito ma non è niente di grave. Ci faremo carico di te finche' ti sei recuperato* (Don't worry. You are injured, but not too seriously. We will take care of you until you have recovered)" the young lady said with a sad smile.

"*Nell'incidente ho perso l'orientamento. Dove siamo?* (I lost my bearing in the accident. Where are we?)" Armando queried.

"*Siamo in Svizzera* (We are in Switzerland)" the lady explained which made Armando breathe a sigh of relief. He was safe.

Armando went back to sleep and when he woke up next time the same lady was there with food for him. A bowl of overcooked porridge, a miso soup and a glass of bitter tea. With an inner smile he realised that he had escaped the deportation to Xinjiang but he had landed, actually *crash landed*, into a vegan community, nevertheless.

Chapter 3
The Era of Gretinism

Greta Thunberg crosses the Atlantic on a sailing boat to avoid the CO2 emissions that a fossil fuel propelled engine would generate. However, both the boat's hull and the technical gear she uses are derived from petroleum products that, if her proposals of keeping the fossil fuels in the ground would take effect, would not be available anymore.

When the protests had started in the US in the early 2000s, they had been presented as the natural extension of the civil rights movement that had been so important in the previous decades in improving the condition of the *Blacks*, a term now considered non politically correct and that has been replaced with the words *African-Americans.*

Eventually, however, this new protest movement, made up of several loosely connected groups, had expanded and incorporated into its manifesto also ecological issues. This included, from 'climate change' that was purported to be solely due to human impact on the planet, with a particular focus on the use of fossil fuels, to the animal rights movement, which included the promotion of vegetarian and vegan food, and indeed, many more issues.

Occupy Wall Street, *Black Lives Matter*, *Extinction Rebellion*, *Planned Parenthood*, *Antifa*, *BAMN*, *Friday for Future* and many others of these, so called 'activist' groups represented the far left of what in the US and the UK were referred to as the *Liberals*. In truth, these groups had very little of what could be called *liberal* in their agendas and modus operandi. Indeed, theirs was more of a religion or cult than a political movement. And like all new religions it was intransigent and often violent in its acts. Whoever did not agree with their views had to be marginalised. And to this extent the so-called *liberal media*, from *The New York Times* to *CNN* to the *Guardian to the BBC*, just to mention a few examples, helped them gain an exposure far greater than the percentage of population that identified with these movements in the Western democracies. It is important to stress the words *Western democracies*, because none of these movements were allowed to function in the *autocratic regimes* of China, Russia, North Korea and so on. And they couldn't care less.

It was as if *racism* and *environmental problems* existed only in a relatively small portion of the planet, the one where, across the northern Atlantic, democratic governments were routinely elected by the population.

Had a *Martian* scouting team landed by chance in New York to identify a safe place where to establish a new colony, based on the superficial impressions gathered after looking at the news for a week, it would have certainly decided on a desert spot in the Xinjiang province, where everything appeared orderly and peaceful thanks to the Chinese repression of the local population. Alternatively, a part of the vast swaths of Siberia inhabited by tamed political prisoners, or, if the *Martians* had been keen on mass folkloric dances, they might have chosen the bleak but safe outskirts of Pyongyang in the, so called, Democratic Republic of North Korea. These were the places where people appeared to be content with their condition, unlike the areas where the masses were rebelling against all the evil done by the democratic governments of the West.

By 2030 these various groups had coalesced into the *Gretinism* movement. The name was derived from Greta Thunberg, who, as a Swedish teenager in the early 20s, had led the hard core of the environmental fringe, shaming the Western governments for not acting promptly on her agenda. She often travelled from Europe to the US using a sailing boat to symbolize how her journeys had zero carbon impact. Obviously, looking at the details of her trips, someone with preconceptions could have pointed out that the fiberglass hull of her boat and the high-tech gear she was wearing were produced using petrochemicals, which without the oil industry would not be available. Letting alone the fact that the change of the captain and crew of the vessel was managed across the Atlantic by planes propelled by fossil fuel. Another observation that could be made of her trips was that for her demonstrations she never travelled to China or India, that at the time produced 50% of the total CO2 air pollution. This was probably because the winds propelling her boat never blew in that direction.

A natural evolution of *Gretinism* had been the *cancel culture*. In the1960's, at the time of the Maoist's Red Guard revolution in China, anything that had taken place previously was deemed to have been wrong and evil; likewise in the early 2020s the *Gretins* discredited and wished to remove anything that reminded them of the heritage of the Western world. In all of the main Western metropolis spanning the Atlantic, the US, the UK, France, Italy and many more, statues of individuals, who until then had been revered for their important role in the building of the societies of their times were defaced and eventually forcibly removed by *Gretins* mobs protesting against racism, injustices etc. Museums displaying artworks of periods deemed to be not-politically correct were invaded by the *Gretins* and centuries old paintings or sculptures were destroyed in the name of the so-called *civil rights* movement in a way not dissimilar to the Taliban in Afghanistan during all the periods they have been in power.

But societies need heroes, even the *Gretinist* society. And approved *Gretin* heroes would eventually replace the ones removed. Among them George Floyd had a significant prominence. His statue had been erected in many important places in the Western world, from Times Square in New York to Parliament Square in London, from Place de Vendome in Paris to Saint Peter square in Rome. Indeed, the likes of Washington, Roosevelt, Churchill, Napoleon and Garibaldi, just to mention a few of the outdated heroes had been removed and left their places to new figures, like George Floyd, who had become famous in 2020 for his horrible death caused by a white policeman who murdered him by pressing his knee to Floyds neck for over nine long minutes. Before that terrible death, however, George Floyd had enjoyed a quite colourful life. He had been jailed several times for crimes ranging from drug possession to theft, to trespass and also aggravated robbery with a deadly weapon. It appeared however, at least this was the line imposed by the so-called *liberal media*, that his martyrdom at the hands of a white policeman had cleansed him of any previous crime. In the years following his death, miracles attributed to George Floyd were reported across the Western world (apparently his only sphere of influence) and as a result, Severus XX, the recently appointed Pope, who, to suit the times was of Black-African origin and gay, had even started the process of beatification of George Floyd.

Destroying the past has never been a way to learn lessons, it has only helped substitute a form of fanatism for another, but this was the least of the problems for the *Gretins*. Their unreserved condemnation of the Western democracies and neutral position towards the dictatorships of the East (Russia, China, North Korea to mention the most important) was a reminder of what the Left (of the West) had set out to achieve during the cold war of the 1960s-80s: demonstrating against the wars (of the West) and the arms race (of the West) because by definition the wars in which Russia and China were engaged were for the freedom of their peoples and nations, how could it be otherwise.

Mr Lin Zing, the CEO and the major shareholder of *Silk Road Friendship Industriess*, was in his office waiting for the augmented reality meeting with his Big Brother, the Supreme Leader Xin Zing. The office was on the 69th floor of a sky scraper in the Central district of Honk Kong from which he observed with joy the lights of the buildings illuminating the area across the bay. Had the sky not been dark, the intensity of the illumination would have made it difficult to know whether it was day or night.

"This year we have more than achieved the CO2 emission target set by our Supreme Leader for Honk Kong" explained, with great satisfaction, Mr Lin Zing to his Deputy Mrs Tia Ping.

"A great achievement!" concurred Mrs Ping.

"We have managed to increase the strength of the illumination used in the territories belonging to the *Han empire* outside mainland China" continued Mr Lin Zing, referring to the Popular Republic of China by the name used by the Communist elite "and our CO2 emission level has doubled relative to last year."

"Fantastic!" intervened Mrs Ping.

"Indeed. The more CO2 our empire produces" explained Mr Lin Zing "the more stringent are the regulations implemented by the decadent West to reduce theirs."

"I know" replied Mrs Ping "the West is trying hard to balance our increase in CO2."

"They *just try* Mrs Ping" continued Mr Lin Zing smiling "because between us and India we are currently generating the majority of the total worldwide CO2 emissions, around 80% in fact. Therefore, any reduction of CO2 emissions by the West has virtually no impact on the total CO2 emitted into the atmosphere of the earth."

"A deep observation that the decadent politicians of the West have missed or at least they pretend to ignore for short term goals, like winning elections" concurred Mrs Ping.

"You are actually making a very important point. Our stable political system, where elections are rare and in any case are piloted from the top" continued Mr Lin Zing "gives us a great advantage relative to the West."

"Our government can look at the big picture and plan for the decades ahead" concurred Mrs Ping.

"And this palaver on the CO2 is more of the same" explained Mr Lin Zing "for us it is a win-win strategy."

"Yes, I know" commented Mrs Ping.

"We have a solid control of the *so-called* renewable energies market" continued Mr Lin Zing, "I say *so-called* because they depend on the mining of minerals which are not renewable. In any case we control directly or indirectly, the mining of the vast majority of these key minerals, like *Rare Earths*, *Lithium* and *Cobalt* and we also produce, using fossil fuels, the vast majority of the *Photo Voltaic Panels* and *Wind Turbines* used by the West."

"*Renewable Energies* is what the West has been increasingly using to reduce their CO2 emissions" commented Mrs Ping smiling.

"But most of the *Renewable Energy* systems are not reliable. For instance, it is difficult to predict the strength of the wind in any particular season and in any case, it is almost impossible to store large quantity of energy produced by either the *Wind turbines* or the *Photo voltaic panels*. The net result is that the West has a chronic shortage of electricity which is also more expensive than when they contented themselves by using simple and dependable fossil fuels."

"It sounds like we have the decadent West by the balls" exclaimed Mrs Ping who for once, due to the excitement of the moment, had expressed herself without any filter.

"Indeed. Their economy shrinks year on year and it is totally dependent on our economy that is thriving, supported by our reliable supply of fossil fuels" explained Mr Lin Zing with a big smile.

Eventually the meeting with the Supreme Leader, sitting in his Beijing office, started. They used the *Zing-Reality Meeting Platform* which, in the darkness of the meeting room, rendered into 3D the bodies of the participants, floating in the air like phantoms. Mr Lin Zing and Mr Xin Zing could almost touch each other although they were two thousand kilometres apart.

"Good evening Big Brother" exclaimed with joy Mr Lin Zing.

"Good evening to you my Small Brother" replied Mr Xin Zing.

"I was just discussing with Mrs Ping our outstanding achievement for the CO2 emissions in Honk Kong this year" commented joyfully Mr Lin Zing.

"And that is only the beginning, my Small Brother" replied Mr Xin Zing before continuing "I have just approved the construction of another 1,000 coal fired power stations in our Xinjiang province."

"Great news" commented Mr Lin Zing "but why specifically in that remote region of our great empire?"

"The prevailing winds will blow most of the hideous smoke toward Kazakhstan" explained Mr Xin Zing with a smile, "as you know we get a lot of our coal from that vassal nation and I think it is right we give them back some of the by-product. In reality, they cannot complain because coal for them is a major component of their exports."

"You are very sophisticated my Big Brother, as always" commented Mr Lin Zing "as indeed you have been when you decided to launch the *Operation Climate Change*."

"Yes, I have to admit that it has been a complete success, beyond my expectations" shyly confessed Mr Xin Zing.

"We never expected that the West would buy in to it to the point of destroying their own economies" commented Mr Lin Zing.

"And it cost us very little seed money" clarified Mr Xin Zing "a little bit of fake news in Facebook, a few hundred thousand dollars to give visibility to some of the extreme leftist groups in the US and Europe…"

"…and then the Western governments did the rest" continued Mr Lin Zing, "they felt guilty for the pollution, most of which *WE* are responsible for, and they started financing green parties and applying their suicidal policies."

"And now they have no way out" concluded Mr Xin Ling "the Western governments are controlled by our allies of the *Left*, including the *Greens* and the various groups that together form the *Gretinism* movement."

"More than allies these are our business partners" clarified Mr Xin Zing "thanks to the success of *Silk Road Friendship Industries* that you have so wisely led, Small Brother!"

"Thank you, Big Brother. I could not have done it on my own" continued Mr Lin Zing "your leadership has shown the path that I have just followed."

"Do you remember the initial period of our *Silk Road* initiative?" asked Mr Xin Zing.

"Sure, I remember well when we were not sure how the Leftist parties and movements of the West, the ones always on the front line to defend the human rights of the minorities and underprivileged, would react to our crackdown on the democracy in Honk Kong or the ethnic cleansing of the Uighurs in Xinjiang" replied Mr Lin Zing.

"By then, however, the *Silk Road* initiative had made these same Leftist groups our financial partners" interjected Mr Xin Zing.

"Yes, I remember as if it was yesterday when in the early 20s LeBron James, the *NBA* star who made millions from merchandising in China, silenced one of the *NBA* managers who had condemned our crackdown of the Honk Kong protests by saying that *freedom of speech can carry a lot of negative*" commented Mr Lin Zing smiling hysterically "and this LeBron was the same guy who few months earlier had joined the *Black Lives Matter* demonstrations against the US government."

"The *NBA* and LeBron had learned the lesson from how we handled the complaints of *H&M, Adidas, Nike and Zara*, to mention a few brands that had the arrogance of trying to shame our highly productive use of prisoners in the cotton camps of the Xinjiang that at the time accounted for 40% of all the cotton produced worldwide" interjected Mr Xin Zing.

"Yes we closed their shops in our malls and convinced the Han people, our people, to boycott their brands" commented Mr Lin Zing.

"Eventually all these Western brands realised that they could only be 'politically correct' in the West, condemning the racism and inequalities of their own decadent democracies" continued Mr Xin Zing.

"Ours is a society that values the law, order and rights. Therefore, by definition is devoid of racism or inequalities" commented Mr Lin Zing smiling.

"And we never heard any of the Feminist movements of the decadent West complaining about the rapes and forced abortions we have practised against Uighur women" said Mr Xin Zing with a big smile.

"Yes, by then we became confident that our economic growth and joint ventures with the West had silenced their Left when it came to human rights in China and our territories outside the mainland" commented Mr Lin Zing.

"After all our middle-class accounts for the majority of the electronics sold by *Apple*, just to give one example" explained Mr Xin Zing.

"Talking about the present" continued Mr Lin Zing "as you know *Silk Road Friendship Industries* has a solid grip of important nations of Africa and Latin America. Our colonization of these foreign regions, whose mineral wealth is key to the Renewable energies of the West, is extremely advanced."

"Indeed...we are getting to the point where we have control of the full cycle of the Western economies" commented with satisfaction Mr Xin Zing "we give them all the raw minerals and a significant portion of the final products that they need for their generation of electricity through the *Renewables*, which as you know are both inefficient and unreliable. And we buy certain products, from wheat to the smartphones, which are critical for the survival of their economies."

"Like our COVID virus and vaccines business with Latin America and Africa" reflected Mr Lin Zing "the virus produces damage that our weak vaccines only partially control so that they need more of our vaccines and they become dependent on our *friendly* help, so to speak, year on year. We barter our vaccines for their Uranium, their Cobalt, and their Lithium, to mention only a few of the goodies."

"Indeed, my Small Brother, the West is like a *drug addict* and we are the *drug*" triumphally concluded the meeting Mr Xin Zing.

Chapter 4
Sixteen years earlier (December 2019)
The suspicious death of Pasteur Sauveterre
DRC (Congo) and Paris

Artisanal Cobalt mining in DRC (Congo)

The body of Pasteur Sauveterre had been found hanging from the ceiling light of his spartan room at the Venus hotel in Kinshasa.

By the time the maid had made the discovery, Pasteur Serge Sauveterre (PSS to friends) was dead with a broken neck.

PSS was a 40-year-old Congolese of medium height and strong build who had escaped the tribal wars of the DRC (Democratic Republic of Congo), the ex-Belgian colony, and taken refuge in France ten years before. This was the time in which Joseph Kabila was the strong man in charge of the DRC. In Paris, he had been accepted as a refugee, and eventually given a French Passport. Coming from a religious Christian family and being entrepreneurial it had been natural for him to set up an Evangelical Church of his own, called *L' Église de la Dernière Espérance* (*The Church of the Last Hope*) in *Château Rouge*, a neighbourhood located in the *18th arrondissement* of Paris. This was often referred to, informally, as the *African district* of the French capital, although this nickname was due to the type of shops dominating the markets and wares traded in the area rather than its inhabitants. The area was frequented, though, by African and Caribbean immigrants, often coming from different neighbourhoods, rather than necessarily, the racial mix of *Château Rouge* proper.

PSS had lived for most of his French exile in *Château Rouge* with his numerous family members, that aside from his wife Isabelle, included four young children. His Church, supported by funds from the French government, was the point of reference for many African immigrants who felt marginalised and sought solace in God (and Pasteur Sauveterre as the intermediary). In the last three years, however, PSS had returned often to DRC and opened branches of his Church in both Kinshasa, the DRC capital, and Kolwezi, located in the south of the country and the capital city of the province of Lualaba which was very rich in mineral resources.

The news of the death of PSS had taken time to reach Paris and his family. Within the Congolese community of *Château Rouge* many contradicting rumours had spread around the death of PSS. Eventually the consensus had been that PSS had killed himself, although no message had been found in his room in the Venus hotel to explain the reasons for such a dramatic act.

The revelation of the death of PSS had eventually also reached Jean-Jacques Nkomo aka JJ, a dear friend of PSS and a freelance journalist mostly working for the extreme left-wing newspaper *La Fraternité*. Being freelance meant that his income was uncertain and often meagre ('irregular but consistently small' as JJ often mischievously explained to his friends) and also totally dependent on the articles that he managed to get printed. His acquaintance with PSS had occurred almost by chance, because he was not a religious person. On the contrary, as the second generation of a Congolese immigrant family living hand to mouth, he had found comfort in adhering to Marxism. After a fashion, this was his religion that, like all faith-based movements, portrayed the existence of a very perfect society at the end of the tunnel, so to speak. A society composed of solidarity, equality, welfare for all of humanity. It did not matter to JJ that this idealised and perfect society had never materialised to date, even in the countries that were run by Marxist regimes. After all, at 30 he was too young to have any memory of the fall of the Berlin wall in 1989, the subsequent collapse of the Iron curtain and the unreserved joy that had pervaded the majority of the population of the nations that had previously been under the USSR juggernaut. Actually, in 2020 that time was so distant, that for many, including JJ, the historical memory had been lost. The Left even claimed the credit for the collapse of the Soviet Union, obviously presented as the natural evolution of a successful Marxist society. The remaining Asian Communist autocracies, like China and North Korea, were depicted by the European Left as not necessarily a *paradise* but still as models of societies that were so fair and advanced that they did not have any internal political opposition. As Claude Signoret, the political editor of *La Fraternité*, had at one time explained, during an editorial room meeting: *"A political system, like the one implemented in China, that is accepted by 1.5 billion people needs evidently to be good."* It was not a surprise that Claude, now 70, had taken an active leadership role during the 1968 protest movement that had rattled Gaullist French society. At the time he had worn long hair and donned military-revolutionary outfits, half way between a French Che Guevara and a local version of Mao Tse Tung. The revolutionary fervour of Claude had certainly attenuated with age; however, he was still keen on outlandish outfits and smoking cigars. Apart from that, and despite the fact that his newspaper had embraced, among other fashionable issues, veganism, he dined often on *steak frites*, which showed in his expansive waist line, what else! In his view any shortcomings of the communist regimes were necessarily due to the *evil West* that was always trying to interfere with the natural development of societies aiming at fairness and equality among its citizens.

Superficially, it was therefore surprising that two so different personalities like PSS and JJ had met and even more that they had become friends. A Union dispute involving a dozen African immigrants who were working, in the black, for a renowned *supermarché* had been the catalyst. The charismatic personality of PSS had attracted JJ and likewise the social commitment of JJ had touched the heart of PSS. With their significant differences, one a man of God, the other an atheist, they were still kindred spirits trying their best to help the impoverished people that surrounded them, not just the abstract concepts of humankind predicted by the *Bible* or *Das Capital.*

But that was then. Now PSS was dead and JJ was walking in *Château Rouge* among the colourful shops selling from cooked to perfection heads of cows to fresh hibiscus flowers, from frozen tilapias directly flown from Lake Malawi to hair extensions made by slave labour in China, from manioc and sweet potatoes to the entry in heaven, or so it was promised in the poster of an upcoming evangelical reunion of the *Commaunaté Chretienne Bethseda.* The exotic aromas of Afro-Caribbean spices permeated the air, still fresh under the early morning sun.

He finally turned into *Rue de Panama*. His objective, at the end of the road, was *La Calebasse d'Afrique*, a shop selling a large variety of African products and food. Or, rather, the flats above the shop. Indeed, two floors above the shop was the small apartment where PSS and his family lived. JJ had gone to visit the widow of PSS.

"Je suis terriblement désolé (I am terribly sorry)" JJ had said to Isabelle while hugging her

"Il n'y a pas de mots (There are no words)" Isabelle had replied with the evident pain in her face. Isabelle was a thirty something, rather plump, Congolese lady dressed in colourful clothes, as if she had not yet processed the death of her husband. The pain was so raw that it appeared to her like a mirage that would soon disappear. PSS would soon knock at the door, returning from his trip to DRC.

"Quels détails de la mort de PSS connaissez-vous?(What details do you know about the death of PSS ?) JJ had asked.

"Très peu je dois admettre (Very little I have to admit)" Isabelle had replied

« Dites-moi tout ce que vous savez s'il vous plait (Please tell me whatever you know) JJ asked.

"Ils l'ont trouvé pendu (They found him hanged)" had commented Isabelle.

"Est-ce que vous lui avez parlé le jour de sa mort ? (Did you speak with him the day of his death?)" had asked JJ.

"Oui, il était en train de rentrer à Paris (Yes, he was in the process of returning to Paris)" had confirmed Isabelle.

"Avez-vous senti qu'il était contrarié? (Did you sense that he was upset?)" JJ continued.

"Pas du tout (Absolutely not)" replied Isabelle.

"Avez-vous eu des discussions dans les jours précédents (Did you have any arguments in the previous days?)" asked JJ.

"Pas du tout, nous ne nous sommes pas disputés (Absolutely not, we did not have any argument) " replied Isabelle.

"Étiez-vous au courant d'un problème grave auquel PSS avait été confronté ? (Have you been aware of any serious problem that might have worried PSS?)" JJ continued.

"Non (No)" had confirmed Isabelle

"Je comprends qu'ils n'ont trouvé aucun message pouvant expliquer sa décision de se suicider (I understand that they did not find any message explaining his decision to commit suicide)" had queried JJ.

"C'est quelque chose qui n'a aucun sens (Something that does not make any sense)" commented Isabelle

"Je comprends (I agree)" said JJ.

"PSS était un chef d'église vibrant et charismatique et je ne peux pas imaginer qu'il puisse se suicider (PSS was a vibrant and charismatic church leader and I could not even fathom that he could consider to kill himself)" explained Isabelle.

"D'accord cela n'a aucun sens. Je veux vraiment en savoir plus. Je me rendrai en RDC pour enquêter (It is true, it does not make any sense. I really want to know more. I will travel to the DRC to investigate)" concluded JJ, before hugging for a final time Isabelle and leaving the apartment.

JJ informed Claude Signoret that he would be away for a few weeks, travelling to the DRC. He tried to justify his absence from Paris with the aim of gathering information for a scoop that he said, "*would make the front page of the newspaper.*" He knew that he was lying, his trip was purely for personal reasons, his friendship with PSS. But he hoped that, if an article of any sort could come out of his trip, and DRC had many potential news angles, there was always something interesting to report on, he could get not just a fee for his writing but also his travel expenses reimbursed.

The Air France mid-day flight from Charles de Gaulle, that was scheduled to reach Kinshasa in the late evening, was full. JJ was crammed into a middle seat in the economy class. Indeed, the cheapest seat he had been able to find on the internet. He was flanked by two large Congolese men, their bodies far exceeded the space available in their own seats and invaded, without pity, what should have been the personal space of JJ. JJ pushed them gently away a few times but eventually gave up, the physics of body mass overcame any principle of etiquette when flying economy, unfortunately.

He gulped down the snack served shortly after taking off, but due to his uncomfortable seating he gave up on the idea of having a nap and, to pass the time, focused his mind on PSS and his mysterious death. PSS was both vibrant and positive; the last person one would think capable of committing suicide. JJ smiled inwardly: remembering how PSS had been a *coureur de jupons* (a womanizer), especially when in DRC and away from his controlling wife. JJ would have been less surprised if his death had been due to an enraged boyfriend or husband of one of the young ladies that PSS had *exorcised* (that's how PSS presented his dalliances). But a suicide did not make any sense, of this JJ was sure. His thoughts were suddenly interrupted. In the darkness of the cabin, he watched a Congolese lady sitting in the row in front of his taking a young child to the toilet. While she was away, JJ became aware of the existence of another baby, much younger than the one taken by the mother to the toilet, probably less than one year old in fact, and who until then had been sleeping on the floor. He or she, JJ could not tell, had suddenly woken up, discovered he was alone, and started crawling under the rows of seats in front of his. JJ promptly jumped up from his seat and scooped the child up with feline grace, holding him in his arms until the mother returned.

Approaching Kinshasa International Airport in the night always made JJ feel bitterly sick. From the sky he observed the vast dark body of water of the Congo River that separated Kinshasa, the capital of DRC, the Congo that had at one time had been a Belgian colony, from Brazzaville, the capital of the ex-French Congo. While the latter showed an abundance of light, the former, the place where JJ was planning to land, was dark and menacing, even from the sky. A reminder that if the Belgian colonialism had been one of the worst, probably the worst seen in Africa with its cynical harvesting of the vast mineral wealth of the Congo and the treating in the most inhumane way of the Congolese, the subsequent governments, all in the hands of local strong men, had fared no better. They had pocketed the material wealth of the country and delivered nothing to its citizens, not even the basic infrastructure on which to build a modern country.

Despite the fact that he had a valid multiple entry visa, he felt obliged to tip the immigration officer with 10 euros. This was the law of the country; to get anything done one always needed to pay a form of *backsheesh*.

Exiting the airport, the darkness enveloped JJ. He walked to a crush of cars, mostly private, that could be rented as taxis. He negotiated a price and was driven to the Hotel Venus, in the Gombe district of central Kinshasa. For most of the journey, aside from the car lights, the only illumination was provided by the flickering kerosene lamps of informal markets spread out all across Kinshasa.

After checking-in at the Venus hotel, JJ realised that he was not only tired but also hungry because, aside from the snack eaten shortly after taking off, he had not eaten any food all day. He had stayed in this hotel before, he even knew the director, and remembered, with pleasure, that they had an African style 24-hour restaurant. A godsend in a place like Kinshasa where, when visiting for business, one would never know when one could have the next meal. At least the Venus restaurant was always open, or most of the time at least, and one could find solace in their fried plantains or, for the more adventurous, a Congo-style carbonara, after a long day of queues, both in the hallucinating traffic and in the government offices, trying to meet government officials and gain their momentary attention, often with an introductory gift. JJ sat alone at one of the restaurant's tables and accompanied his *moambe*, a local delicacy made with chicken, vegetables and rice, with a couple of *Primus*, the local strong lager. He felt better afterwards and decided to go to sleep and start his informal investigations the next day.

The next day, after breakfast, JJ went to meet Aristide, the director of the Venus Hotel. Like true Congolese friends they exchanged ceremonial headbutts before starting to talk business.

"Comme vous le savez j'étais un bon ami du Pasteur Sauveterre (As you know I was a good friend of Pasteur Sauveterre)"

"Oui je sais (Yes I know)."

"Et je me sens bouleversè pour sa perte (And I feel terrible for his loss)."

"Je ressens la même chose mon ami, le Pasteur était aussi un bon ami à moi. C'était un de notre clients habituels. Chaque fois qu'il séjournait à Kinshasa nous avions le plaisir de l'héberger (I feel the same my friend, the Pasteur was also a good friend of mine. He was a habitual client, every time that he stayed in Kinshasa, we had the pleasure to host him."

"Les informations parvenues à Paris, je veux dire la famille du Pasteur Sauveterre, ont été très rares (The information that has reached Paris, I mean the family of Pasteur Sauveterre, are very scarce)."

"Demandez-moi et j'essaierai de combler les lacunes. (Ask me and I will try to fill in with what I know)."

"Je comprends que le Pasteur a été retrouvé pendu mais qu'aucun message n'a été trouvé dans la chambre. Je veux dire quelque chose pour justifier son suicide. (I understand that the Pasteur had been found hanged but that no message had been found in his room. I mean something that might have justified his suicide)."

"C'est vrai. (It is true)."

"L'avez-vous vu la veille de sa mort. (Did you see him the day before he died)."

"Oui et il allait bien. Il semblait plein d'énergie et d'enthousiasme. Comme toujours. (Yes, he was ok. He appeared full of energy and enthusiasm. Like always)."

"Et que pensez-vous de son suicide? (What do you think of his suicide?)."

"Franchement ça me parait très étrange. (Frankly it seems very strange to me)."

"Avez-vous des éléments supplémentaires pour étayer vos soupçons ? (Do you have any additional elements to support your suspicions?)"

"La femme de chambre a dit que quand elle est entrée dans la pièce, la télé était allumée et bruyante, mais la chambre était vide de tout effet personnel du pasteur. Elle n'a même pas trouvé son smartphone (The maid said that when she entered the room the TV was on and very loud but it was empty of any personal effects of the pastor. She did not even find his smartphone)."

"Vous lui faites confiance? (Do you trust her?)."

"Elle travaille chez nous depuis dix ans. Elle n'a jamais rien volé. (She had worked for us for ten years. She has never stolen anything)."

"Et alors qu'en pensez-vous? (And so, what do you think)."

"Que Pasteur Sauveterre a peut-être laissé ses bagages ailleurs. (It may be that Pasteur Sauveterre left his luggage somewhere else)."

"La police est-elle venue enquêter? (Did the police come to investigate?)."

"Comme ils le font tous à Kinshasa. Pasteur Sauveterre n'était pas un VIP. Ils ont juste rapporté qu'il s'était suicidé. Et c'est tout. (As they always do in Kinshasa. Pasteur Sauveterre was not a VIP. They just reported his suicide. Full stop)."

"Et le consulat de France? (And the French consulate)."

"Ils ne se sont pas présentés à l'hôtel. (They did not show up at the hotel)."

"Vous rigolez? (Are you joking?)"

"Pas du tout il est normal ici que les consulats étrangers restent à l'écart des enquêtes policières... à moins qu'il ne s'agisse évidemment d'un blanc ! (Not at all. It is normal here that the foreign consulates remain outside of the police investigation…unless obviously, that a white man is involved)."

"Et que savez-vous de la soi-disant enquête policière? (And what you know of the so-called police investigation?)."

"Rien d'officiel... mais j'ai entendu dire qu'ils avaient classé la mort de Pasteur Sauveterre comme un suicide et ont clos l'enquête. (Officially nothing…but I understand that they qualified Pasteur Sauveterre's death as a suicide and they closed the investigation)."

"C'est étonnant! (It is amazing!)"

"Incroyable en France peut-être... mais normal chez nous. (Unbelievable in France may be…but not here)."

It took the connections of Aristide, a lot of backsheesh and a full week of waiting for JJ to be able to meet with the Chief of the Police who had signed off the report on the death of Pasteur Sauveterre. And even then the conversation did not go anywhere.

"Que pensez-vous de la mort de Pasteur Sauveterre? (What do you think of the death of Pasteur Sauveterre?)" JJ asked the police officer.

"Qu'il s'est suicidé (That he committed suicide)" replied the police officer.

"Et que dites-vous du fait qu'aucun objet personnel n'a été trouvé dans sa chambre. Pas de bagages, pas de téléphone... rien (And what do you make of it that in his room no personal effects were discovered. No suitcase, no phone…nothing)" asked JJ.

"Il était probablement désespéré et a tout jeté dans le fleuve Congo avant de se suicider (He probably was desperate and he threw his belongings in the Congo River before killing himself)" explained the police officer.

"Pourquoi pensez-vous qu'il était désespéré? (Why do you think that he was desperate?)" queried JJ.

"Parce que seul quelqu'un de désespéré se suiciderait (Because only someone desperate would commit suicide)" clarified the police officer.

Typical circular police logic, thought JJ while leaving the police office with an ironic inward smile. He was no wiser on what had really happened to PSS than when he had entered the police office.

As part of the deal Aristide had made with the police, JJ was allowed to see the body of PSS, that was still in the morgue of the Kinshasa Central Hospital, waiting for the completion of the paperwork before being flown to Paris.

The body was in a wooden crate in an air-conditioned trailer parked in the garden of the hospital. Upon payment of a little backsheesh, the morgue employee opened the top of the crate and walked out of the room, leaving JJ alone. JJ tied a bandana around his mouth and nose due to the smell of death and corruption coming from the crate and peeked inside with trepidation, because he had never seen a dead person before. JJ noticed that the face of PSS was not just swollen, but also bruised, as if while hanging himself he had bumped into something hard, deeply cutting his forehead in the process. He noticed the signs of the rope that evidently, he had tied around his neck and also that PSS was still dressed in the clothes in which he had been found hanged. JJ found it bizarre that someone would kill himself formally dressed and with a pink tie. This was the one JJ knew that PSS used when he wished to pick up some young lady for his nightly entertainment. In the crate was also a length of rope, supposedly the one that PSS had used to hang himself with. JJ thought this was somewhat bizarre. Normally, this would be an item the police would store separately. Before closing the casket JJ, took a picture of the corpse of PSS and then left the morgue.

In parallel, during the long week of waiting for the meeting with the police officer, JJ went to visit the local branch of the Church of Pasteur Sauveterre, located in a dilapidated building in *Cité Mamam Mobutu*. The name of this hilly district referred to the 1st lady of Mobutu, the long-lived dictator who had governed the DRC (and pillaged it for his own enrichment) from the country's independence in 1965 until his death in 1997. May be at one time, the *Cité* had been an improvement in the lodging conditions of many impoverished families, but now, many years after its completion and without any proper maintenance, it was just one more *favela* surrounding the centre of Kinshasa with roads marked by potholes, ramshackle buildings, electricity generators used to supplement the limited and precarious electricity provided by the government network.

JJ had visited the Church on several occasions with PSS, in a few instances, actually during some of the Pasteur's religious functions. The inside of the Church was sparsely furnished with rows of cheap plastic chairs and a kitchen table that functioned as the altar. There was no proper floor either, just beaten earth with the occasional pothole. But, JJ remembered, smiling, there was a sort of cardboard office in a corner of the building-cum-church where only PSS was allowed to enter and that he used, among other activities, for *exorcizing* young ladies. Those that, based on his observations and unaudited verdict, had become the prey of the devil. JJ convinced the caretaker of the Church, an old, tall and thin man, of the necessity to break into the office of PSS, which was locked, to check if the missing possessions might be stacked there. But nothing of relevance was discovered. The office, like the Church, had some basic furniture; the most intriguing item being a camp bed with dirty linen, that PSS had probably used for his particular type of exorcism. There was also an open packet of *OK Condoms*, the most successful condom brand marketed in the DRC, which showed, that in his own way PSS had been a prudent man.

JJ spoke with several Congolese belonging to the congregation of *L'Église de la Dernière Espérance*. None of them provided any additional clue to the reasons behind Pasteur Sauveterre's death. They had no idea where his personal effects could have ended up, but one thing all of the parishioners interviewed by JJ confirmed, was that in the days leading to up to his death PSS had been, like always, active, charismatic and looking to the future. Indeed, he had recently returned from a trip to visit the other branch of his Church in Kolwezi, and was planning to travel to Paris. Nobody could believe that PSS had killed himself, although the police report pointed in that direction.

This was the moment when JJ reflected on the fact that his trip to Kinshasa had been a failure. It had not resulted in any better understanding of the circumstances of Pasteur Sauveterre's death which he could report to Isabelle, nor had it provided him with any insight that could be turned into a news worth article of any sort. Had he returned to Paris, he would have had a hard time to have his expenses covered by *La Fraternité*. Still, he could cut his losses and return to his normal life in Paris, but he decided not to. If, in the years to come, you would have asked JJ why he had decided to travel to Kolwezi to further his investigations, he would have told you that he did not know why. He could not point to a precise, straightforward reason. Probably, he would say, a combination of hurt pride and his anguish for not understanding the underlying causes of the death of his friend. But also, he would admit, his hard-headed personality, the fact that he wished to impress Claude Signoret with his investigative skills.

JJ had never travelled in the DRC beyond the greater Kinshasa area. Reaching Kinshasa from Europe, as he had recently done with Air France, was *sometimes uncomfortable* (he still felt the pain of being crammed between two overweight Congolese) but relatively *safe* because only international carriers, recognised for their safety records, were allowed to fly in and out of Europe. However, long distance travelling *within* Africa was in general *not particularly safe*, either because the road conditions were at best patchy and often dreadful, many of the drivers had limited skills and large swaths of land were often controlled by bandits that from time to time doubled as terrorists. But even travelling by plane *within* Africa was not for the faint hearted. Only local carriers were available. And the main risk was not necessarily the pilot's skill and experience, or lack off, but rather the haphazard aircraft maintenance, which was a widespread hazard across the black continent.

JJ sketched out his trip to Kolwezi. First, he had to fly to Lubumbashi, the third largest DRC town, and located close to the border with Zambia. This route was served by *CAA*, a local carrier, after which, he needed to cover around 300 Km by car to reach Kolwezi. He checked on the safety record of *CAA* on Google, currently known as flyCAA, only to learn that due to security and safety issues the airline had been included in the list of air carriers banned in the European Union, along with many other airlines based in the Congo. On the positive side was the fact that, of the many accidents that the airline has been involved in, only one had caused deaths. The other incidents involved overshooting or veering off the runaway and in one instance an engine failure just after taking off. Even so, he bought the plane ticket, economy what else!, with a certain apprehension. For the land portion of the journey from Lubumbashi to Kolwezi, however, JJ managed to organise his car journey through the network of *L' Église de la Dernière Espérance.* They assured him that someone from the Kolwezi branch would come to pick him up.

With over 2.5 million inhabitants, Lubumbashi would have been a large town anywhere in the world. Spread over a vast area that encroached the surrounding savannah, the town had taken its modern shape in 1910, when the Belgian government had established the city of *Elisabethville* (the colonial name of Lubumbashi), named in honour of Queen Elisabeth, the consort of King Albert I of Belgium. The site was selected because of its proximity to the copper mine of *Etoile du Congo* and the copper ore smelting oven installed by the *Union Minière du Haut-Katanga (UMHK),* an Anglo-Belgian enterprise, on the nearby Lubumbashi river. *UMHK* represented a powerful group of global copper producers (although it also produced tin, cobalt, radium, uranium, zinc, cadmium, germanium, manganese, silver, and gold) that by the start of WWII controlled 70% of the Congolese economy.

In colonial times the town had been segregated; it consisted of a central area inhabited only by white people, most of them employed by *UMHK*, surrounded by shanty neighbourhoods where the black labourers camped in insalubrious conditions. Those times were obviously gone but the town's footprint still reflected the colonial era, with its long perpendicular avenues, oriented NW-SE and SW-NE, the city centre marked by the Catholic Cathedral of *St. Pierre and Paul.* The buildings, both ancient and modern, and the roads gave however, a sense of transience, common to many towns and villages of Africa; the lack of maintenance, the garbage and dust littering even the main thoroughfares had marked the evolution from a relatively small colonial town to a metropolis in the independent DRC. Still, the thread that linked colonial to post-colonial times, was the fact that Lubumbashi remained a very important mining centre.

JJ landed in Lubumbashi at around midday with one of the Fokker 50's of flyCAA. The sun was shining but he knew that, as happened every afternoon during the rainy season, a huge monsoon rain would soon arrive. Indeed, he could already see large dark clouds forming on the horizon. He had hand carried, rather than checking in, a rucksack with a few clothes and his laptop to avoid the risk of arriving without luggage, a common occurrence when flying within the DRC with a local carrier. He was soon out of the airport and looking for his contact from the Kolwezi branch of the *L' Église de la Dernière Espérance*. He was expecting someone holding a placard with his name but this was because JJ had been living most of his life in France and had only a limited understanding of the Congolese rituals so to speak, where few things are planned and even fewer carried out in a professional manner.

After realising that nobody had a sign from which he could identify his driver, he stood outside the airport exit hoping that someone would somehow show up soon and, more importantly, recognise him. His eyes were attracted by the looming monsoon rain that would find him otherwise unsheltered. Eventually a thin, tall black man with an elegant posture arrived calling the name *Jean Jacques*. It turned out to be just in time before the sky broke out in a heavy rain. JJ waved his hand and the man signified to follow him to the car parked nearby. The driver of the car, a battered Peugeot 404, helped JJ load his belongings while another man, already sitting in the car, introduced himself to JJ.

"Bonjour Monsieur Jean Jacques, je m'appelle Chef Célestin. Je viens de Kowelzi (Good morning, Mr Jean Jacques, my name is Chief Celestine. I come from Kowelzi" said the man.

"Bonjour à vous Chef Célestin, merci d'être venu me chercher (Good morning to you Chief Célestin, thanks for having come to pick me up" replied JJ.

"Je suis en retard car les conditions de la route sont terribles avec tant de pluie (I am late because the road conditions are terrible due to the rain)" explained Chief Célestin.

"Je comprends (Understood)" replied JJ while taking the passenger seat.

JJ did not know who Chief Celestine was, although the charm that exuded from his persona suggested someone with a high position within the Kolwezi community, and decided to postpone any questions about the death of PSS until their arrival at Kolwezi.

The first drops of rain resonated on the windscreen while they started their journey to Kolwezi, 300 Km away. The condition of the road was fine within the greater Lubumbashi area, except for the occasional pothole that the heavy rain quickly filled with muddy water. However, beyond the town limits the conditions of *Route Nationale 1* (N1) worsened. JJ could not tell if this was due to the lack of maintenance or the rain starting to flood the length of the road which crossed the lowlands. The driver drove carefully, which for JJ, accustomed to the standard of driving in Kinshasa, was a relief. However, progress was slow, very slow.

N1 runs North-Northeast. Chief Célestin's plans were to follow N1 as far as the small village of Guba, 180 Km from Lubumbashi, and then take the N39, running East-West, to reach Kolwezi, 120 Km from the N1-N39 junction. However, when they reached the natural reserve of Lufira, only 70 Km after starting their journey, they found themselves in a savannah that had been flooded by the nearby river. There was no way to drive through the flood, so they had to wait in the car, parked on a small hill, until the rain stopped. By then the flood had receded enough to allow the driver to see the tarmac road but it was late evening and dark. In normal circumstances, whatever *normal* meant in the DRC, the total trip would have taken 4 to 5 hours. However, they could resume driving from Lufira only late in the night, 7 hours after leaving the airport, and by then darkness had descended and driving was even less safe than before.

"Nous devrions nous arrêter dès que nous trouverons un endroit convenable. Il est trop dangereux de conduire la nuit (We must stop our journey once we find a suitable spot. It is too dangerous to drive in the night)" Chief Célestin informed them.

A few kilometres after exiting the reserve of Lufira, they found a dry spot on the side of the road where they stopped for the night. The driver made himself comfortable in the front seat while Chief Célestin and JJ did the same in the back seats. Luckily it was not cold.

Accustomed to these types of unforeseen events, both the driver and Chief Célestin had carried a few plastic bottles of water and some food provisions. The driver started eating *fufu*, a dough-like food made from mandioca flour, which JJ remembered from the Sunday lunches prepared by his mom in Paris when he was still living at home, as tasting like a gelatinous plastic foam. When forced to eat it by his parents, he always thought of chewing one of these silicone implants certain ladies use to enlarge their breasts. *Fufu* was used in Africa as a stomach filling starch for the poor, at best accompanied by a spicy soup of some sort that ennobled its taste. The difference in status of Chief Célestin was reflected in his food provisions that consisted in a meat dish, something JJ thought would have been more to his taste. Not having any food of his own JJ was pleased that Chief Célestin offered him a morsel of meat. JJ grabbed it and while chewing it he noticed that the meat had a greasy flavour and a hard, indeed very hard texture. Cooked without salt, which is a very precious commodity in the DRC, JJ thought that it was like eating a piece from a leather belt. All things considered it still represented an improvement relative to the plastic texture of the *fufu*. He did not want, however, to appear impolite or, worst, antagonise his host, so he smiled, as if he had been offered some caviar, and limited himself to ask what cut of meat it was.

"Cul de macaque (Monkey arse)" explained Chief Célestin with a smile before adding "cuit au vin de palme, le meilleur délice de la jungle (cooked in palm wine, the best bush delicacy)."

Luckily by then JJ had already swallowed the *delicacy*, so the etiquette was not breached. However, when offered more meat he refused to take it by saying that he was full. He slept, dreaming of angry monkeys.

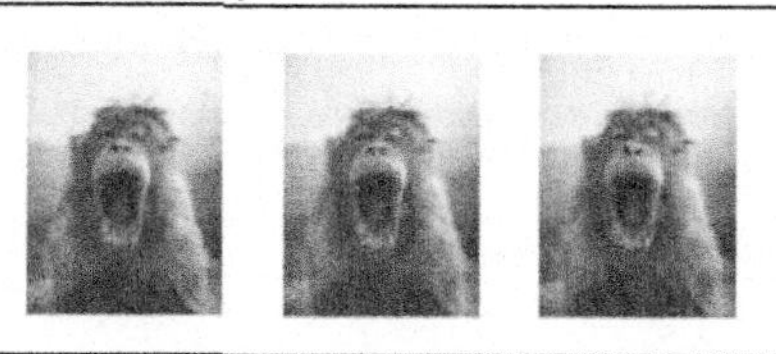

They resumed their trip early the next day. Going through some of the villages and hamlets JJ noticed that the biggest potholes had been marked by dropping into them a piece of furniture or a concrete post or a broken washing machine. These items emerged from the potholes to guide the driver away from them during the day. JJ reflected how dangerous they would have been during the night, when these hazards would have been difficult to identify.

Eventually, after no more adventures, they reached the outskirts of Kolwezi by midday, just before the afternoon of rain and flooding.

Kolwezi, located on the Manika plateau of the Katanga province, is an important mining centre in the DRC, founded for this sole purpose in 1938 by *UMHK*. The land here is very rich in minerals which are excavated in the copper and cobalt mines that can be found in the vicinity of the city. These *formal* mines consist mostly of a large open crater where; besides copper and cobalt, other minerals are excavated as well. There are also *informal* mines, totally unregulated, existing in many locations of the region. Because of its mineral wealth the city had been an important strategic point in the conflicts, armed and otherwise, that have taken place over the past several decades in the DRC.

They had prepared a room for JJ in the building used by the congregation of *L' Église de la Dernière Espérance*. The building was a large, old structure that, however, had been repainted recently in light blue, the colour of the sky and by religious extension of heaven. The room shown to JJ, although spartan, included, apart from a small bed, a table and chair and, more importantly, had electricity provided by a generator. This was a considerable luxury in the DRC. The only drawback was the lack of running water in the small bathroom of the building. JJ later discovered that the premises belonged to Chief Célestin who was the head of one the largest Luba tribes of Katanga.

The following day Chief Célestin organised a meeting for JJ with the senior members of the congregation. Among them was an oldish white man, sticking out from the crowd not just for his skin colour but also for his obvious, and very large, beer belly and long grey hair. JJ remembered that, on the contrary, PSS and his religious affiliates did not drink alcohol and most of the time stuck to *Maltina*, a fortified malt drink that was rumoured to enhance sexual prowess. As he had done in Kinshasa, JJ queried how was the mood of PSS during his stay in Kolwezi and the answers he received were not dissimilar to those he had heard in the DRC's capital. PSS had oozed a positive energy that could never be drained by the many practical problems he faced, lack of sufficient funds being the most serious, that he had running his own church in three so different locations, Paris, Kinshasa and Kolwezi. JJ explained the little he knew about the death of PSS, that all his possessions had disappeared, that he had even visited the morgue and upon insistent requests, reluctantly showed the graphic images of the body of PSS that he had captured with his smartphone. At the end of the session, he realised that the trip to Kolwezi had been probably an unnecessary waste of time and money. When the meeting ended, JJ started walking to his small room. He was planning to check when next he could fly out of Kolwezi, the asshole of the world if one existed thought JJ, and back to Paris as soon as possible. However, the white man approached JJ and spoke to him in English.

"I would like to introduce myself, JJ" he opened, "My name if Bob Rare and I have been a close friend of PSS for a few years."

"Nice meeting you Bob. May I ask what brought you to DRC and, of all its vast territory, to Kolwezi?" queried JJ.

"Mining" replied Bob.

"You mean you work in a mine?" queried JJ.

"Not anymore. I am a mining engineer and used to work at the Musonoi mine. I did that for thirty years." explained Bob.

"So, you have been here for a very long time" remarked JJ.

"Indeed. Obviously from time to time I travelled back to the UK. I come from Lancashire and my father was a coal miner. It is in the family blood" explained Bob with a smile.

"You said that you don't work anymore?" queried JJ.

"Yes, I am sort of retired… for the past three years. At 60 I was feed up of the daily chore of mine working, although lately it was an office job, and instead I bought a small bar in Kolwezi, called *Triangle de la Mort*" explained Bob.

"Not a very auspicious name" said JJ smiling.

"The bar already had that name when I bought it and was also well known in the area, so I did not want to mess around" clarified Bob.

"And how did you get to know, and become friends with PSS?" asked JJ

"It is a long story" started Bob "but let's say that I rescued a young girl from the street and that girl eventually linked me with PSS."

"A good action then" said JJ "very good."

"I want to be frank JJ. I run a bar-cum-brothel, but my girls are protected in many ways though" explained Bob.

"Many ways…" JJ left the sentence uncompleted.

"Before, they worked in the streets or in the outskirts of Kolwezi which is even worse from a safety point of view. They were often beaten, not paid by their customers who also liked to have unprotected sex" explained Bob "My place is safe for them."

"I understand now Bob" said JJ.

"I thought it was important to give you the full picture, before telling you something more about my recent relationship with PSS" continued Bob.

"So, you have something that you can add to the picture of the death of PSS?" queried JJ.

"I'm not sure, but it is worth putting on the table everything I know" explained Bob.

"I am all ears" JJ said eagerly.

"You see JJ, PSS was taking care of my girls. I mean their spiritual needs. But my friendship with PSS had also exposed him to the terrible conditions in which most of the mining occurs in and around Kolwezi" explained Bob.

"I see" proffered JJ. "And what might that have to do with the suicide of PSS?" asked JJ.

"I am just connecting the dots. And I may be mistaken JJ" continued Bob, "but you said that the possessions of PSS were not found, neither in his room at the hotel, nor in the building of the church in Kinshasa."

"Correct" confirmed JJ.

"Well…it just so happens that I know that PSS had got hold of some documents showing the dirty side of how the mining game is played. Something that PSS was planning to take to Paris and release to the press. He actually mentioned your name JJ" explained Bob.

"That's certainly an interesting angle to try and understand the suicide of PSS" agreed JJ.

"Suicide or murder?" exclaimed Bob.

"Murder?" repeated JJ, shocked.

"Come to my bar tomorrow morning, when it is quiet, and I will tell you the full story" explained Bob.

JJ did not sleep much that night; he could hear in his mind time and again the word 'murder' as it had sounded in the reedy accented English of Bob. He had always considered suspicious, inexplicable, the suicide of PSS and this new piece of information that Bob had provided, the incriminating documentation that had disappeared, provided an alternative explanation, a murder, that, however outlandish, could justify the many bizarre elements of the death of PSS. For instance, the head wound suffered by PSS may have been the result of violence inflicted before being 'suicided.' His smart dress, the pink tie, which JJ had found incongruous for someone preparing to commit suicide, would make sense in this context. He had probably been trapped by his assailants while in on one of his girl hunting evenings. The disappearance of his phone from which he would never part, as well as all his luggage that had probably included the documents Bob had described, probably the result of a commissioned theft-cum-homicide.

The following morning Chief Celestine's driver took JJ to the *Triangle de la Mort.* Located in a small road off Boulevard Kabila, the main thoroughfare of the town, the two-story building was rather discreet by DRC standards. Indeed, although painted in fluorescent pink, it did not explicitly display on the outside, any images of the human fare sold inside its premises, as typically done to attract clients in most of the other night clubs of the country. Posters with the names of the hostesses and the related price list of services provided were however shown on the side of the entrance of the venue. Noticing that the writing was in incongruous gothic characters, JJ thought that a German should have been the author. The name of the bar was illuminated by flashing lights of different colours to make sure that the building could be easily identified in the night in what would otherwise have been a dark road.

As soon as JJ stepped inside, noticing that the interior walls and ceiling were painted in the same blue sky as the church. He was welcomed by Bob who showed him around. At 10:00 am the venue was very quiet and almost deserted. Half of the ground floor was occupied by a bar area, on the right of which was a disco with all the trappings, while on the left of the bar was, of all the things unlikely to be found in such a venue, a chapel, the entrance of which was marked by a pink cross that JJ noticed had the same colour tone as PSS tie.

"In poor countries like the DRC" explained Bob, with a wry smile "sex and religion often go hand-in-hand. They help people cope with their many predicaments. Sex provides an immediate gratification, while religion, let me use a business expression, is the *long-term incentive.*"

"*Long term incentive...*" repeated JJ with astonishment.

"Religion promises heaven...but only in the afterlife. That's the *long term* I was referring to JJ" clarified Bob.

"I understand... well, sort of understand now. I guess that you and PSS had the whole thing covered, no?" said JJ smiling.

"You've got the point JJ. I knew you were an intelligent young chap" confirmed Bob "PSS would spend entire evenings and sometimes nights comforting both the customers and my girls."

"What is on the second floor of the building Bob?" queried JJ.

"My office and the girls' rooms. Ten rooms in fact, where they take care of their clients. From time to time, when they were alone, PSS would climb the stairs and provide them with one-to-one comfort sessions" explained Bob "that the girls enjoyed thoroughly."

"An impressive, well organised establishment" commented JJ.

"A German architect helped me out with the renovations" explained Bob.

JJ, with an inward smile, thought of the gothic writing. It all made sense, eventually. Will his visit to that bizarre bar-cum-brothel-cum-chapel make some sense also of the death (or murder?) of PSS? JJ hoped so.

Bob walked JJ to his office on the second floor. It was extremely well organised. It gave the sense of being a place where business was run efficiently, with a modern double screen laptop connected to a laser printer. A large TV, tuned to CNN, adorned one of the walls. The office table was in dark mahogany and the accompanying chairs were in real leather. Bob invited JJ to sit, offered him a strong Americano and for the next two hours talked him through the situation of mining in the DRC, and the documentation he had given PSS the day before his death.

Bob explained that: "Like many African countries, the DRC have been reaching out to China for many years, asking for help to build their infrastructure, like roads, factories, mines, etc. Usually, this has involved using loans relating to their natural resources. This was what Joseph Kabila did in 2005 when he was the president and the strong man of the DRC. Chinese companies, most of which Bush's US administration thought were *just* private enterprises, started flocking to DRC. Their investments, however, were paid for with Chinese government money, a lot of money. Just the five biggest Chinese mining companies had lines of credit worth over $120 billion from banks backed by the Chinese government. A good example of this *trojan horse* approach is well exemplified by China's *Molybdenum* mining company that, despite being funded by the Chinese government, describes itself as 'a pure business entity' and trade on two stock exchanges."

"With time, the Chinese state-backed mining enterprises took control of 15 out of 19 cobalt-producing mines in the DRC" Bob continued, "For many years cobalt was a not particularly valuable by-product of the mining of copper. However, for the last twenty years or so, with the advent of the *clean energy politics*, that is reducing dependence on fossil fuels and replacing it with renewable energies, like solar, wind, etc., the cobalt has become a highly valuable strategic chemical element. Its main use is in the Lithium-ion batteries needed, amongst other things, to propel electric cars."

"China's goal has always been to control the global supply chain from the metals in the ground to the batteries themselves, no matter where the vehicles were made" explained Bob "and the US was stupid enough to let them do it. Many important western mining outfits, like Anglo-Swiss Glencore or Arizona based Freeport-McMoRan, sold their DRC cobalt mines to the Chinese. The big picture is that the Chinese now have control not only on the production of most of the cobalt mined in the world, but also of its processing and marketing."

"In the process, what was already an only partially regulated business, because a lot of artisanal mining was occurring, had become even less regulated, because the Chinese like to keep their business away from public scrutiny" Bob stressed.

"And that's where the interest of PSS started. His concern was about the environment and human impact of cobalt mining, not the geopolitical side of it" explained Bob.

"I see" said JJ.

"You know JJ, PSS used to often tell his audience that DRC was at the centre of the universe because it is the only country with nine different international boundaries" continued Bob smiling "and I always found it amazing how PSS managed to excite his congregations through this nonsense."

"I remember one of his sermons on the subject while we waited to be received by the Chief of Staff of Kabila. It did not make any sense" said JJ. Then he remembered to have taken a picture of that sermon with his smartphone.

He immediately scrolled his gallery of images until identifying a grainy shot. PSS's right arm projecting to the audience something that probably was only in his mind, like the centre of the universe.

"Madness" commented Bob "Unless…unless you talk about Renewables. DRC really is at the *centre* of the *Renewable Universe*, so to speak. Its cobalt mines account for seventy per cent of all cobalt being produced globally."

"*Merde*!" said JJ "I really had no idea about this!"

"Many villages, located over good mining sites, have been first encroached on by the Chinese and then, with the complacency of the DRC authorities, have been bulldozed" explained Bob.

"What about the inhabitants of these villages?" asked JJ, rather naively.

"Obliged to move. No compensation" clarified Bob.

"Amazing" exclaimed JJ.

"Not in DRC my friend" explained Bob.

"I know, I am a French-African, and have lost touch with the ways of the black continent" admitted JJ.

"Obviously the environmental impact of many of these mining sites is disastrous. Especially now that the Western companies are out of the way. The Chinese have no share holders to worry, aside from the Chinese government, which is only interested in increasing production" continued Bob.

"I can imagine" replied JJ.

"And also, the safety of the employees is not a concern for the Chinese mining companies" explained Bob.

"Are there work injuries and deaths in excess of what was taking place when *Glencore* or *Freeport-McMoRan* were in charge?" asked JJ.

"Yes indeed. This is the case. More injuries and deaths" explained Bob "however it is difficult to prove it black-on-white because the Chinese oblige the injured employees to keep a low profile, lest they fire them, and make the bodies of the dead disappear."

"And so, what documents have you given to PSS" queried JJ "such that someone had an interest to kill him and make it seem like a suicide?"

"Have you ever heard of the *Tenke Fungurume* mine?" asked Bob.

"Not really Bob. Mining had never been an interest of mine…until today I mean" replied JJ with a smile.

"It is a very large cobalt mine. Eighty per cent of which was bought in 2016 by Chinese's *Molybdenum* from *Freeport-McMoRan* for $2.65 billion. The other 20% belongs to *Gécamines,* the state mining enterprise" Explained Bob.

"Shit!" said JJ "we are talking about big money."

"Also, big production. The mine currently produces around 15,500 tons of cobalt per year. For comparison the total cobalt production of the USA is 600 tons" explained Bob.

"Even more shit!" commented JJ.

"In a way, the history of this mine exemplifies the mining problems of DRC, the fact that what people living in Europe or North America call *clean energy*, is everything but *clean*, or *ethical* for that matter, when it comes to the mining of the minerals needed for the process" continued Bob.

"I am all ears" commented JJ.

"To start with, when the mine was still operated by *Freeport-McMoRan,* they forced out 1,500 villagers that lived within or in the proximity of the mining site. They just bulldozed their poor dwellings, no compensation or any plan B for where they would relocate."

"So even the gringos are bad!" commented JJ.

"Nobody in this, and indeed many other businesses, is an angel. However, subsequently *Freeport-McMoRan* had a very positive impact on the community. They built hospital, schools, etc. Not out of generosity, mind you, but because being publicly listed they were under the continuous scrutiny of their shareholders…and the free world's press which often, when China is involved, prefer to look the other way" explained Bob.

"Not all the press is muzzled, Bob. For instance, the magazine I work for is totally independent and if, from this inquiry I am conducting, comes something press worthy I will have no problem to get that published, irrespective of the political angle that I will need to take" said JJ "I will send you a copy, Bob."

"Let's go back to *Tenke Fungurume* mine" continued Bob.

"You see JJ, before completing the deal, the Chinese had a problem. *Freeport-McMoRan* had a Canadian partner that needed to be bought out. A Shanghai-based private equity firm bought this partner on behalf of *Molybdenum*" explained Bob.

"Sounds like a routine commercial transaction" commented JJ.

"Not so routine JJ. None of the $1.14 billion raised to buy the partner's share came from private investors. The filing shows that the money was funnelled through Chinese state-controlled entities" explained Bob.

"I start to understand now, Bob" commented JJ.

"The best is still to come though. The board of this so-called private equity firm, known as BHR, included three Americans: Devon Archer, a businessman who was later convicted of defrauding the Oglala Sioux tribe. James Bulger, the son of the former president of the Massachusetts State Senate and…this is the real gem JJ…Hunter Biden, the son of the then US vice president!" explained Bob.

"Great stuff Bob. You mean that not only is the US losing the commercial battle against Chinese dominance of the cobalt market, but also some of its elite, so to speak, considering the CV of the individuals you mentioned, are taking advantage of the deals made by the Chinese" commented JJ.

"Indeed" replied Bob "but let's go back to what happened once the Chinese started operating the mine."

"Cannot wait to hear" commented JJ.

"One problem that all mines in DRC have, is the stealing of minerals. Generally, this is not huge quantity, but enough to make feel some of the thieves rich enough to come to my venue to enjoy the profits of their scavenging" said Bob

"But often, the theft involves taking serious risks, like digging tunnels within or around producing mines. They often collapse and people are injured or die" explained Bob.

"So not just sex and religion, Bob. Also, sex and cobalt" laughed JJ.

"When the Chinese took over, they *hired,* so to speak, the army that then became their security outfit. And you know how the Congolese army is. They are not shy about using violence. And they did. They opened fire against trespassers or supposed trespassers and killed quite a few. The Chinese made sure to pay for the funerals and to give the family some backsheesh to keep them quiet" continued Bob.

"What a story" commented JJ.

"And the employee safety arrangements went south as well" explained Bob.

"I had no doubt about that. The Chinese lack of HSE commitment is well known" commented JJ.

"There have been many cases of accidents that could have been preventable. Lack of helmets, or safety harnesses for example. Something that *Freeport-McMoRan* would have never accepted and that, on the contrary, the Chinese encourage because it speeds up the production of cobalt" explained Bob.

"All this is interesting Bob, but still we do not have a smoking gun to explain why PSS would have been murdered" said JJ.

"Usually, it is difficult to get witnesses, reliable witnesses, willing to share their experience of working for the Chinese. But one of my customers turned out to be one of the security officials of the mine. He came one evening and was very distressed. He had witnessed a car crash between a truck hauling copper sheet and a truck carrying acid, which is used in the cobalt extraction process. He led a team to recover many bodies and many more seriously injured staff. Apparently both drivers had no experience with big trucks. Something he told me would never have happened before the Chinese took over" explained Bob.

"You mean that you found a whistle-blower?" asked JJ.

"In a way" replied Bob "someone who was fed up with covering up the truth, preparing false reports."

"By chance, was PSS in your venue that night?" asked JJ with a smile "I mean, taking care of the spiritual needs of his flock."

"Indeed. He was on the second floor with Lulu. I interrupted their… prayers and asked PSS to join me in my office where I had Papa Basinkiza, the security official of the mine" explained Bob.

"And how did it go?" queried JJ.

"They spoke until early morning of the next day. Papa Basinkiza was both distressed and afraid. He needed to unload his pain, but was afraid that if the Chinese discovered his leaks they would punish him, he could even lose his job" explained Bob.

"So, this Papa Bakinza…" said JJ

"Basinkiza, JJ" Bob corrected him.

"Whatever, he just hinted at a few vague incidents…and then was afraid to provide any concrete evidence, I guess" commented JJ.

"You know enough PSS…he used his charisma and…charm, like the one of DRC being the centre of the Universe, to convince Papa Basinkiza to empty the bag of his troubles, so to speak. And his bag contained not just hundreds of examples of incidents that could have been prevented if the Chinese had taken care of their employees, but also many of these were documented with pictures he had taken with his phone" explained Bob.

"Ah ha, I guess that these are the documents that have disappeared, along with the other possessions of PSS" commented JJ.

"Correct" replied Bob.

"Can we get hold of Papa Basinkiza and get a new set of copies?" asked JJ.

"Gone" replied Bob.

"What do you mean by 'gone'?" asked JJ.

"Papa Basinkiza disappeared a few days after his momentous visit to the *Triangle de la Morf*" explained Bob.

"Merde!" commented JJ "so we are left with only what you heard of his *confession,* so to speak, to PSS. Nothing that I could use to publish and further the investigation."

"I did not invite you to this blessed place just to chat of unsubstantiated rumours" commented Bob.

"??" JJ made a double question mark face.

"I have a digital copy of what Papa Basinkiza gave to PSS" explained Bob with a smile "here is the USB drive with pictures, documents, and the write up of his *confession*, to use your expression."

JJ plugged the USB drive into his laptop, but before he could have a glance at its content, Bob gestured to wait.

"Before you dig into it, let's have some lunch first" said Bob. He pressed a button from a contraption resting on his desk and a few minutes later the famous Lulu arrived with hamburgers and fries from the local equivalent of a McDonald's, and also a few bottles of Primus. To the relief of JJ, the hamburgers were made of beef.

JJ, always attracted by ladies, noticed that Lulu could have not been defined as beautiful, or certainly not beautiful by the current western standards, where models needed to be *size zero.* She was neither tall nor short; in any case, the first thing JJ observed was Lulu's cleavage, which was generously exposed by her skimpy and colourful shirt. Her ample hips filled the tight trousers and contrasted with a thin waist. Her meaty and protruding lips were a promise of some sort. 'Not beautiful then, but attractive; no surprise that PSS had spent time comforting her spiritual needs' thought JJ smiling.

With lunch finished, and with Bob's guidance, JJ spent several hours reviewing the pictures and documents contained in the USB drive. Some of the pictures were very graphic, showing Congolese who had died or had been badly injured as a result of the mining activities. There was a full section dealing with child labour. Children as young as 3 working in informal mines carrying heavy sacks containing the precious cobalt ore, the mines mostly consisted of deep and unsafe tunnels carved for tens of meters into the ground around the mines produced industrially. The picture showed an environment where holes, mud and humanity were mingled. 'A modern representation of Dante's *Inferno*' JJ thought.

"Technically, the Chinese corporations have nothing to do with this aspect of mining" explained Bob "however the traders that buy the ore from informal mines sell it to the major corporations; hence they are all in the game."

JJ noticed several pictures showing the environmental disasters caused by the disposal of the acid used for the extraction of the minerals from the ore. Land areas devastated and water bodies contaminated. Most of the written documents were internal memos and emails in which some of these accidents had been reported by Papa Basinkiza, either without getting any response from his boss or much worse, just being told to shut up.

"This is serious stuff" commented JJ "I could prepare an article or actually a series of articles about this. A scandal of no interest to the western press. It is a dark paradox that the so-called clean energy of the west comes from the pollution and exploitation of labour and children of the third world."

"The west has a tradition of outsourcing their work to emerging countries with a cheap labour force; now they have also outsourced the pollution needed for their so-called green energy" commented Bob.

"...and they close their eyes in the face of the environmental disasters and human exploitation so as not to feel guilty!" concluded JJ angrily.

"I trust you now understand why I think there is a link between the death, which I think is a murder, of PSS and the information he had gathered from Papa Basinkiza" asked Bob.

"Absolutely" replied JJ.

"What about if we were able to identify who killed PSS and have a confession of some sort?" asked Bob.

"That would be the nail in the coffin, sorry for my unintended pun" replied JJ.

"Well, I have asked Chief Célestin to help in that part of the investigation" explained Bob, "he has a prominent position in our society and enough of a network to scout for clues that the police would not even be able to recognise."

Several days passed before Chief Célestin came up with some leads. During this period Bob gave JJ one of the upstairs rooms, so as to avoid having to pick him up every day from the church. As a result, JJ became acquainted with the hostesses; other than the famous Lulu he could also observe the business routine of the *Triangle de la Mort*, where most of the action started after dark. Business was anything but continuous and relied mostly on *creuseurs* (mineral diggers) having achieved the jackpot. Or what they considered to be a jackpot …pocketing $100 in a day, in a country where that often represented the income of one year. This made them feel rich enough to spend some of the money in drinks and relaxation at venues like the bar-cum-brothel of Bob.

Eventually Chief Célestin showed up with a few of his guys escorting a young Congolese, bruised from head to toe.

"Nous l'avons eu (we got him)" said Chief Célestin before continuing "Comme on dit: un secret c'est quelque chose qu'on dit à une personne à la fois (like they say: a secret is something you tell one person at the time)."

"C'est l'idiot qui a tué PSS? (that's the idiot who killed PSS)" asked Bob.

"Il l'a fait tout seul ? (He did it alone?)" asked JJ.

"Non mais l'autre a disparu comme ton papa Basinkiza (no, but the other one has disappeared, like your Papa Basinkiza)" explained Chief Célestin.

"Et qu'en est-il de lui ? (And what about him?)" asked Bob.

"Il a eu peur et se cachait chez des parents à Tambo (He got scared and was hiding with relatives in Tambo)" explained Chief Célestin.

"Et comment l'as-tu attrapé ? (And how did you get hold of him?)" asked JJ.

"Nous avons envoyè un message aux aînés tribaux. L'un était lié à la famille hébergeant Gnugu, c'est le nom de ce type (we sent a message to the tribal seniors. One was related to the family hosting Gnugu, that's the name of this guy)" explained Chief Célestin.

"Et ensuite tu l'as battu pour avouer le crime ? (And then you beat him to confess the crime?)" asked JJ.

"Nous ne l'avons pas battu. C'est la famille qui l'hébergeait lorsqu'elle a découvert ce qu'il a fait. Il a eu de la chance que nous l'ayons éloigné d'eux. Ils l'auraient tué (We did not beat him. It was the family hosting him when they discovered what he had done. He was lucky we took him away from them. They would have killed him)" explained Chief Célestin.

"Je comprends (I see)" replied JJ.

"Qu'allons-nous faire de lui Bob? (What shall we do with him Bob?)" asked Chief Célestin.

"Nous avons besoin d'un aveu, je doute que le gars sache écrire cependant, enregistrons simplement ce qu'il a à nous dire (we need a confession, I doubt the guy knows how to write though, let's just record what he has to tell us)" replied Bob.

Which Gnugu eventually did, lest he would be returned to his relatives in Tombo, which was a deadly option for him, literally. He had been working in one of the informal mines, part time illegal diggers, part time thieves, and had been recruited together with his now disappeared accomplice by another Congolese miner working at *Tenke Fungurume* mine. They had been paid for the job, an advance of 350 Euros and the same amount, for a total of 700 Euros (a fortune by DRC standards) after they proved with pictures that the murder had been accomplished simulating a suicide. PSS had resisted being constrained and they had to beat him, which explained the bruise on his head. While it showed a connection between the murder of PSS to the information he had received from Papa Basinkiza, the confession of Gnugu did not demonstrate any direct Chinese connection. The minds behind the murder had been smart enough to create a spiderweb to make their connection to the actual killers opaque. In any case they had probably planned to make the two killers disappear afterwards.

Having completed the recording of his confession, the wretched Gnugu was taken away by Chief Célestin and his men.

"I think I now have enough information to write a series of articles" said JJ, pleased that he now knew for a fact how PSS had died "make sure, however, that Gnugu does not die. He may well need to come to France as a witness once the French government is informed of the murder of PSS."

"No problem" said Bob "we will take care of him."

The evening had descended on Kolwezi and the sound of business being taken care of permeated the *Triangle de La Mort.*

"We need to celebrate the success of the investigation" said Bob.

"What do you mean, Bob?" asked JJ with a wry smile.

"You just go up to your room, JJ" replied Bob "I will take care of the organisation of a small party and join you shortly."

Half an hour later led by Bob, the girls, food and drinks arrived. Lulu, Evelyn and Princess dressed in their most revealing outfits and started teasing JJ. And then they partied, and what a party, lasting until the early hours of the next day.

On his flight back to Paris, JJ daydreamed. However sad he felt for the murder of PSS, he was pleased that he had uncovered the plot behind his death. And even more than that, he was enjoying the expectation of surprising his boss with his piece of investigative journalism. While on the plane he had finalised the draft of his article that included some of the most poignant pictures he had retrieved from the Papa Basinkiza USB drive. The write-up was divided into three chapters; at first glance the first two appeared unconnected. The last chapter, however, provided the link between all the elements previously described making the story compelling, or at least that's what JJ thought of the result of his work.

He started with the description of the discovery of the bruised body of PSS. The police report that classified the death as a suicide. The incongruence's: the fact that PSS could have dressed *formally* before taking his own life, the bruise in his forehead, the missing personal effects, which could not be located even in his churches of Kinshasa and Kolwezi. In the second chapter JJ summarised the story of the colonization of the original Congo. He briefly described how King Leopold of Belgium had used it as his own personal colony for decades, condoning in the process, some of the most horrendous atrocities against the local population ever enacted in black Africa by a colonial power, only to eventually let the Belgian concern UMHK take over the mining and trading of ores. Until, in modern times, when certain minerals, like cobalt, had become critical for the world's renewables technological advances. Katanga, the richest part of the DRC, from a mineral wealth standpoint, had seen the arrival of US, UK and Swiss mining giants that eventually had been, by and large, replaced by Chinese mining companies acting on behalf of and funded by the Chinese government. The unsafe working conditions that had resulted, the child labour, the pollution and other environmental disasters were all documented. Finally, in the third chapter he presented the case history of the *Tenke Fungurume* mine and linked it, like in a good thriller novel, to the death, actually the murder, of PSS. The decision made by PSS to reveal to the press the misdeeds that had occurred and on which Papa Basinkiza had provided a comprehensive documentation. He did not have the smoking gun to directly connect any of the Chinese companies to the actual murderers of PSS; JJ left the reader to jump to his own conclusions about who would have benefitted from silencing PSS.

When he landed in Paris early in the morning, he felt the urge for a good black *espresso* and a few *pains au chocolat*, the delicacies he had longed for during his time in the DRC. Then he took a taxi and went straight to the office of *La Fraternité*.

"Tu ne peux que plaisanter JJ (You can only be joking JJ)" said Claude Signoret after having reviewed JJ's draft article "Ce que vous avez ramené de près d'un mois passé en RDC, ce ne sont que des bribes, qui d'un point de vue enquête sont inutiles. Vous ne pouviez pas les amener devant un tribunal pour prouver quoi que ce soit (What you brought back from almost a month spent in DRC are just bits and pieces, that from an investigative point of view are useless. You could not take them to a tribunal to prove anything)."

"Nous devrions au moins faire savoir au gouvernement français qu'un de leurs citoyens a probablement été tué en RDC, sous la direction d'un gouvernement étranger (We should at least make the French government aware that one of their citizens has probably been killed in DRC, under the direction of a foreign government)" replied JJ.

"T'es fou, personne ne s'intéresse au meurtre d'un putain de Pasteur noir en RDC (You are crazy, nobody is interested in the murder of a fucking black Pastor in DRC)" exclaimed Claude Signoret with an angry face.

"Eh bien, au moins vous avez commencé à parler de *meurtre* plutôt que de *suicide*. Évidemment, j'ai touché une corde sensible… (Well, at least you have started talking about *murder* rather than *suicide*. Evidently, I struck a chord...)" replied JJ raising his voice.

"Juste un lapsus JJ. Il n'y a aucune preuve que votre maudit Pasteur ait été tué par les Chinois (Just a lapse JJ. There is no proof that your bloody Pasteur was killed by the Chinese)" stated Claude Signoret.

"Les Chinois avaient toutes les motivations pour garder secrète leur ingérence en RDC. Le fait qu'ils contrôlent désormais pratiquement toute la production et la fabrication du cobalt. Leur absence de procédure de sécurité. La pollution qui détruit les rivières et les forêts. Ils ont l'Ouest par les couilles, pardonnez mon français, mais pas nous (The Chinese had all the motivation to keep secret their meddling in DRC. The fact that they now virtually control all the production and manufacturing of cobalt. Their lack of safety procedure. The pollution that destroys rivers and forests. They have the West by the balls, pardon my French, but not us)" replied JJ, his voice still raised.

"Notre magazine ne peut rien publier qui puisse être considéré comme négatif par les Chinois (Our magazine cannot publish anything that could be considered negative by the Chinese)" commented Claude Signoret.

"Que voulez-vous dire? (What do you mean?)" asked JJ with a dismayed face.

"JJ, pensez-vous vraiment que nos ventes couvrent les frais d'édition de *La Fraternité*? (JJ, do you really think that our sales cover the cost of publishing *La Fraternité*?)" Claude Signoret asked rhetorically with a thin smile.

"Je ne sais pas, tu es l'homme d'affaires (I don't know, you are the business man)" admitted JJ, his face showing the delusion that had taken hold of his soul.

"Bon, je peux vous dire que mon salaire, mon pot de retraite ainsi que les indemnités de merde que vous recevez de temps en temps sont essentiellement dus à la gentillesse de nos amis chinois (Well, I can tell you that my salary, my pension pot as well as the shit compensation that you receive from time to time are essentially due to the kindness of our Chinese friends)" explained Claude Signoret.

"Vous voulez dire que nous sommes financés par le gouvernement chinois? (You mean that we are financed by the Chinese government ?)" asked JJ.

"Non, ils ne sont pas si stupides JJ (No, they are not so stupid JJ)" replied Claude Signoret.

"Et alors, comment obtenez-vous l'argent? (And so how do you get the money ?)" asked JJ.

"Je voulais dire que plusieurs sociétés fictives, enregistrées dans divers pays du monde, nous soutiennent avec des subventions. J'ai enquêté sur qui se cache derrière ces entreprises… après tout, je suis journaliste d'investigation et j'ai découvert qu'elles sont toutes liées à une société privée enregistrée à Hong Kong, du nom de *Silk Road Friendship Industries* (I meant that several shell companies, registered in various nations worldwide support us with grants. I did investigate who is behind these companies…after all I am an investigative journalist, and discovered that they are all linked to a *private* company registered in Honk Kong, by the name of Silk *Road Friendship Industries)*" explained Claude Signoret.

"Donc, je suppose que les Chinois ne peuvent pas être touchés (So, I guess that the Chinese cannot be touched)" said JJ with an angry face.

"Cher JJ, il y a beaucoup de scandales et de corruption en Occident. C'est le pain et le beurre de notre magazine. Et je vous recommande de vous concentrer sur cela, oubliez votre truc avec la Chine et je m'assurerai que vos dépenses en RDC seront prises en charge (Dear JJ, there is plenty of scandal and corruption in the West. That's the bread and butter of our magazine. And I recommend you focus on this, forget about your China thing and I will make sure your DRC expenses will be taken care)" explained Claude Signoret with a smile.

And that was the end of the investigation into the suspicious death of Pasteur Sauveterre. The only long-lasting legacy of JJ's inquiry was the antibiotic resistant *clap* Lulu had given him, on-the-house as Bob would have wryly remarked, due to a defective Chinese condom.

Chapter 5
Geologists Anonymous
Switzerland and Northern Italy, Fall 2035

He dreams of being twenty-three years old again, working on a rig off the Adriatic coast.

Armando longed for the symphony of the summer rain splashing on the greasy rig floor; the joy of the early morning breakfast with warm, just baked bread and Parma ham, after a night spent *coring* (why did all *coring operations*, the collection of rock and sediment samples with a coring drill bit designed with a central opening, occur at night, this was a mystery that no scientist had ever completely unravelled.) The simple satisfaction of picking up the hydrocarbon pay zones in the preliminary log runs undertaken by Schlumberger, followed by the eager devouring of the mussels gathered by the rig divers from the submerged legs of the nearby production platforms that would be served for lunch, cooked in white wine. The wonderful inebriating whiff of gasoline brought by the chopper landing on the rig, which signified the end of his offshore shift accompanied by the rising anticipation of romantic adventures ashore, that so often remained just dry dreams. These, after all, were the memories of his youth, not just of his profession. But it was difficult for the old Armando to distinguish one from the other.

Every night before a *Geologists Anonymous* meeting, he always relived in his dreams, and sometimes nightmares, the often-conflicting emotions related to the work he had carried out for many years across the world. Every night, a different dream would morph into a nightmare after which he would wake up and realise, not only that he had aged but that for being in hiding, he had to limit his diet to seasonal vegetables and fruits, rather than the simple but rich fare he had consumed during his working days. In the right seasons, the berries that the vegan community gathered from the nearby woods were a pleasant change to the otherwise monotonous and limited diet. Once a month, however, he would ride his horse across the Italian border to Gerola Alta for his *Geologists Anonymous* meeting.

Means of transportation were limited in this new world. Combustion fuel vehicles had been completely banned in 2030 and only rich people could afford to buy and maintain electric cars. And even for them, having to continuously change the cotton/metallic tires that had replaced the traditional ones, whose rubber required among other components the use of petrochemical resins, was so expensive, that many electric cars were now found abandoned on the side of the road. Indeed, the stealing of *traditional tires* from the old car models had become so rampant that *Neighbourhood Tire Vigilantes* had been born and lynching was common for thieves caught in the act. The thieves apprehended by the regular law enforcers fared no better in the US, where a law had been passed to punish them with death by hanging, in a strange way, very similar to what had happened in the American west with the rustling of horses and cattle two centuries before. Therefore, horses and donkeys were the typical means of transportation; only the wealthier few among the impoverished population could afford even horse drawn carts.

Strolling in the village, negotiating the acrid fumes of the wood stoves which were the only source of energy left, and crossing from time-to-time other horse or donkey riders reminded Armando of an Amish community in Bolivia, where he had done some geological mapping. But at least the Amish compensated for their lack of electricity and modern comforts with an intense sex life, as evidenced by the numerous children each family had. His vegan community, conversely, was largely sexless because it was so hard to produce and gather enough food to just survive that any sex drive had virtually disappeared with the permanent exhaustion. The implementation of organic cultivation on a massive scale, that is to say without pesticides and other treatments to protect the crops, had dramatically reduced the harvests. In the old times, more than twenty treatments were routinely required to maximize the apple harvest and preserve the crop from its natural enemies. Now, with no treatment legally allowed, only 10 percent of the harvest survived nature and was still edible. In times past, the organic products were expensive and available only to rich people. Now it was the same, however *traditionally grown products* had been banned and therefore the majority of people did not have enough to feed themselves properly.

Actually, on deeper reflection Armando realised that rather than an Amish village, the world in which he lived was like a post-nuclear war society, except no nuclear war had occurred. The hardship had just been self-imposed. And only in the western world.

He remembered that, for a while at least, the Engadin valley where he was hiding had plenty of electricity produced by hydroelectric power stations. Their steel turbines powered by the gravity flow of the water of the many man-made dams that dotted the valley. As green an energy as Armando could ever think. But then the *Super Grün* party had won the election and their leader, Annete Wilken, *une dur and pur ecologiste*, had realised that most of the spare parts needed to keep the hydroelectric plants working were produced in China using coal fired power plants, the least green of the fossil fuels. As a result, new legislation had been passed in Switzerland prohibiting the importation of any product made in China. Within a few years this had resulted, among other things, in the hydroelectric power stations stopping working for lack of spare parts. Idle and rusting they were now monuments of a time gone by. School children were taught of the times, *the bad times*, when the Swiss hydroelectric network contributed to worldwide pollution, and not having lived those times of plenty, they passively accepted the narrative. That *today's times are better*, that was the government's narrative; although everybody knew that the cutting down and logging of trees, however illegal, was rife in order to keep warm in the long and harsh winters. The increasingly barren mountain sides would often source deadly landslides that, together with the limited access to energy, was presented by the *Super Grün* as a small price to pay for the progress that would eventually result in a better world.

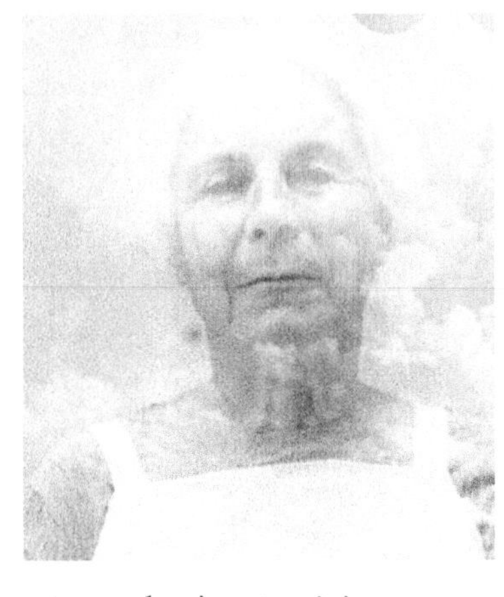

They were not sure who had first recognised a kindred spirit in the other. They had met, by chance, in the hills at the boundary between Italy and Switzerland (is there really *chance* in life or maybe what we call *by chance* should be called *by courage* because it happens only when we have the *courage* to go out of our *zone of comfort*?). They both, independently, were gathering *porcini*, a very precious type of wild mushroom, to spice up their otherwise bland diet. Armando had noted Annabelle's mastery of maps (she even knew how to orient them, which he knew was an acquired skill), the nervous tic in her right finger often associated to the users of Petrel, an interpretation software used by the oil industry and as such, now banned. He had known immediately that she was a geoscientist of some type. Conversely, Annabelle had noted a range of small, but special traits of Armando that had been sufficient to unravel to her keen eye his past profession. His oil rig swagger, the swearing that he could hardly contain when faced with idiotic problems, his jittery plucking of a beard long gone. She had immediately classified Armando as a *recovering geologist*, someone who was suffering from *geological abstinence*. Annabelle had also realised that Armando was like a spiky fig, that below his hard and pungent skin, was hidden an intense sweetness.

She wished to invite him to the monthly secret meetings she had organized for individuals affected by *geological withdrawal syndrome*, but she needed to be sure that she had not misinterpreted his body language.

"Paleozoic" Annabelle nonchalantly said, with the same intonation she would have used to cheer a stranger with a "Good Morning."

Armando was taken aback. This was a dangerous word that he had not heard for many years. Maybe he had misunderstood what she had said, possibly her strong French accent was the culprit of the misunderstanding.

"Paleozoic" Annabelle repeated, this time as a sort of imploration but with a broad smile.

Armando was now sure he had heard her well the first time and smiled back.

"Trilobite" he replied.

They hugged. The felt the safety of being at home, of touching each other without fear.

When later, they had enjoyed a moment of intimacy among the birches and the pines, Armando had noted with surprise, that Annabelle's back was fully covered by a large tattoo with a detailed rendition of the *Three Graces* of Botticelli.

'A lady of the Renaissance' thought Armando with pleasure.

The zone where the *Geologists Anonymous* meetings were held was considered safe. Or as safe as anything could be for a recluse *Fossil Fuel Professional.* The majority of the population were just vegetarian, not vegan, and reared cattle to prepare cheese, also keeping chickens for their eggs. However, from time to time, the *No Cheese - No Eggs*, a violent far-left fringe of the vegan community, would roam down the valley and into the village on their war horses to punish the individuals who did not follow their strict vegan-communism. In the name of ecology, they would then slaughter any cow or chicken that they came across. Farmers were killed and their properties burnt down. Criminals, that in their view were guilty of the sin of rearing animals. Nothing like this had been seen in Europe since Attila's times.

It would take a couple of days for Armando to reach his destination and he used his solitary time on horseback to reflect on the changes he had experienced in the last period of his life, well the last ten years or so at least.

The arrival of green energy in Europe had been initially accepted with joy by most people. The farmers had given away large swaths of arable land to install solar panels. Obviously, the EU had provided subsidies that made it more profitable for them to *plant* Photovoltaic Panels than growing maize or wheat. Wind turbines had also popped up on every slope and mountain, mainly on land that had been confiscated by the EU, replacing large orchards of apple, pear and cherry trees among others. This had caused some initial resentment by the landowners, that however had subsided quickly thanks to the large bonuses that the EU bureaucrats had eventually agreed.

All had worked fine for a couple of years. Until the food supplies had started running out due to the greatly reduced amount of arable land. The EU had insisted that people needed to change diet, lose weight, become vegetarian or, even better, vegan. The EU had indeed stressed that the problem was with people's insistence on sticking to their old-time diet, and absolutely not with the food chain. Multimillion Euro advertising campaigns had been run to instil the politically correct view to the masses.

Switzerland, not being part of the EU, had followed its own approach to energy transition. However, at a certain point, the electricity supply had started to falter. The ban on Chinese imports had not only affected the hydroelectric power stations but also the Wind turbines (whose steel was mostly produced by China) as well as the fields of Photovoltaic cells, that required *polysilicon,* that was also mostly produced by China. Armando remembered, that once the oil products had been totally exhausted (and could not be replaced because oil and gas derivatives had been banned) among other problems, the Wind Turbines could not be defrosted in winter and eventually had remained on the hills and slopes like monuments reminding the old people, the ones that had lived before the *Super Grün* took power, of the wrong choices made in the name of ecology.

Armando decided to call it a day. He left the main road, trekking uphill until finding a comfortable place where he could set up his tent among the golden larch trees. In a few weeks they would become completely bare but at that moment the foliage underneath was colourful and soft. Like his sleeping bag, the tent also was a relic of the pre-Energy Transition era. Both were made of a combination of nylon and polyester, that is oil products, they could not be produced anymore, in the western world. And therefore, Armando treasured them like gold. From time to time, he would need to mend them but he knew that the alternative, the silk and wool sleeping bags currently produced, were expensive and beyond his means, and indeed the means of most of the population. Also, his windcheater, made of warm and impermeable microfibres derived from oil, was something for which there was no proper replacement. The pure wool raincoats promoted by the ecologists were not really water proof, let alone that they were heavy and not really practical for Armando's journeys by horse.

He was aware of the smuggling from China of many products that the west could not produce anymore without hydrocarbons. For instance, *traditional medicine* required drugs, like analgesics, antihistamines, antibiotics, antibacterial gels for which petrochemicals were essential. *Silk Road Friendship Industries* produced an Aspirin equivalent that was a big hit on the black market of Europe and the US, just like in the old times had been cocaine or heroin. Those who had no money for black market medicines or were ecological purists resorted to the *green medicine* of yoga, meditation or plant infusions. The result was that infections that would be preventable using *traditional medicine* were now ravaging entire communities to an extent last experienced in Europe in the Middle Ages.

Once upon a time, dentures had been made of acrylic resin, which was derived from hydrocarbons; now only expensive metal work was allowed. As a result, many people were going without teeth, which forced them onto a strict plant and fruit-based diet, that was considered a win-win by the *Greens* and the left leaning parties.

Sixty-year-old, heavily built, *Mastro* Giuseppe, as he was known locally, manufactured one of the best *Bitto* cheeses of the Valtellina valley. He made the cheese from whole cow's milk produced in the summer months when the cows feed in the high alpine meadows. To which, he later added 20% of goat's milk to allow for a long aging that could easily take 10 years or more. This cheese was the mountain equivalent of the more famous *Parmigiano Reggiano* that was, on the contrary, produced in the Po Valley and was equally as expensive.

But the production of cheese, though done with love, was only a cover for the real activities of *Mastro* Giuseppe. His son had been a *Fossil Fuel Geologist,* one of those that had been snatched up by the *Green Jackets* and now was either dead or living a life of forced labour in China. There had been no information, so no one knew where he was. From that moment, *Mastro* Giuseppe had declared war on the *Greens*, albeit a subtle war, which included hosting the monthly sessions of the *Geologist Anonymous* charter of Northern Italy and Switzerland in a cave that he had especially prepared under his home, built on the slopes of one of the hills of the area.

Each attendee had his own password to access the cave. For Annette and Armando, these were 'Paleozoic' and 'Trilobite', respectively, but others had more exotic passwords that provided a direct link to where they came from. For instance, Hussain used 'Zagros', a mountain chain from his country, Iran. Two Italian geologists also regularly attended the meetings: Nicoletta used 'Rosso Ammonitico'; a reddish limestone typical of the Apennines, while Ubaldo, from southern Tuscany, had adopted the password of 'Travertino', a hydrothermal limestone which was abundant in his region.

That particular evening was the first time that Hussein, an Iranian national with a US passport, after having been extensively vetted by Annette, had joined the group, and it was his turn to introduce himself and lead the conversation.

"I was 15 and living a privileged life in Tehran in 1969, although I did not know that at the time" Hussein explained to the audience, "when the first lunar landing occurred. The TV images were just black and white and probably grainier than in more advanced countries, like the US or Britain. I was fascinated by the *ingenuity* and *science* that had driven and made possible that feat and thought that the future of humanity depended on these two complementary qualities."

"I see that you are taking us through a long journey Hussain" Armando, commented smiling.

"In a way, I am Armando" conceded Hussain, "but it is important to understand the roots of my predicament."

"Feel free to take all the time you need Hussain" said Annabelle who knew the importance of unburdening for recovering geologists.

"I had to escape from Iran, my beloved country, shortly after Khomeini took power in 1989. His regime, supported by bigots and people taking advantage of the religious aspect for their personal interests and even, sometimes, obsessions, was as opposite to my view of the world as could possibly exist. The US gave me a refuge. I did my utmost to integrate in that society. I had already my degree in geology from the Tehran University, which was eventually recognised in my new adoptive country. I used my expertise in structural geology, matured while working in the Zagros mountains, to help with finding oil and gas in the 'Rockies'. Denver, after all, had a climate similar to Tehran but with less pollution. I loved it. I must confess that I converted in the process..."

"From being Muslim to become Christian?" Armando asked with curious eyes.

"No. Not that" laughed Hussein "I meant that I converted from being a *honey eater* to discover and absolutely love the *maple syrup*. The real one though, collected from the bark of the maple trees, not the sugary stuff to which they add some maple flavouring."

"That may explain your belly" commented Annette with a sardonic smile.

"You see" continued Hussain "I thought that this was my dream country. Not perfect by any standards, but where I could express myself freely."

"And then what happened?" asked Armando who sensed that Hussein's experience in the US had turned sour.

"Gradually a new mood and view of the world, pushed at the time by the *greens* took over the stage" explained Hussein before adding "and you could sense that the world in which we were living was changing, gradually, but irreversibly. And not for the better."

"What was your first experience of the changes" queried Nicoletta.

"I could give you many examples but one that crystallises the concept I am trying to explain is the food evolution at the *Galleria* in Houston you know the place, the upscale mall" pointed out Hussein.

"Explain please" asked Annabelle.

"You see, even though based in Denver I travelled often to Houston, the capital of the international oil industry at the time," explained Hussein, "I would stay at the *Westin Galleria* and go for breakfast at *Zucchini's*, a friendly Italian place on the upper floor of the Galleria."

"I have actually heard of that place" commented Annabelle "I understand they serve quite gargantuan breakfasts."

"They did in the old times" explained Hussein, "I used to eat there for breakfast what they called the *Texan pancakes stack*. Three thick pecan pancakes, so large that they would not fit on the large plates used for serving them, plenty of real butter and maple syrup until they dripped with the golden liquid."

"I can visualise the scene" commented Armando sucking his teeth longingly.

"But then, gradually, things changed" continued Hussein, "the size of the pancakes reduced, then there were no pecan nuts to be seen anymore. Later, there was margarine replacing the butter which was just 'pour le cinema' as the French say, because margarine is not really any healthier than butter. Eventually, also the maple syrup was replaced by a golden liquid that did not contain either maple nor sugar."

"A terrible evolution" commented Annette.

"And then even the pancakes were not *pancakes* anymore" continued Hussein.

"What do you mean?" asked Armando.

"Instead of flour they started using a batter made of zucchini, banana and eggs. Then even the banana was removed because of the sugar content. Finally, the Vegans obliged even the removal of the eggs from the batter. They were renamed *hot zucchini cakes*" explained Hussein frowning.

"At least the name was appropriate for the venue" joked Armando.

"And what happened next?" Annette asked with curiosity.

"Zucchini's went bankrupt, and that's it" concluded Hussein.

"I suppose, however" intervened Ubaldo "that you did not leave the US only for the *failed evolution* so to speak of the Zucchini's pancakes."

"The *mutations* of the pancakes were the symptoms of a much bigger disease that eventually spread across all of US society and culture, and then, I must say, from the US eventually to most of the so-called free world" explained Hussein.

"You mean the cancel culture?" queried Annette who was always one step ahead of the audience.

"Exactly Annette, you got the point" replied Hussein with a sad smile "hundreds of years of culinary traditions were destroyed in the space of a decade. They even tried to make people feel guilty for their innocent gastronomic pleasures. Eating a steak became either a crime or an act of courage, depending on the points of view, rather than simply an individual dietary choice."

"And that was enough for you to consider leaving the US?" asked Nicoletta with a whimsical smile on her face. For the record Nicoletta had been a vegetarian even before the *new world* frowned up the *meatarians* and therefore, had not been a fossil fuels geologist, she would have adapted without any difficulty to the imposed food restrictions.

"Again, all of these events were symptoms of a much bigger malaise" continued Hussein "that eventually led a minority, however vociferous but still a minority, to impose their idealistic view of the world."

"Idealistic?" asked Annette.

"I did not mean *idealistic* as a compliment; I meant in the sense of *not practicable*" explained Hussein "or at least *not practicable* if the wellbeing of the people was considered."

"I understand now" confirmed Annette "obviously the cancel culture was not just restricted to food choices but extended to denying the nation's history."

"For me, an Iranian who had fled Khomeini, it was like as if this devil had conquered the US. Nobody could express an opinion that was different from *theirs* without being accused of being fascist or worse" Hussein pointed out.

"The additional problem was, and is, that the general level of education of the children has gone down the drain" commented Annette "the children born in the last 10 years belong to the *No Books* generation. The natural evolution of the *No Everything* groups. Their opinions are not based on facts; that would require studying. Their attention span is less than that of a gold fish on acid. They only believe what is posted on *Zingtube,* the *metaverse* application of the Joint Venture between *YouTube* and Mr Zing of *Silk Road Friendship Industriess.*"

"And you can be sure that these very short, full immersion videos make the point well. I mean the Chinese point" commented Hussein "Their view of the perfect world. For them and the *No Books*, this is the world we live in now, obviously. They have even released a tutorial on how to send a rocket to the moon. The *No Books* felt empowered. Even such a technical feat could be achieved without wasting time, having to attend a university, wasting money to obtain a technical degree. You could just watch an enhanced reality tutorial on *Zingtube* and wow!...you knew enough to put a man, a Chinese man, on the moon again."

"And then the witch hunt against the oil industry started…" commented Armando.

"Indeed, Armando" said Hussein "and if for you guys in Italy it was just a nuisance, simply because you have a very small oil industry, for the oil professionals in the US it was a real nightmare. After the Democratic party took power in 2020, they did their best to demonise and demolish an industry that had provided wealth and energy to the country for centuries."

"Yes, in thrall to the green lobby, I remember they stopped the construction of several pipelines and the issuing of new exploration leases…" Annette commented.

"And, as a result when the economy picked up after the Covid scare we did not have enough domestically produced energy. Fuel prices went off the scale and Biden asked the Saudi's to increase their oil production so that the US ecologists driving their large SUV's would stop complaining about the increase in the fuel bills" stressed Hussein before continuing "that was the time I started planning to leave the US."

"You realised that next thing would be the witch hunt against the oil people, correct?" asked Annette.

"Yes. To me, a survivor of Khomeini, it was obvious what would happen, but not for many of my colleagues that had not lived the extremes that dictatorial regimes end up imposing to their citizens" explained Hussein.

"Dictatorial regimes?" asked Armando.

"The democratic party in the US is led by a group of leftists that could have made the Soviet Union proud during the cold war" explained Hussein.

"I think you are exaggerating" commented Armando who still had a positive view of the US.

"Well…when Senator Redondo Cortez took charge of Homeland, the US security department, the first thing she did was to require all the oil industry professionals to register in, what at time, we referred to as *the black oil list*" explained Hussein "Much like the KGB and its successor FSB have done in Russia with the dissidents."

"I did not know that" admitted Armando.

"One day I discovered that my phone had been tapped" continued Hussein "and realised that it was time to leave."

"Was this before or after the *Hydrocarbon Cessation Act*?" asked Annette who was very much into the legal side of things.

"Before" confirmed Hussein "I managed to leave the US before that legislation had been implemented."

"Good for you" commented Nicoletta.

"I once read a book called *The Survivor Club* by a guy called Ben Sherwood" continued Hussein "in which he states that in moments of serious danger the majority of people react by ignoring the problem. A small portion do the wrong things and only a few, 10 per cent of less, not only understand the situation but also do the right things to survive."

"You certainly were one of these few" commented Annette.

"Indeed Annette" confirmed Hussein "most of my colleagues took the stance that the US, being one of the cradles of democracy could not possibly start discriminating against individuals based on their profession, let alone race etc. How wrong they were. The ones that are not dead are mostly being re-educated by the Chinese, of all people!, in Xinjiang province."

"But why, of all places, did you decide to hide in Italy?" asked Nicoletta.

"I thought it was a safe bet: a small oil industry in the country, so most people have no idea what a geologist looks like, and also it is a very bureaucratic state that I doubted would implement effectively the *Fossil Fuel Professional Act* issued by the EU, the law requiring the arrest or *neutralisation* of the oil industry people" explained Hussein.

"You have a good point, actually two" admitted Nicoletta "the other day I saw the government science video course for high school, and I stress it is a video because books are not allowed anymore. In this video the geologists are represented as some sort of monsters with one eye like the cyclops of Ulysses."

"These are the *normal* geologists" wryly commented Armando "in Switzerland they are typically represented with spiky tails, like devilish characters."

"It is no wonder that parents tell their naughty children that if they do not behave a geologist would come to seize them in the night" said Ubaldo.

"It has been so many years since geologists have been legally present in society, that young people started believing that they never existed. For them, we are like unicorns, mythological characters" commented Ubaldo, "and in a way that is good for us, the geologists in hiding I mean, because they have stopped looking for us, at least in the same active and aggressive way that occurred a decade ago."

"And why did you choose the region of Piedmont, the hills around Barolo?" asked Annette.

"On clear days I can see the Alps. This is something I love, aside from the fact that I can support myself by selling paintings of the mountains" explained Hussein "after all it is just an extension of my skill at drawing geological cross-sections."

"Is the market for that type of paintings good?" asked Ubaldo who had a structural geology background himself.

"It is seasonal" explained Hussein "and mostly relies on the Chinese tourists. They are the only ones left now with enough money to go around and splash it out on good wines and…my paintings."

"And aside from painting, how is life?" asked Armando.

"In the small community in which I live it is relatively relaxed. One of the farmers even secretly produces and sells sausages so that people can buy them without having to be listed in the *meatarian* register."

"Slurp!" was the comment of Armando, always keen on meat, particularly considering his long-lasting abstinence.

"I also love soccer and had been a fan of Juventus, the team based in Torino, which is not far from Barolo, ever since I was a child in Iran. Unfortunately, the Italian *Serie A* is not what it used to be" commented Hussain.

"I am not a sport person" commented Annette "so can you explain in simple terms what has happened to *Serie A*?"

"Several compounded problems" Hussein started to explain. "To start with it is inconvenient travelling with electric vehicles such that they now play *regional* rather than *national* tournaments. Also, the Chinese have bought all the good teams, the world over. In Italy, they started with Inter some twenty years ago and later expanded their empire to include Milan, Roma and Juventus. As a result, the only really important soccer tournament is the *China World Cup* which is held once a year in China or in one of their territories. For instance, in 2029 they held the tournament in Taipei, which used to be the capital of Taiwan before the Chinese invasion of

2028. They did this to prove how safe and organised it is now, after their annexation. The Chinese provided the full package for the teams including transportation on *traditional* aircraft, the ones still propelled by jet fuel I mean."

After a brief pause, Hussein continued:

"And the new soccer kits are a joke. Due to misplaced political correctness the footballs are now made only of natural leather, like in the 50s, and they are very heavy and cause a lot of concussions. Also, the shirts and shorts are made either of wool for the winter season or cotton for the summer, none use modern microfiber technology because this would require a petrochemical source. As a result, the kits are very heavy, ill-fitting and impractical to play professional soccer. Obviously, the teams are allowed to use proper high-tech gear when they play in China, but it takes them a few weeks of adjustment to perform at a high level again after changing back to natural fabrics."

"It seems like madness" commented Nicoletta before changing subjects "How easy or otherwise was it for you to come here from Barolo?"

"I had a horse ride to get to Torino, which took half a day. I then took the weekly electric bus that connects Torino to Venezia. The old fast trains like *Frecciarossa* or *Italo* are unfortunately gone because not enough electricity is produced through the wind turbines and solar panels to keep them running on a regular basis. The electric bus is fine, but it takes three days to reach Venezia because of several concurring issues. To start with, its maximum speed is 50 Km/hr. Also, the road conditions are in a terrible state because they are not maintained any more using petrochemical products, like bitumen for instance, that would be necessary to repair the tarmac. This means that the damage caused by wear and tear cannot be properly repaired. The holes on the roads are now only filled up with stones. Finally, the bus needs to stop at several charging stations on the way because of the limited life of the electrical batteries" explained Hussein "and being just a weekly thing, you need to book well in advance to find a place."

"Where did you leave the bus?" asked Annette.

"I got out in Bergamo. A full day of travel from Torino to cover less than 200 Km" explained Hussein "and from there I hitch-hiked several horse and cart rides to get here, an additional two full days. Quite a long but worthwhile journey."

"I think is time to wrap up the session" said Annette, while Mastro Giuseppe stepped into the room with a tasting of his cheeses and wine. The cheeses consisted of three different levels of aging of his best *bitto*, while the wine was a *sforzato,* a dry *passito* red wine made from *Nebbiolo* grapes, the powerful but refined soul of Valtellina, a magic creature fortified by the sun, wind and time, as all good field geologists are as well.

Chapter 6
Fifteen years earlier (June 2020)
"El progreso" in the desert of Atacama (Chile)

Lithium extraction plant.
Image courtesy of SQM

The lithium brine evaporation ponds occupy vast swathes of what used to be the dry land of the Atacama Desert.

"Este es progreso, abuelita (This is progress, granny)" said Paco to Maria Soledad Contreras, pointing to the evaporation ponds created by SQM, the second largest company producing lithium in Chile. *Abuelita* frowned, showing her disapproval for such a *progreso.*

Paco was the first of his family to go to university and indeed, he was the first from the town of *San Pedro de Atacama.* He had attended the prestigious *Universidad de Chile* in Santiago, and had graduated in mining engineering. Now, back in the Atacama *salt flats* of his youth, he was a low-level manager employed by SQM and working in the production of lithium.

Maria Soledad measured just 1.6 metres in height. Her body was thin, wrinkled and dry like the desert in which she had lived all her life. The skin of her face was dark and smooth though, as if her features had been moulded and caressed by the desert winds, hot in summer and cold in winter. Like her mother, she was a *yatiri*, as medical practitioners and community healers are referred to in the highlands across Chile, Peru' and Bolivia. She was also a leader of her community, respected but also feared. The 'bad tongues' of the community, in private, said that her determination and assertiveness was the result of the rape of one of her ancestors by the *conquistadores** that had brought *bad blood* into her lineage. The same maligns sustained that, on certain days, she would act as a *layqa*, one of those shamans who use frogs and snakes in rituals to do harm to others, rather than 'someone who knows', the literal meaning of *yatiri*. And, on the few occasions that a light rain briefly interrupted the monotonously dry weather, Maria Soledad was always away from the village, setting a solitary tent on the *Pukara' de Quitor*. This 'archaeological' hill side, overlooking the salt flats, was where she conjured a mournful music with a *magical drum*, these were her 'words', created from the skin of an albino guanaco. Everybody naturally related the rain to Maria Soledad's witchcraft for which, for once, they all were pleased. In reality, the sudden pain in her old arthritic bones was a clear signal that a storm was in the making and she would purposely set up her shaman tent a distance away, but still visible from the village, as a means to enhance her standing with her own people. Most of time, her face was an inscrutable mask that concealed how much she relished the power projected onto her community by her *real* magical skills but also by the rumours on her witchcraft.

**The Spanish soldiers and explorers that, following the discovery by Columbus of America in 1492, had subdued a great portion of the 'new' (new to them because the continent had existed for millions of years!) continent to the Kingdom of Spain.*

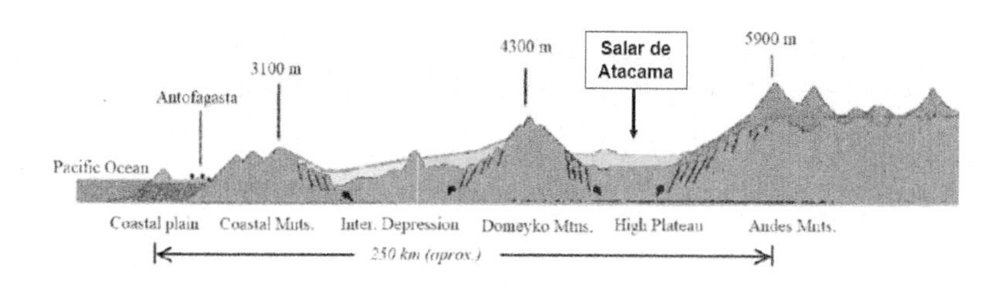

The Atacama Desert, made up of rocks and salt flats, is a 2,400-metre-high plateau bounded by the *Cordillera del Sal* to the West and the *Cordillera de los Andes* to the East. The driest plateau of its kind, it had been shaped by the uplift of the Andes that have caused a dry climate for at least the last 10 million years. Its distinctive climate is the result of several concomitant factors: a subtropical high-pressure zone, the cold Antarctic Humboldt current on the Pacific coast that creates a fog on the landward side, but very little rain and, finally, the Andean rain-shadow effect. But this would have only been of interest to the few adventurous travellers that from time to time had come across the *cordillera* to watch the herds of llamas on the *Salar de Tara*, the pink flamingos standing on one leg in the lagoon of *Chaxa* or the cougars hunting in the *Los Flamencos National Reserve.* What, however, makes the *salt flats* of the Atacama Desert so economically important for Chile is the lithium dissolved in their fossil waters, which, after several processing steps, reaches as high as 6% of the resulting carbonate ore, a very high grade by world standards. And even more important, is the fact that 60% of all the known lithium reserves of the world are contained in the *salt flats* of this desert. Lithium being as precious as gold in the manufacture of electric batteries which, of course, are the foundation of the *Renewable Energy Industry.*

Chile is a country where the mining industry had traditionally provided 10% of the national GDP and 50% of its export volumes. In old times, the copper mines had been the kings of the mining industry. While many large copper mines were still producing a commercial quality of ore, even having been exploited for a long time, the supply of high-grade ore has now diminished. Copper miners are increasingly forced to exploit copper sulphide deposits, using a process that is extremely water intensive. Accordingly, the exploitation of the lithium reserves of the country has become of outmost importance to replace the state income previously mostly gained from copper mining.

All the alpacas of Juan *el bizco*, so nicknamed for his *lazy eye*, sported red and yellow head-ribbons. He used this trademark to recognise his herd even from far away. Despite being only in his mid-40s, Juan was already an old man, weathered by his harsh living conditions as an *alpaquero*, his limited access to medical care and Chiva, his aggressive and unreasonable wife. The wife, who did not condone his drinking and dalliances that, at most, took him away from home for a week at a time. This at least, was his justification to himself.

Indeed, rumours circulated to the effect that Juan was more affectionate, almost more in love, with his animals (indeed he would have never referred to them as such) than his wife. And this, after all, might have even been true. However, for the last several months his passion for his alpacas had made him a sad person. Not because he ever had a change of heart; however, he had noticed that the pastures were not as vast and green as in the old times and that his flock was suffering. But he could not pinpoint the reason or reasons for these adverse changes.

Juan was not an educated person, indeed he was basically illiterate; just able to scribble his given name *Juan* to which he would often add not his family name which was very common in the region, but rather his nickname *el bizco* which, like the red and yellow ribbons of his alpacas, was his trademark, his way of providing irrefutable evidence of whom had signed. Despite his limitations, of what educated people would call *culture*, he was aware that something big was happening, a change in nature that was not linked to specific seasons or years. Something that grew worse year on year causing a significant number of his alpacas to suffer, and then die.

On Saturday evenings, many of the *alpaqueros* of San Pedro liked to meet for a drink at *Conchita*, a *figón*, as the *greasy spoons* are referred to in Chile. This bar, or cantina, lay in the northern outskirts of the town. The next day, Sunday, was their only day of the week free from work, and they would take advantage by having a late night out.

When Juan reached *Conchita* a few of his friends were already in the venue, busy downing shots of *pisco sours* (the Chilean version that's is, made from *Chilean Pisco* brandy, lemon juice from *Pica*, sugar, and ice, but with no egg white as they do in Peru'). They varied this with some *terremotos* (pineapple ice-cream, mixed with a sweet, fermented white wine called *Pipeño* and grenadine). A few Evangelicals, that is, those that did not drink alcohol, were savouring their *motes con huesillo*, a drink made from husked wheat (*mote*) and dried peaches (*huesillo*) soaked with sugar, water and cinnamon, a drink so popular in

Chile, that it has led to the saying *More Chilean than a mote con huesillo.*

"*Que tal compinche*? (How are you mate?)" asked Ramiro *El cojo*, his nickname deriving from the fact that his right leg had been broken beyond repair by one of his alpacas and as a result he now had a permanent limp.

"*Compadre, estoy muy cansado* (Buddy, I am very tired)" replied Juan, while ordering the first of his many *pisco sours* of the evening.

"*Es cierto, fue una semana larga* (It is true, it was a long week)" commented Rodolfo *El indio* who liked to participate in any discussions, although most of the time, as in this particular case, his sentences were at best nebulous, and driven by the level of alcohol in his blood. He liked to keep this as high as possible, usually by the consumption of his own powerful moonshine.

Mercedes was sipping her *terremoto*, sitting at a table with three male friends, but as soon as she saw Juan entering the venue, she went to say hello and embrace him. Everybody knew that they had dated before Juan had married Chiva and that Chiva, who was luckily at home that evening, was very jealous of Mercedes, whose nickname was *La Negrita.*

"*Que tal mi amor*? (How are you, my love?)" jokingly asked Mercedes.

"*Cansado Negrita* (Tired *Negrita*)" replied Juan using the nickname he used to call her when they were a couple.

Mercedes knew that farming the alpacas was a hard job requiring early morning starts to bring the herd to the pastures. The animals were segregated by sex, because the male alpacas are quite aggressive and can only be allowed to visit the female herds only one male at a time. She knew that the alpaqueros needed also to keep a constant watch on their grazing herds because they could easily be snatched by the cougars which roamed the plateau. But all this was normal for Juan. She had never seen him so exhausted and gloomy before.

"*No te achaques. Decile a tu mamacita que paso', Juan* (Don't be sad. Tell your mummy what happened, Juan)" she teased him.

"*La labor me hace mal* (Work makes me sick)" replied Juan, typically taciturn in a way that always drove Mercedes crazy. He had proffered a few enigmatic words without explaining what the real problem was.

"*Que te pasa mi pajarito*? (What happen to you, my little bird?)" insisted Mercedes.

"*La Niña y la Pinta estan mal, de hace tiempo no estan comiendo bien* (Niña and Pinta are sick, it is a while since they have eaten properly)" Juan eventually admitted. He had named the oldest of his alpacas after the caravels used by Columbus in his voyage of discovery to America.

"*Pachamama* nos abandono'* (*Pachamama** abandoned us)" commented *Carlos El Loco* who, when had drunk more than his normal share of *pisco sours* would typically become mystical and often speak in a language, that most of the times were of his own making.

"*¡Andate a la chucha Loco! No quiero hablar más contigo* (Go to hell Loco! I don't want to talk to you anymore)*" Juan* shouted at *Carlos El Loco* to stop his babbling nonsense.

"*No te preocupe Juan, mañana te acompañaré al pasto y chequearé que pasa con tus alpacas* (Don't worry Juan, tomorrow I will accompany you to the pastures and check out what may have happened with your alpacas)" said Mercedes who was a renowned animal *curandera* (healer).

The rest of the evening passed melancholically for Mercedes and Juan, remembering past times that had been better and not only because the alpacas had been healthier.

**The earth goddess revered by the Indians of the Andes, that presides over planting and harvesting, embodies the mountains, and causes earthquakes*

Juan had spent the night with Mercedes, hoping that Chiva would not discover it. He would invent an excuse, like he always did. That he got drunk at the *Conchita* and his *compinches* had convinced *el padron* to let him sleep in the venue to avoid freezing to death on his way back home in the case that he passed out due to his blood's alcohol level.

The early morning was cold, just above freezing, although in the course of the day the temperature was expected to rise up to 20C. Mercedes saddled two horses. Hers was a white mare that she had decorated with black and red ribbons, while Juan took a brown stallion, *nature* so to speak. A red-backed hawk that Mercedes had tamed with her soothing songs would always accompany her long rides, enhancing her powers of *curandera*, or so she said. Against the morning cold both Mercedes and Juan wore colourful *chamantos*, ponchos typical of Chile.

"*Para alla* (In that direction)" said Juan, indicating the general direction where the alpacas would pasture that morning. His young assistant Pedro *El agil* had already guided the herd to the grass land where Mercedes and Juan would meet them.

"*¡Vamos al toque!* (Let's go right now)" shouted

Mercedes to the hawk, her command to put the bird in to motion. In the stark morning light, they rode east. The blue sky and the surrounding mountains were reflected in the many lagoons that they skirted on their way toward the mountain pastures. In the distance, the border between Chile and Bolivia was marked by the *Licancabur* volcano, a perfectly circular mountain 6 Km high, a holy site for the Atacameño. Its magical powers were seen at best during the solstices when it would interact with its neighbour volcano *Quimal.* They would be seen to overshadow each other and according to the local mythology this copulation would fertilize the earth.

After riding for about one hour, they reached the lower slopes of the volcano and the cushion plants and shrubs where the alpacas of Juan were grazing under the sleepy supervision of Pedro *El agil.* The herd recognised Juan and started *clucking*, the noisy suction of their soft palate with the tongue, a sign of friendship and submission. The alpacas of Juan were of the *huacaya* breed, whose fibre, short, dense and crimpy gave a woolly appearance. Their fleece would be sheared in the next couple of months and sold to a local trader. A long line of middlemen taking their cut before precious wool clothes would be sold at a premium in the luxury shops of the world, from New York to London to Shanghai.

"*Te quiero caleta* (I love you so much)" Juan whispered in the years of *La Pinta* and then repeated the same with *La Niña.* They both increased their *clucking* showing their appreciation of Juan's affection.

Mercedes however, was a more pragmatic person and, while Juan was talking to his dearest alpacas, she examined them like a *curandera* would do. She touched their hind and then introduced her expert hand into their fleece.

"*Estan jodidas* (They are fucked)" was Mercedes simple but abrupt diagnosis which was not of the liking of Juan.

"*Te mandaste un condoro, Mercedes* (You made a mistake, Mercedes)" shouted back Juan, tears of anger and impotence wetting his face.

"*Queria estar equivocada, pero' te estoy diciendo la firme Juan* (I wish I was wrong, but I am telling you the truth Juan)" replied Mercedes. Then she continued:

"*Ya he visto varios rebaños en estas condiciones. Ninguno deles se recuperó* (I have already seen several herds in this condition. None of them recovered)" Mercedes explained.

"*¿Qué pasa?* (What happens?) asked Juan, who wished to know the cause of the disease in his herd.

"*Mira, no sé a ciencia cierta* (Look, I do not know for a fact)" replied Mercedes.

"*Dime que sospechas* (Tell me what you suspect)" asked Juan.

"*Creo que los mineros tienen a que ver con tu problema* (I believe that the miners are responsable for the problem)" explained Mercedes.

"*Y porque' proprio los mineros? Las minas de cobre están bien lejas de aca'* (And why the miners? The copper mines are far away from here)" replied Juan.

"*Escucha Juan, me refiero a la extracción de litio* (Listen Juan, I am talking of the extraction of lithium)" explained Mercedes.

"*Y que tiene a que ver el litio? Las zonas de producción están en las planicies. Cerca de los salares.* (And what is the relationship with the lithium production? That all takes place in the plains, close to the salt flats)" commented Juan.

"*Eso es* (Exactly)" replied Mercedes.

"*No entiendo* (I don't understand)" replied Juan.

"*Mira Juan, yo soy una curandera de animales y a veces de hombres, como tú sabes talvez me dicen brujas. Pero... me han hablado de un grupo de gringos, les dicen los gringos fantasmas, que han venido de Estados Unidos. Hablan español muy bien.* (Look Juan, I am an animal healer and sometimes also can heal men, as you know sometimes they call me a witch. But...they told me of a group of gringos, they are called the 'ghostly gringos' who came from the United States. They speak Spanish very well)" explained Mercedes.

"*¿Gringos fantasmas?* (Ghostly gringos?)" queried Juan.

"*Les llaman así porque no beben alcohol, ni café, ni coca cola. La gente no sabe cómo se sustentan sin estos elementos esenciales de nuestra dieta.* (They name them like this because they don't drink alcohol nor coffee or coca-cola. The people do not know how they can sustain themseves without these essential elements of our diet)" explained Mercedes.

"*¿Y cuál es la relación entre los gringos fantasmas y el sufrimiento de La Pinta y La Niña?* (And what is the relationship between the ghostly gringos and the suffering of La Pinta and La Niña?)" asked Juan.

"*Están visitando un lugar tras otro alrededor de las salinas. Han sido enviados por las empresas mineras para decirle a la gente que la extracción de litio es excelente para la economía de Chile y, lo que es más importante, no afecta el medio ambiente.* (They are visiting one place after another around the salt flats. They have been sent by the mining companies to tell the people that the extraction of lithium is excellent for the economy of Chile and, most importantly, has no impact on the environment)" explained Mercedes.

"*Mejor* (Better they do this)" commented Juan.

"*Juan no lo entiendes. Si la producción de litio no afectara el medio ambiente no mandarían unos gringos a decirnos.* (Juan, you don't understand. If the production of lithium had no impact on the environment they would not send the gringos to tell us)" explained Mercedes.

"*Tienes razón. La cosa es sospechosa.* (You are right. The thing is suspicious)" conceded Juan.

"*Los gringos fantasmas incluso han propuesto abrir pequeños centros médicos en la mayoría de los pueblos alrededor de las salinas.* (The ghostly gringos have also proposed the opening of small medical centres in the majority of the small villages around the salt flats)" continued Mercedes.

"*¡Excelente!* (Excellent!)" commented Juan.

"*No te haga ilusiones. A lo mejor los hacen solamente para monitorear el efecto dañino de su minería en la población. Para tener datos de antemano para prepararse para futuros casos legales.* (Don't have any illusions. They probably only do this to monitor the damaging effect of their mining on the population in order to be ready for future legal cases against them)" explained Mercedes.

"*Eres lista como un zorro* (You are smart like a fox}" admitted Juan.

When they left the pastures, Juan was still very confused. A *bruja* like Mercedes was probably right about the fate of his beloved La Niña and La Pinta. And in his heart, he knew that Mercedes probably had a point about the *mineros.* But what could he do? And how could he learn more about the relationship between the drying out of the pastures, the diseases of his flock and the extraction of lithium from the salt flats? Riding back home he thought of Maria Soledad. If the magical powers of Mercedes were good with animals, then Maria's witchcraft was at a different level altogether. Juan felt confident that she would know about the *gringos fantasmas* and whatever the mining companies were doing in Chile. And maybe she could even stop their evil spell on his herd.

Finding Maria Soledad was not an easy task for anyone. She would disappear from her village for weeks at a time to perform her magic in the desert, or so she liked to pretend. However, the few sceptics, who normally were those who had a minimum of formal education, who had attended at least a few years of school before having been sucked into the unskilled workforce to support the meagre income of their families, these doubters suggested that the disappearances of Maria Soledad were just her way of increasing her charisma. Her way of increasing the mystery and raising expectations around her persona. Who knew if these doubters were right? In any case Juan *el bizco* was not one of them.

As it turned out, Juan's anxiety about locating Maria Soledad was soon over. She, in fact, went to find him in the late evening, while he was riding home from the day's pasture.

"*Se que me estabas buscando* (I know you were looking for me)" said Maria Soledad.

"*¿Quien te lo dijo?* (Who told you?)" asked Juan with a quizzical face.

"*La luna* (The Moon)" Maria Soledad explained.

"*¿La luna?* (The Moon?)" repeated Juan.

Maria Soledad pointed skyward and picked out the *Mare Nubium*, one of the largest of the Moons craters, that to her skilled eyes appeared like an open mouth, Juan did not know what to say. He was even more confused, as was the case when he stepped outside his strict sphere of work.

"*La luna me dijo que tienes un problema con tu rebaño* (the Moon told me that you have a problem with your herd)" explained Maria Soledad.

"*Es verdad* (It is true)" admitted Juan.

"*Y que te gustaría saber más de los gringos fantasmas* (And that you would like to know more about the ghostly gringos)" continued Maria Soledad.

"*Es verdad también* (True as well)" replied Juan.

"*Para empezar estos gringos no son fantasmas de verdad. Resultan ser mormones* (To start with these gringos are not ghosts at all. They are mormons)" explained Maria Soledad.

"*¿Mormones?* (Mormons?)" asked Juan who had never heard of such a word.

"*Es una religión donde los hombres no beben alcohol, ni toman ningún estimulante, como café o té o cualquier bebida carbonatada que contenga cafeína* (It is a religión where the people cannot drink alcohol, nor any kind of stimulant, like coffee or tea or any carbonated drink containing caffeine)" explained Maria Soledad.

"*¿Y? (And?)*" Juan was waiting for the next line.

"*Pueden casarse con varias esposas* (They can marry several women)" continued Maria Soledad.

"*Ah…esto tiene que ser una compensación. ¿Y las mujeres, pueden tomar?* (Ah…this has to be a compensation. And their women, can they drink?)" commented Juan.

"*No seas estúpido* (Don't be silly)" replied Maria Soledad.

"*¿Entonces también las mujeres pueden tener más de un marido?* (Is it the case therefore, that the women can also have more than one husband?)" asked Juan, showing a logic that baffled Maria Soledad.

"*Eres realmente un idiota* (You really are an idiot)" shouted Maria Soledad whilst she also quietly recognised that Juan had a point.

"*En fin, ¿qué hacen estos gringos aquí?* (To get to the point, what are these gringos doing here?)" asked Juan.

"*Vinieron a decirnos lo bueno que es la minería del litio para nuestro país... y nuestros pueblos* (They came to tell us how good the mining is for our country…and our villages)" explained Maria Soledad, her voice rising to falsetto.

"*Mercedes no le cree* (Mercedes does not believe in them)" said Juan.

"*Esa puta bruja... por una vez puede ser que tenga razón* (That bitchy witch…for once she may be right)" admitted Maria Soledad.

"*Y tú María, ¿qué piensas de ellos?* (And you Maria, what do you think of them?)" asked Juan.

"*No me gustan* (I don't like them)" Maria explained.

"*¿Cuáles son tus planes?* (What are your plans)" asked Juan knowing that Maria would not stand aside in such a situation.

"*¿Te acuerdas de Paco, mi sobrino?* (Do you remember Paco, my nephew?)" commented Maria Soledad.

"*Claro que sí, lo que trabaja con los mineros* (Obviously, the one who works with the miners)" replied Juan.

"*Le pedí que me organizara una reunión con los gringos fantasmas. Te mantendré informado* (I asked him to organise a meeting with the ghostly gringos. I will keep you posted)" concluded Maria Soledad, who disappeared into the darkness without even leaving time for Juan to reply.

Eventually, Paco was not able to organise a meeting between Maria Soledad and the *gringos fantasmas*. They had already left Chile and returned to Utah, their home base where the best foreign language schools of the US are located. This is not by accident. The Mormons form a significant portion of the population of Utah. And young men, between the ages of 18 and 25, within the congregation, and who meet the standards of worthiness, are strongly encouraged to consider a two-year, full-time proselytizing mission. This expectation is based in part on the New Testament passage "Go ye therefore, and teach all nations" (Matt. 28: 19–20).

Latin America, where Spanish is spoken, with the exception of Brazil, is their natural playground, so to speak; hence it is relatively easy to find Mormons who have been taught and can speak fluently, Spanish.

The mission of the *gringos fantasmas* in the desert of Atacama was not particularly religious however, unless one took account of the zealous attitude of many of the individuals promoting Renewable energies. From time-to-time, entrepreneurial individuals within the Mormon congregation would offer their services to the industry, much like mercenaries. This had been the case for the group contracted by the *mineros* to spread their words of wisdom, so to speak.

Maria Soledad was not, however, the type of person who would give up at the first hurdle (or second or third for that matter); indeed, overcoming what other individuals would have considered *stumbling blocks* was her specialty. She remembered her distant relative Boto *el aguacate* Gonzalez, so nicknamed because of the large plantation that he managed, located along the coastal plain three hours north of Santiago, where he grew high-quality Haas avocados. She asked him to pay her a visit.

Like her nephew Paco, Boto was also the first of his village who had attended a university. As a result of his intellectual brilliance, however, he had managed to win a scholarship to study agricultural engineering at the prestigious *La Sorbonne* in Paris. After a life spent abroad supporting agricultural projects all over the world he had come back to Chile, and now was highly considered within his extended community, both for his wisdom and experience. A sort of intellectual *campesino* to whom everybody referred to when something complex needed to be sorted out or at least understood.

On meeting, they hugged and remembered the old times, when Boto was a toddler and Maria Soledad his mentor. But those were past times, and now the situation had reversed. She needed help from him. Maria Soledad explained to Boto the poor situation of the pastures, the illness among the herds of alpaca and the poor quinoa harvests. All that had occurred in the last few years, certainly after the exploitation of the lithium from the salt flat had started. Whilst considering the time frames in her mind, she began to see that the mining of lithium and the environmental problems were indeed related, even if she didn't understand exactly how?

"*Es una posibilidad Tia* (It is a possibility Auntie)" explained Boto.

"*¿De qué manera?* (How's that?)" asked Maria Soledad.

"Se' que la minería de litio requiere la extracción de mucha agua del subsuelo (I know that the mining of lithium requires the extraction of a lot of wáter from the subsurface)" explained Boto who, indeed, had to manage similar issues with his avocado farming.

"¿Y luego? (And then?)" asked Maria Soledad, who still could not put all the elements of the puzzle together.

"El agua extraída es fósil (The water that is extracted is fossil water)" continued Boto who was perhaps a little too academic in his phrasing.

"Que significa eso (What does that mean?)" asked Maria Soledad, becoming a little anxious.

"Que como el petróleo que se extrae no puede ser reemplazada por la naturaleza. Además, casi toda el agua fósil se evapora en los estanques de litio (like extracted oil, it cannot be replaced by nature. Its worse, almost all the fossil wáter is evaporated in the lithium ponds)" explained Boto.

"¿Y cuál es la relación con nuestros pastos? (And what is the relationship of that with our pastures?)" asked Maria Soledad.

"El agua dulce, la que normalmente alimentaría tus pastos y animales, se aleja de su curso natural para llenar el espacio dejado vacio por el agua fósil extraída (The fresh water that normally feeds your pastures and animals, is removed from its natural environment in order to fill up the voids left by the extraction of the fossil water)" explained Boto.

"¿Es por eso que nuestros pastos se están secando? (Is that the reason why our pastures are drying up?)" asked Maria Soledad who had finally connected the dots.

"Es algo muy probable (It is very likely)" concluded Boto with the same detachment as he would have done at the end of one of his academic presentations at *La Sorbonne.*

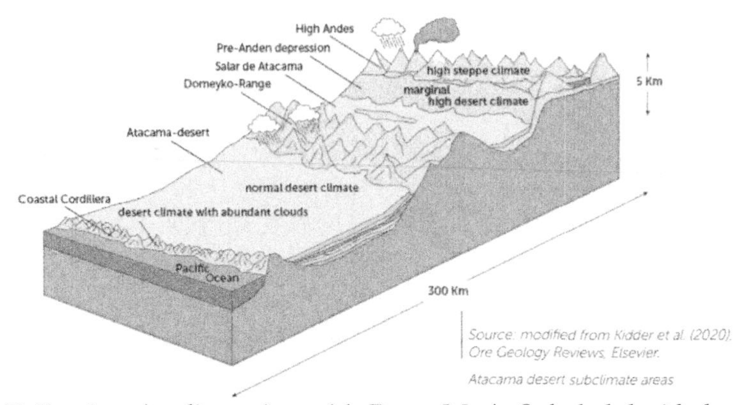

Source: modified from Kidder et al. (2020). Ore Geology Reviews, Elsevier.

Atacama desert subclimate areas

Following the discussion with Boto, Maria Soledad decided to travel to Antofagasta, the regional capital, and confront the local representatives of the government. Boto decided to travel with her, and they were not alone; Maria Soledad enlisted a full team to accompany her in the mission. There was Alvaro *bicho* Hernandez, the veterinarian, and Teresa *doctora* Rojas who owned the *Cruz Verde Pharmacy* on *Caracoles 359*. Although most of the people of the village who needed help with their animals, would prefer the services of the *curandera* Mercedes, Maria Soledad knew that she needed to have more presentable characters representing *the science*, when meeting with the officials in Antofagasta. Also coming along, was Martin *alpaca* Fernandez, the single largest owner of an alpaca farm in the region, and Pedro *el brujo* Cardozo with Conchita *la rubia de farmacia* Suarez who were not wealthy and notable like the others, but they knew how to cook and so they were engaged by Maria Soledad as the *cocineros* of the party.

And, finally, joining the group was Domingo *Chevrolet* Martinez because he was the only one in the region owning a large enough truck that, however old and poorly maintained, could carry them all to Antofagasta.

The distance from San Pedro de Atacama and Antofagasta is 350 Km, a distance that on many other trips, could have been negotiated in a full day of travel. But Maria Soledad's trip was a *special* trip. To start with, her party would travel southwest to Tocoano for the first of her meetings with the local Indian communities. She wanted to convince them to join the trip using their own means of transportation. Then they would go back to San Pedro de Atacama and travel towards the north east until they reached the town of Calama, where the second and final meeting would take place before the final leg, to Antofagasta.

They started the trip early in the morning, heading southwest along route 23. Maria Soledad, her normally grey hair now dyed with red stripes that, in her mind, represented her war colours, sat in the front of the truck along with the driver Domingo, and Martin, the alpaca farmer. In the back of the cabin was the *science community*, that is to say, Alvaro, Teresa and Boto. The *cocineros*, however, made do with the open air at the back of the pick-up. They were young, and so, accustomed to the cold, but also the sun of the early mornings in the desert. They made the best of their situation by sitting on a thick blanket, covering themselves with wool ponchos and resting their backs on pillows that they had brought from home.

Together with them, in the open air of the back of the pick-up, were their cooking tools, including a large pot, and the basic food ingredients required to prepare a succulent *patasca*, a hearty soup made from corn, potatoes, pork, beef and onion. They also brought four different types of *pisco*, each one infused with different herbs and spices like green chili, Rica Rica, Coca and Chaña, they hoped this would cheer and warm them on their cold evenings on the road.

As planned by Maria Soledad, they met the leaders of the Tocoano Indian community outside the *Campanario de San Lucas,* a bell tower that is an historic landmark of the small town, built in the colonial times of the 1700's.

"*Como les expliqué por teléfono, necesitamos reunirnos con los funcionarios del gobierno regional y quejarnos sobre la situación de nuestros pastos* (As I explained to you over the phone we need to meet the officials of the regional government and complain about the situation of our pastures)" explained Maria Soledad.

"*Estamos todos contigo María Soledad. Aquí también sufren nuestras alpacas y llamas* (We are all supporting you Maria Solead. Here as well, the alpacas and llamas are suffering)" replied Mateo *tres dedos*, the community leader who was missing three fingers of his left hand due to a work accident many years before.

"*Sospecho que la minería del litio está dañando nuestros pastos* (I suspect that the mining of the lithium is damaging our pastures)" pointed out Maria Soledad.

"*Tú eres muy inteligente María Soledad y de estas cosas tú sabes más que nosotros* (You are very intelligent Maria Soledad and of these things you know more than we do)" Mateo admitted.

"*¿Están listos para unirte a nosotros?* (Are you ready to join us?)" asked Maria Soledad.

"*Somos diez María Soledad. Y tenemos un camión grande. Los seguiremos* (We are ten Maria Soledad. And we have a large truck. We will follow you)" explained Mateo.

By the time they reached Calama, the evening darkness had engulfed the desert around the town. Their meeting with the local community took place outside the *Capilla Sagrado Corazon de Jesus,* a Catholic church. The meeting ran very similar to the one they had in Tocoano and a dozen individuals including the chief, Lucas *el chino,* so called for the oriental features of his face, joined Maria Soledad's party with two cars.

They stopped for the night at a magical spot, a waterfall along the River Loa, Chile's longest river, around which the town of Calama had been built many hundreds of years before.

Alvaro and Teresa, with some help, produced a marvellous *patasca* that was downed by the team with many glasses of *pisco.* The food, the drinks, the Andean music played with *quena, zampoña and ocarina* was both languid, and yet full of expectation. It left the party feeling happy and confident that the next day their complaints would be heard by the government officials in Antofagasta.

Unfortunately, the morning light, like the warming sun dispersing fog, would eventually diffuse the expectations raised by the magical night of food, drinks and music.

They reached Antofagasta, a port city and the regional capital of the mining area in and around the Atacama Desert. Their caravan of cars and trucks negotiated the heavy traffic until reaching *Plaza Colon,* in the centre of the city. This was close to the regional government building, arriving exactly when the clock of the tower, that marks the centre of the square was signalling mid-day. They had to wait well into the afternoon before the government offices reopened. However, when they did open the main entrance, they would not allow the delegation, composed of Maria Soledad, the other two community chiefs and Boto, visit with the government officials.

"Ustedes deberian haber reservado una cita (You should have booked an appointment)" the janitor at the entrance of the building told them with a stern face.

"¿Podemos reservar una ahora? (Can we book one now?)" Maria Soledad asked.

"No es tan simple. Primero necesitamos entender el motivo de su visita. Para dirigirle al funcionario adecuado (It is not that simple. We

first need to understand the reason for your visit to send you to the right oficial)" explained the janitor.

"Estamos aquí para protestar por el desastre ambiental que la minería de litio en los salares de Atacama le hace a nuestros rebaños y agricultura (We are here to protest about the environmental disaster that the mining of lithium in the salt flats of Atacama has on our herds and agriculture)" explained Maria Soledad.

"Eso es un problema. El funcionario encargado de registrar las quejas está de vacaciones, me temo (That's a problem. The oficial in charge of receiving the complaints is on vacation, I am afraid)" explained the janitor, rolling his eyes.

"¿Y cuándo volverá? (And when will he be back?)" asked Maria Soledad.

"Esa información es confidencial (That information is confidential)" explained the janitor, indicating that he wished to stop the conversation right there, particularly with these low cast Indians coming in from the desert.

"¿Qué podemos hacer para encontrarnos con un funcionario? (What can we do to meet any government oficial?)" asked Maria Soledad.

"Le dije que está de vacaciones. Por favor, abandonen el local inmediatamente o llamaré a la policía (I told you he is on vacation. Please leave these premises immediately or I will call the pólice)" shouted back the janitor.

And so they were left on their own, disappointed and angry, and with no foreseeable chance of meeting with the government in the near future. They set up camp in the central portion of the square, which was pedestrianised, what else could they do? Maria Soledad, Mateo, Lucas and Boto had no intention of travelling back to their communities without first having presented their complaints.

It didn't take long for mattresses, blankets and cushions to dot the area around the watch tower. A little later, the music instruments started playing under the skilled guidance of the group of Mateo. And, finally, Alvaro and Teresa organised themselves to go shopping, buying whatever supplies they felt were missing to prepare another of their heavy delicacies for the group's late dinner.

The police eventually came along, but Maria Soledad and her group looked like a folkloristic group playing indigenous music and that was fine with the guardians of the town's order. They even enjoyed the fact that, for once, the central square of Antofagasta had become a cultural hot spot, the music and songs covering the otherwise noisy traffic. It was only on the second day of the peaceful occupation of the square that people started realising that the group had not come to entertain them but rather to press complaints on the regional government.

Banners appeared, prepared by Boto *el aguacate*. They bore the mark of his culture and sophisticated mind, to the point that some were actually difficult to understand for the participants of the rally and passers-by alike.

"*La minería mata a nuestras alpacas* (Mining kills our alpacas)" one of the banners pointed out, leaving many of the bystanders in doubt about what that really meant.

"*El gobierno esta hecho de corruptos* (The Government is made of corrupt people)" said another banner that had much more success with the onlookers.

"*Nuestros pastos son más importantes que los coches eléctricos* (Our pastures are more important than their electric cars)" a third banner asserted, which appeared quite an obscure statement, that, however, probably because it was so difficult to understand for the non-initiated, elicited so much interest that many passers-by stopped and started asking questions.

By the time the police returned, this time to drive Maria Soledad and her party out of the square, they found themselves confronted by hundreds of protesters and decided to give up trying to disperse the gathering.

In the following days, left leaning anti-government groups descended on the square to support the protest; some of these political movements had rebranded themselves into *Movimiento de las Alpacas Revolucionarias* (The movement of the revolutionary Alpacas) and their banner stated "*El oro blanco no se toca. Gringos afuera!* (The white gold cannot be touched. Gringos out!)" referring to the lithium rich carbonate that was the final product of the evaporation pools and the idea that the foreign forces were behind its exploitation.

While all these events occurred Boto *el aguacate* prepared a technical report and an accompanying PowerPoint presentation summarising the damaging environmental impact of the lithium mining on the Atacama Desert.

Eventually, the regional government decided that the best course of action was to meet with the leaders of the protests. Not because they intended to follow up on any of their demands; only to stall their action and, more importantly, convince them to leave the square and return to their desert dwellings, well away from the keen eyes of the city people, the ones that really counted when the results of the next political election would be decided.

And so, Maria Soledad, Mateo *tres dedos*, Lucas *el chino* and Boto *el aguacate* were finally allowed to meet the deputy complaints manager, Mr. Sergio Barullo, on the second floor of the government building.

"*Buenos dias señora y señores* (Good morning lady and gentlemen)" said Mr Barullo.

"*Buenos días a usted señor Barullo* (Good morning to you Mr. Barullo)" Maria Soledad replied on behalf of her team.

"*¿Qué puedo hacer por ustedes?* (What can I do for you?)" asked Mr Barullo.

"*Aquí está un informe, elaborado por Boto el aguacate... quiero decir el Ingeniero Boto González sobre los efectos nocivos de la minería del litio en nuestros pastos, rebaños y agricultura en el salar de Atacama* (Here is a report prepared by Boto *el aguacate*...I meant Engineer Boto Gonzalez on the damage produced by the mining of lithium on our pastures, herds and agriculture)" explained Maria Soledad.

"*Muchas gracias doña María* (Thank you so much doña Maria)" replied Mr Barullo making sure however, not to pick up the document that Maria was pushing toward him.

"*El ingeniero González, con su permiso, les presentará los elementos clave de su informe* (With your permission, Engineer Gonzalez will present to you the key elements of his report)" explained Maria Soledad.

"*Adelante* (Go ahead)" replied Mr Barullo, who was taken aback by these *Indios,* that dared to present a document to him, rather than just waving their hands and shouting as he had expected. This was what he had hoped, because that would have given him the excuse to call the police and cut short this nonsense spectacle of a meeting, with people that he considered marginally better than troglodytes. In this, Barullo was only following his ancestors, the way they had acted with all those indigenes' rather than *uncontaminated* white Spanish blood.

Boto's presentation was slick, maybe even too polished for Mr Barullo who as a mid-level government official without any technical background, was just an administrator more accustomed to passing papers from one office to another without ever having to take a decision. With the presentation finished, they tried to hand over both the presentation and the report to Mr Barullo whilst asking him to provide a receipt proving that he had received the documents.

"*No es posible. Ese es un nivel de autoridad por encima del mío. Como saben yo solo soy el subgerente de quejas...* (This is not possible. It requires a level of authority beyond mine. As you know I am only the deputy complaints manager)" explained Mr Barullo, refusing even to touch the documents prepared by Boto *el aguacate.*

They pleaded many times but to no avail, until they realised that they were stuck in a rut.

"*Vamonos a la prensa* (Let's go to the press!)" shouted Boto *el aguacate* realising that they needed to find someone not linked to the government to lodge their complaints and get attention. On second thoughts, he also realised, however, that their noisy presence and protest in the main square of Antofagasta had not even been reported by any mainstream newspaper, radio or TV station. And indeed, later on, when they tried to organise a meeting at *El Mercurio* or *La Tercera*, the most important of the Chilean dailies, they did not even manage to get an appointment. Finally, Boto *el aguacate* began to understand that these newspapers and indeed most of the radio and TV stations in Chile were part of the establishment; furthermore, the *white* establishment that considered with contempt, any issue involving indigenous tribes. Eventually the only media outlet that lent them an ear so to speak, was *Radio Che Guevara*, a radio channel operated by one of the extreme left wing political groups. Sonia Braga, a twenty-year-old, beautiful, and fervent revolutionary who came to interview Boto and Maria Soledad, was not particular interested in their plight as such but she liked to broadcast any news that embarrassed the government and that their supine media outlets would not pick up. Her commentary on the issue of the water uses and abuse by the lithium industry as opposed to the needs of the farmers took an anti-American tone, what else? Her narrative was that American-led industries pushed for the extraction of lithium with total disregard for the local population and their economic activities, even though the processing and marketing of all the lithium of Chile was carried out by the Chinese, not the Americans. But, as all left leaning persons knew, talking bad of the capitalist *Gringos* is much more palatable to the masses than badmouthing the Chinese *compañeros*. In any case she did nothing that would really bring forward the agenda set out by Maria Soledad and her friends. The only thing they really achieved from their efforts in Antofagasta was a better

understanding of their situation in the big scheme of things. And this occurred through a chance encounter with Pete, who was a *gringo,* but not a *gringo fantasma,* because he loved his pisco and more.

Pete was a 50-year-old, burly, US journalist whose political views were liberal but not leftist by any stance. He was in love with Sonia though, so from time to time he would visit her in Chile. And this was the case when the upheaval brought to the centre of Antofagasta by Maria Soledad and her group took place. Pete did not speak Spanish, or not sufficiently well to communicate with Maria Soledad, whom he immediately realised was the leader of the group. So, he asked Sonia and Boto to be the go between, the persons he trusted to translate the important message he wished to pass on to Maria Soledad.

"Let's start from the basics" said Pete "the lithium mining process involves pumping lithium rich brine, which by the way is a fossil water that cannot be replaced, from a depth of 20-40 metres below ground, into evaporation ponds. The brine contains originally only around 0.15 % lithium. This is then pumped through a cascade of ponds where impurities or by-products are precipitated by solar evaporation, wind, and chemical additives, until the lithium ore reaches a commercial grade, let's say 5%."

"And what happens to the fossil water?" asked Sonia, who was not familiar, as Boto was, with the process.

"Up to 95 per cent of the extracted brine water is lost to evaporation and so not recovered" explained Pete.

"That's a lot!" exclaimed Sonia.

"Yes, but the real problem is that the *brine water* is in hydrodynamic balance with its surroundings, the water-intensive mining process, in this extremely arid region, causes *fresh water* aquifers to deplete and affects the water equilibrium" continued Pete.

"*Fresh water*...That's why the pastures are drying out and the herds are suffering" commented Boto.

"Yes, this has an impact, a big impact. The water withdrawal affects, among other activities, the farming of quinoa, llama and alpaca" admitted Pete.

Boto summarised the substance of Pete's talk to Maria Soledad. Her face showed the rage that had taken possession of her soul on hearing the confirmation of the damaging impact on her community that the mining in the salt flats had.

Pete waved his hand. He looked at Maria Soledad eye-to-eye.

"You see doña Maria, you are protesting against the wrong thing. If, *Pachamama* forbid, an oil pipeline had been crossing your sacred land and disturbed your ancestors...then I am pretty sure the *salt flats* would have been flooded, not only by the autochthonous brine, but also by foreigners, I mean white, politically left-leaning people, including politicians and journalists from the US and Europe. They would have financed your protest and staged it in a way that could be captured in smartly arranged video clips. This would have been sufficiently long to tell the story, but short enough to be interspersed among the TV adds that generate their cash flow. But, as I said, you are fighting the wrong battle. You are fighting what they call *progress*. You see doña Maria, to appease the *Native Americans*, the ones that in the old times were referred to as *Red Indians* for lack of politically correct imagination, the US's left-wing would like to stop the construction of the *Keystone XL pipeline* that brings oil from Canada into the US, strengthening US energy independence from the Middle East, while supporting thousands of high-paying jobs in the US and Canada. And you bet now that Biden is fully installed in power, he will stop this project to appease his left-wing audience, which is a minority even within his party, but it is very vocal. Because that is what they call a *just cause* doña Maria. You have to admit that you may be a *Native American* much like your *Red Indian* cousins, but you are an *Indian of a lesser God*, doña Maria, because the lithium extracted from your sacred land feeds the *clean energy* madness of the West. *Clean* for them, that are thousands of kilometres away from the environmental and cultural disasters they take advantage from. For them you are just a collateral damage, an acceptable collateral damage and that's it I'm afraid!"

And that was the moment when Maria Soledad realised that even her magic powers were not match for the evil spirits of environmentalism.

Chapter 7
Energy Transition's Geopolitics in 2035

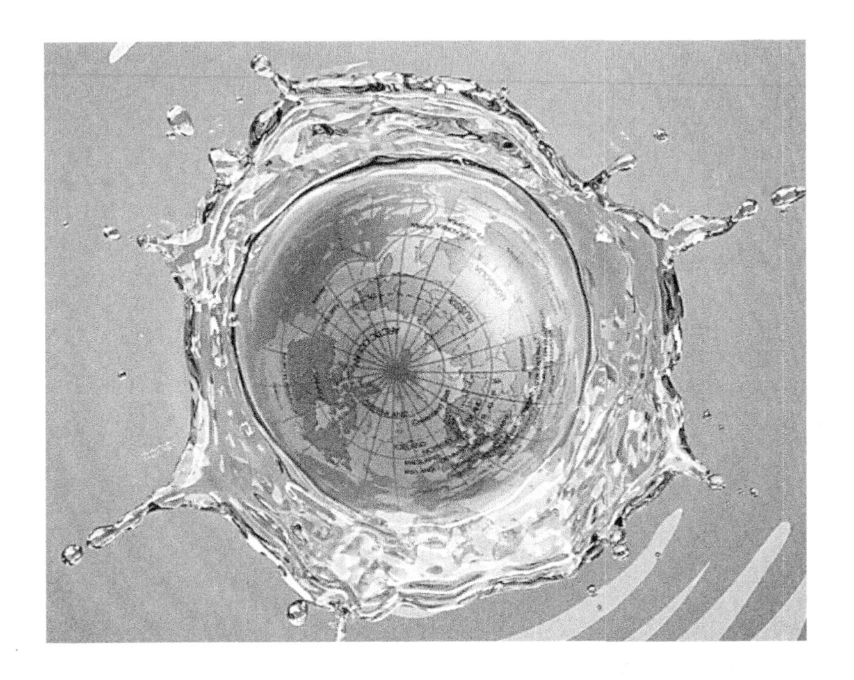

The waves had eventually wrapped the entire world.

It had all started with two small ripples, one originated in the US and the other in the EU. These had perturbated the currents of the oceans. But then, when the two ripples had encountered each other, they had morphed into a tsunami that had reached every corner of the world, modifying and often destroying the boundaries that had been known before.

The US, Canada, the EU and Australia since the early to mid-20's had been governed by left-leaning parties that, depending on the nation, were referred to with different names, Greens, Liberals, Democrats. With some subtle nuances, they had all however, pushed for similar reforms with a strong focus on the controlling of what they referred to as *climate change* and the protection of the environment in general. Probably, the cornerstone of the above was the *Combustion Engine Deactivation Act* (*CEDA*), which prohibited the use of any type of vehicles which were not powered by electric engines by 2030. Obviously, the pact had been signed *only* by the US, Canada, the EU and Australia. It should be noted that the Supreme Command of the US Army had warned Madam President that this Pact would dramatically affect the capability of the western armies against the always present expansionistic menace of Russia and China. The left leaning parties of the West, however, had historically been *pacifist*, in the sense that wished to reduce and ideally eliminate the military capability of *their* national armed forces and therefore, what the military saw as a problem, a big problem indeed, for the Western governments of the time was actually a major achievement. Initially the *CEDA* boosted the economies of the West (and China) because a massive number of electric vehicles had to be produced (mostly in China) in a very short timeframe to match the self-imposed deadline. Among these, were the first generation of armoured trucks and tanks that supplanted the traditionally armoury previously used by the Western forces. Their large and heavily armoured frames now dotted large swaths of territories, aptly referred to as *Tank Cemeteries.* The new trucks and tanks were small and light, because anything bigger or heavier could not be moved by their electric motors and they were aptly named *Smart Tanks.* In return they were also slow compared to the traditional tanks and were required to recharge the batteries of their engines every two hours of engagement, thus, they were *ideally suited* for short, slow and small battles.

Unfortunately, these were not the types of battles envisaged by China and Russia, with imaginable consequences that will be described later on. Indeed, these new electric weapons were both *eco* and *enemy friendly*.

China had slowly started its worldwide imperialism implementing industrial scale fishing off the coast of Africa since early 2000's. This had been followed with a progressive encroachment strategy. Chinese restaurants had sprung up in most African cities and then, gradually, the Chinese had swept into even the jungles and savannahs of most African countries with their plastic chopsticks. Actually, this included only the countries that had mineral wealth. Niger for their large but barely developed Uranium resources, DRC-Congo for its cobalt mines that needed further developments, Nigeria and Angola for their oil reserves that, following the termination of the use of fossil fuel in the western world would have been otherwise mothballed. *Silk Road Friendship Industries* was the corporation, that through its many subsidiaries, operated the commercial Chinese conquest of new territories and resources. Technically, the corporation was a private enterprise, registered in Honk Kong, but everybody knew that the major stake older was Mr Xin-Zing, the brother of Mr Lin-Zing, the Supreme Leader of the Popular Republic of China.

The Chinese restaurants in Africa acted as listening posts, often manned by the Chinese secret service. Eventually the fishing fleets were paired with aircraft carriers under the excuse of protecting the fishing from the menace of 'pirates', even though no incidents had occurred to justify this. In due course the Chinese had also sent onshore many armoured divisions of the Great Popular Army to protect the Chinese restaurants from local customers that had angrily refused to use the chopsticks. Mr Lin-Zing was careful to explain that this was a purely defensive measure.

But the next steps of the Chinese expansion had been executed much more swiftly. After the release from their Wuhan biological warfare lab of what would eventually be known as COVID-19, the Chinese had flooded Africa and Latin America with their vaccines. They were provided for free so as to create a captive market for products that were otherwise inferior to the vaccines produced by the free world. Sinovac only had a 50% capability of combating the COVID-19 virus as opposed to the 90+% of the Pfizer or AstraZeneca vaccines; this lack of efficacy had been purposely engineered by the Chinese. Indeed, a new dose of the Chinese vaccine was needed every few months to build the immune system against the ever-changing strains of the COVID virus that the Chinese were spreading worldwide (by 2035 covid-25 was the latest engineered strain of the virus). These new vaccines were also provided for free under the *Friendship Vaccine Program* (FVP), a pharma-diplomacy program designed to hook many countries of the world to China. The west referred to this policy as the 'infection stick and vaccine carrot' program.

Since the beginning of the Energy Transition Program the Chinese had maintained a significant stake in the mining of Rare Earths Elements (REE), 95+% of which were extracted in China, mostly in the Xinjiang province. These minerals were essential for the production of, among other key products, Wind Turbines,

Solar Panels and Electric Motors. Through their African and Latin American expansionism, the Chinese had created various Joint Ventures (JV's), such as the ones in the DRC-Congo, which allowed them to control by 2020 around 70% of the worldwide cobalt production and processing, or the ones in Chile, where they could hold a controlling equity on the worldwide production of 75% of Lithium by 2028. Cobalt and Lithium were metals essential for the production of Electric Batteries, Fuel Cells, Photovoltaic Panels, Robotic Drones, 3d Printing and ICT. Everything that was required for the production of so-called *Renewable Energy.* The sad irony that had been missed by most of the western world, was that the raw materials needed for the *Renewable Energy* required *Non-Renewable Minerals*, minerals that were themselves *finite, i.e., Fossil Minerals.*

Even more troubling (for the western world) was the fact that the mining and processing of most of these minerals were controlled by China, which, however, continued using fossil fuels and whose economy was growing exponentially, as opposed to the situation of the western world where the implementation of the Energy Transition had resulted in the not-so happy, *economic de-growth.* By the late-20's, through a variety of companies operating under the umbrella of *Silk Road Friendship Industries*, China had bought major stakes of the most important infrastructures of Western Europe, including all the major harbours, thus closing the commercial loop: from the mining, to the manufacturing to the marketing of all the minerals the West needed for their *Renewables.*

Not only had the Chinese Army created large military bases in various foreign countries to protect their national, commercial and strategic interests, but over 300 million Chinese labourers had been forcibly relocated to selected countries in Africa and Latin America, such that the long-term demographic implications would make it impossible to revert to pre-colonisation times. *Sinoblacks* (in the Nigeria-Congo region), *Sinobrown* (in Angola) and *Maurichino* (in the Sahel) were rapidly becoming the predominant races of large swathes of Africa. While in Latin America the new race was referred to as *Latchinos.* The relationship between these new mixed races was not always smooth though. For instance, the *Maurichino*'s had taken to encroaching on the *Sinoblacks* territory to enslave their population. Something that the Sahel Arabs had been doing to the black Africans for generations, anyway.

Ecological disasters of a proportion never seen before had resulted from the intensive and unscrupulous mining of Cobalt in the DRC-Congo. Landslides the size of a medium sized city had occurred, killing hundreds of labourers, both locals and those of Chinese heritage. The waters bodies of Katanga, the region where most of the cobalt mining was taking place, had reached such a level of industrial pollution, including a high content of Lead, that blindness and other pollution related illnesses had become the norm among the local population. On the other side of the world, extraction of Lithium from the salt flats of the Atacama Desert, at the rates required by the Chinese production targets, had resulted in a massive shortage of fresh water supplies, that until then had supported the ecosystem and local communities.

But China had not stopped at only this. After many years of skirmishes with Taiwan, and having realised that the West would never intervene militarily to protect their ally, China had invaded and annexed Taiwan in 2028 through a short but bloody war. Officially this was only a military operation to reunite the island to China proper, but there was a strong economic agenda. Indeed, Taiwan produced 90% of all the advanced chips manufactured in the world through their *Taiwan Semiconductor Manufacturing Co. (TSM).* This component is required by virtually all electronic products. Thus, the annexation of Taiwan had provided the last piece to build the Chinese puzzle of world control.

Like China, Russia also had not implemented any significant reduction to its use of fossil fuel. Its economy, however, had slumped due to the reduction of exports of hydrocarbons, particularly gas, to the EU. This reduction had initially started as a result of the sanctions imposed by the West on Russia for its bloody invasion of Ukraine in 2022 and it had subsequently been integrated into the overall bans on the use of hydrocarbons irrespective of their provenience.

Therefore, as opposed to China which was thriving, riding the wave of both the inefficiencies of the western world's Energy Transition, and the dependence of that transition on minerals and products mostly controlled by China, Russia found it was now suffering, and had initially tried to cover its internal malaise with foreign wars. From the Caucasus mountains to the plains of Ukraine, Putin's Russia had waged wars since 2008, encroaching into countries that during the soviet era had been part of the old USSR and that now were independent and friendly with the West. The occupation of Ukraine's Crimea peninsula in 2014 had been swift and unopposed both by the Ukrainian army and the West, a situation that had led Putin to think that he would have a free hand continuing with expansionism. He was even more encouraged after the disastrous retreat of the USA and the West in general from Afghanistan in 2021. As a result of the perceived weakness of the West, Putin had decided to remove the Ukrainian pro-Western government and completely annex that otherwise independent nation. However, Russia's 2022 invasion of Ukraine had been strongly and successfully resisted by the Ukrainian army that had taken advantage of both the training and sophisticated weapons provided by the USA and the UK since 2014. The EU had provided initially only some moral support to Ukraine and avoided material aid because of its, at the time, dependence on Russian gas. It had taken months of bloody war and carnage before the EU had agreed to cut its umbilical cord to Russia and its hydrocarbons.

As a result, what Russia had assumed to be a smooth and quick occupation of Ukraine turned into a long-lasting conflict in which Russia had lost thousands of soldiers together with a significant amount of military gear. Among this the Ukrainian Army had managed to sank the most important vessels of Russia's Black Sea fleet. Indeed, the photo depicting Putin inspecting his fleet during Russia's *day of the sailor* became the symbol of the poor military performance of Russia.

Russia would have eventually lost (a new Afghanistan) if not for the changes imposed by the new Western environment driven governments to their own armies. The light eco-friendly Western armies and their smart tanks subsequently proved no match even for the obsolete Russian tanks. In the first skirmish the Russian heavy tanks with combustion engines had smashed the foremost line of defence formed by the NATO's *Smart Tanks* like a knife penetrating into warm butter. It was like as if a Ferrari had been competing on a F1 circuit with a *Smart Car*, pun intended: the outcome was very predictable. Following that initial battle NATO had simply retreated, ceding living space to the Russian army. They could occupy whatever Western European territory they desired. This appeasement stance of NATO had been exacerbated by the fact that, following the disengagement of the US from any foreign intervention, which had been sanctioned by amending the constitution, NATO was now run by bureaucrats rather than soldiers. They preferred to issue notes and complaints, in detailed memos, supported by complex spreadsheets, but would never commit force to protect any of the NATO partners. If Russia had not completely invaded Western Europe, this was only because of their ineffectual logistics marred by corruption at all possible levels. As a consequence, Russia had eventually occupied (or re-occupied) Ukraine, Lithuania, Latvia and Estonia without any serious military confrontation with NATO.

Russia had also made strides in Latin America, sending troops and missiles to Venezuela and Nicaragua, nations that would have otherwise have imploded because of their dire economic situation. And North Africa had been, initially, another fertile ground for Russian expansionism following the US retreat from Syria in the early part of the 20s. This had resulted in a strong position across Syria, Lebanon, and Libya that provided Russia with access to the sought-after Mediterranean region.

However, following the Taliban take-over of Afghanistan in 2021, and their subsequent invasion, supported by Pakistan, of neighbouring countries (Tajikistan, Uzbekistan, Turkmenistan, part of the Caucasus, the northern portion of Iran and part of Kazakhstan) an Islamic Emirate Confederation had sprung up that represented a threat to the southern boundary of Russia. Therefore by 2030 Russia was fighting for its survival against the Islamist movement as well as China in various parts of the world.

Israel, UAE and Saudi Arabia had started collaborating against Iran many decades earlier. Eventually the Iranian nuclear threat, that no treaty or sanctions could properly address, had been resolved by the US with a series of tactical nuclear strikes. This had occurred in 2028, before the *Disengagement Act.* Actually, the nuclear attack on Iran had been part of a bipartisan agreement to prepare for the *Disengagement Act.* The Democratic Party, which was still in power, had sold to its *peace loving – vegan – eco-friendly* section, the idea that UAE and Saudi Arabia would stop producing hydrocarbons only if the Iranian threat could be taken out of the picture. The Republicans liked to bomb things anyway, so for once there had been implicit and explicit support from all sides of US politics. As long as no US military boots had to be employed on the ground. The rapid war against Iran had been referred to by the *New York Times* as the 'War to end all wars', a slogan that was a reminder of the one used to justify WWI, a name that, however, had not prevented any subsequent wars; but the generations living in the US in 2028 had never Googled WWI in their smartphones and therefore were not aware of the fallacy of the slogan. After all, if you don't see it on Google, it does not exist.

The war had ended swiftly with the complete destruction of the Iranian nuclear facilities and some collateral damage, that depending on who you believed, included between 5 and 15 million civilians.

Convincing the UAE to stop oil production had not been easy though. The US had to actually cover all their hydrocarbon installations with mine fields, both onshore and offshore. With the Saudi's it had been even more difficult and eventually the US had to resort to painting all their oil infrastructure with a special, and deadly irradiating coat of paint. The sweetener for both the UAE and Saudi Arabia, aside from the elimination of the Iranian threat, had been their participation with Israel in a high-tech Joint Venture which included US private money coming from Halliburton and Schlumberger, the most important oil service companies before fossil fuel had become a bad word. This JV, called *Techfuture*, was involved in many high-tech programs, from medical to the aerospace industry. Lots of their endeavours were quite secret, others less so. Among the latter, was the production of the *Faisal-Cohen anti-covid pill* that from time to time was re-engineered to counteract the new strains of the virus manufactured and spread by China.

ISAUAE was the military organisation set up by Israel, Saudi Arabia and UAE to protect each other against the ever-present threat by the Islamic Emirate Confederation and its allies. Israel, with its high-tech weaponries, was by far the greater 'muscle' of this organisation because both the Saudi's and UAE militaries had demonstrated during the war in Yemen that they could only fight in a properly air-conditioned environment and that even from their air-conditioned plane cockpits they had been responsible more of collateral damage than military successes.

The Taliban had been an invention of the Inter Service-Intelligence (ISI) of Pakistan, and that link had always remained strong. Pakistan had indeed provided shelter to the Taliban when many of them had been driven out of their hideouts following the Afghanistan invasion by the US (and other Western forces) following 9/11. In the following years Pakistan had provided financial and military support leading to the return of the Taliban to Afghanistan and eventually had rejoiced when the Taliban had taken over the country in 2021.

By 2025 the Taliban/Pakistan alliance had expanded their influence on other Central Asian countries forming an *Emirate Confederation* that among other areas, now covered large swaths of northern Iran and Kazakhstan. This confederation antagonised Russia in Central Asia, both commercially and militarily. In addition, Pakistan had started a war with India in the disputed Kashmir region.

India's population had grown to 2 billion by 2035 and as such it had matched that of China, helped in this by the fact that the Chinese had, for many decades, constrained their population growth through government imposed strict family planning. However, India had much less territory to spread its massive population across than China.

This was especially so since India had missed out on the African and Latin American 'colonies' of China to export its excess head count to. If pollution had been a problem for India and its surrounding region for a long while, by 2035 the problem was off the scale. There was no apparent solution, because most of the energy needed to keep the nation moving and population fed was still derived from coal, the worst source of pollution. Indeed, the Indian subcontinent could hardly be seen in satellite images, most of its land area covered by a thick smog, that depending on the wind direction, spread to the neighbouring countries.

However, the Indian alliance with Israel, the UAE and Saudi Arabia (after they found they all had the same common enemy, represented by the Islamic State and its allies) had provided some breathing space to its population density issue. Starting in 2032, a quota was set at 50 million Indians a year, that could relocate to the vastness of the desert between the UAE and Saudi Arabia, originally known as the *Empty Quarter* and now renamed *The-Not-So-Empty Quarter*. Jungle plants, like the *Euterpe precatoria*, a relative of the *açai* palm, the Brazil nut, and the nutmeg plant were now grown throughout the desert through a *dry air* technology developed by *FuturTech*. This technology did not require water to grow these plants, as opposed to n their original environments in Amazonia.

Accordingly, vast stretches of the UAE/Saudi Arabia deserts were now green and populated. Fruit was the main staple produced in these green areas by the imported Indian labour, that was then exported, for hard cash, mostly to China. This was the only remaining country rich enough to be able to afford such expensive delicacies.

The economic and military pact between India and *ISAUAE* was rather unusual, in the sense that it included two autocratic states (UAE and Saudi Arabia) run as fiefdoms by their respective royal families and two democracies like Israel and India that had their own nuclear weapons. This incongruous alliance represented, however, the only stalwart defender of the free world against the other autocratic nations and alliances of the East (China, Russia, the Islamist Confederation) and the decadent ecological dictatorships of the West.

The technology and vision of Israel, the funding from the UAE and Saudi Arabia and the sheer population size of India were the seeds of a new, and complex civilization that would in future decades become as strong and expansionistic as the one currently projected only by China.

Chapter 8
The freedom trail, Xinjian – China
January 2027

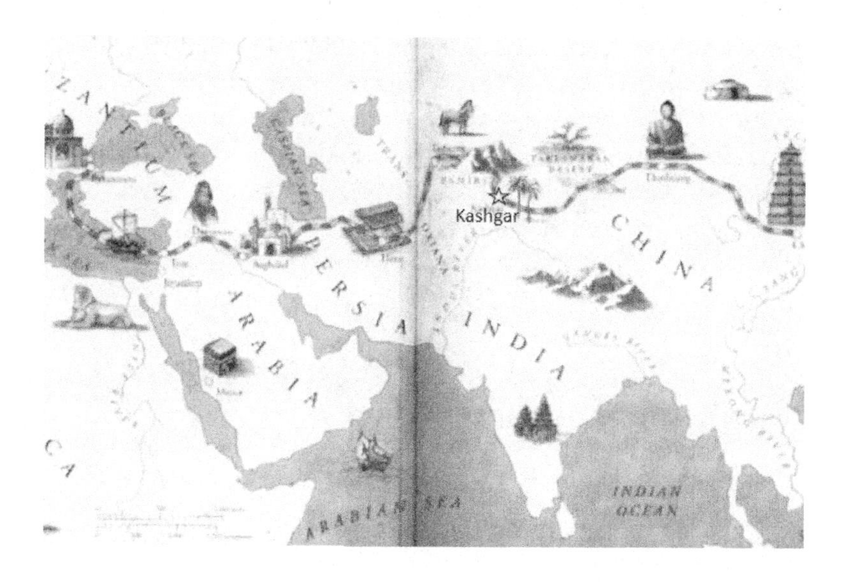

At one time they called it the Silk Road. Nowadays, certain individuals referred to it as the Freedom Trail.

Claire had only recently been deported from France to site 102-R-W, the labour camp not far from Kashgar, located in the extreme north west of the Xinjiang province of China. The camp inmates mostly worked the cotton fields located along the Kashgar River, from which the best cotton in the world was produced. And also much of the world's production, because Xinjiang province accounted for over 80% of the total Chinese production of cotton which in turn represented almost 25% of total world cotton production.

Claire, a British geologist in her mid-thirties, who had specialised in sedimentology, had been snatched up by chance or rather lack of it. She had been visiting the Paris office of BRMG, the French geological survey, when the 'woke squad' had arrived. They had refused to listen to her pleading, to the fact that she did not even work there. For *them* it had been enough that she was present in such a place, a crime scene as the woke party leader had described it; an office that had been dealing with geological issues for many years and therefore, as all the other individuals apprehended in its premises, she had to be considered guilty. As a result, she had endured, together with the French employees of BRMG, the long journey to China and their rehabilitation camp.

Camp 102-R-W was one of the many facilities set up in Xinjiang by the CCP, the Chinese Communist Party, to *re-educate*, that was the term officially used, the Uighur's, a Muslim ethnic group of Turkic lineages. The oppression of the Uighur's by the Chinese government had aimed at taming their spirit of independence and had started many decades before. Among other ethnic cleansing actions, a significant number of Han, the mainstream Chinese race, had been forced to relocate to the Xinjiang, so that by the early 2000's the Uighur's, although still representing the majority of people living in the region, represented only just above 50% of the overall population. Starting in 2017 however, this ethnic cleansing had taken on a much more sinister form with the first prison camps becoming operational.

By 2027, over 2 million Uighur's, that is 20% of the total population, had been detained in the camps, separated by sex. Both men and women were used for forced labour, mostly employed in the cotton industry, and brainwashed, indoctrinated by representatives of the CCP. However, the treatment reserved for the women was much harsher and included the systematic rape by the guards, forced abortions, sterilisations, cutting of their long hair to be sold on the cosmetic market. This ethnic cleansing had resulted in a significant reduction of the Uighur population and therefore some of the facilities had become redundant. This was the case with camp 102 that had been appropriately renamed 102-R-W, where *R* meant that it had been *revamped* at the request of the EU, to host the fossil fuel professionals captured in Europe. *W*, of course, stood for *women*. In the process of refurbishing the installation, all traces of blood and any other bodily fluids and parts had been erased. Once cleansed, to meet the stringent HSE standards of the EU, the camp buildings, both internal and external walls, had been painted in emerald green, the colour of choice of ecologists and vegans. In addition, the vegan EU commissioner had insisted that, as opposed to the pork often served to the Uighur's to offend their Muslim faith, the fossil fuel professionals would only be allowed vegan food, and as such a premium had been agreed with the CCP to cover the additional cost of this *special* diet.

Claire had noticed that a few Uighurs were still present in the camp. These were the ones that had survived the genocide, mainly because they were useful to the CCP by providing general services, from cooking in the spartan canteen, to taking charge of disposing of the bodies of the dead inmates. This was very much like almost a century before, when the Kapo's had served the same function in the Nazi camps where the final solution, the extermination of the Jews, had been carried out. Most of the work force, however, was constituted by oil professionals, and Claire had noted that they appeared resigned to their fate, at least that's what she first thought. She could not say that they were happy, certainly not that, but they were not un-happy either, which puzzled and even shocked the recently arrived Claire, who was by nature an impatient and independent free-spirit. The first week had been the hardest because she had to adjust to the routine and the madness of the place. The wakeup call was at 5:00 am sharp. The *prisoners*, correction, the *trainees* as the Chinese guards referred to them, had half an hour for their early morning ablutions, in overcrowded facilities. After that they were offered what Claire, accustomed to her eggs and bacon, thought was a very meagre breakfast of unsalted, unsweetened porridge and bitter green tea. By 6:30 am, they were divided into classes of approximately 100 *trainees* and they would start a re-education session that would last for 3 hours. Each internee had been given a notebook where they wrote the key sentences that were the subjects to be discussed during the daily sessions. The instructors were middle aged Chinese men who explained, in pidgin English, the virtues of socialism versus the pitfalls of the capitalistic societies.

"Socialism superior. All your needs satisfied" one of the instructors shouted.

"Everybody eats same food. In capitalistic society poor eat shit, only rich eat well" explained a second instructor, a statement that Claire would have called *funny* if it was not for the seriousness of their situation.

"Write the sentence of the day" ordered the first instructor before continuing "*Farming cotton saves lives.*"

The second instructor went into a half an hour explanation of the deep meaning of the sentence of the day, which included a reminder of the superiority of the Han race (the Chinese mainstream so to speak) and the luck that the *trainees* had in being re-trained in Xinjiang rather than being in the hands of the woke parties in the West, that would torture and kill them.

The lesson would always finish with the singing of the *March of the volunteers*, the Chinese national anthem.

Arise! Ye who refuse to be slaves!
With our flesh and blood, let us build our new Great Wall!
The Chinese nation faces its greatest peril.
From each one the urgent call for action comes forth.
Arise! Arise! Arise!
Millions with but one heart,

Braving the enemy's fire, march on!
Braving the enemy's fire, march on!
March on! March on, on!

Finally, they were let out of the facilities to spend the afternoon tending the massive cotton fields that surrounded the camp. Summer was hot, winter very cold and they never had the appropriate or adequate clothing for either of these seasons. As a result, the arrival of spring and early autumn was celebrated by the oil professionals working the cotton fields. For a few weeks a year most of the labour force rejoiced like as if they were free men and women. The truth, for many of them, was that the concept of freedom had *evolved* after several years of re-education. Freedom for them now meant not suffering too much, that's it.

They had divided the oil professionals into three groups: engineers, geoscientists and administrators, the individuals tattooed with the initials of each group, ***E***, ***G*** and ***A*** to facilitate their control by the guards. Every group had specific tasks that matched their previous experience. The *engineers* were good at planting the cotton seeds, in perfectly aligned and spaced rows; the *geoscientists* on the contrary, were very good at picking the cotton and dividing it by quality, easily recognising anomalies in the crop; finally, the *administrators* were in charge of counting the crops, what else? In addition, they had selected across the board, some of the inmates to be trained at producing cotton garments that, prepared with the best cotton in the world, would fetch massive amounts of hard currency for the CCP when sold in the West by the remaining high street brands.

Claire had to get used to the long afternoon and evening in the field, interrupted only for a snack break that consisted in one fried soya filled dumpling in mid-afternoon, brought by one of the other European prisoners working in the camp kitchen. Eventually they would return to the training facilities at sunset.

Dinner was normally unsalted boiled rice accompanied by another glass of bitter green tea. Enough food to keep the trainees from starving but not enough to satisfy their hunger. This helped the Chinese guards to control the masses, that had also learned the hard way that any small act of rebellion, a single poorly planted cottonseed or a bud of cotton that had been poorly separated from its stalk, a small counting mistake, or a garment poorly finished, would result in the entire group going hungry for one or more days, depending on the gravity of the infraction.

More re-training was normal after dinner and then the trainees were allowed to sleep a few hours on hard wooden bunk beds, with no cushions or mattress.

On the first Saturday morning, Claire had slowly noticed that the senior trainees, those that had been in site 102-B-W for many years, displayed, if not joy, then certainly some form of expectation that made them happy. Their faces did not show the tense grin of the other days of the week. Claire summed up all her courage and asked Lauren, a middle-aged production engineer from Wales, what was this about?

"Tonight, will be fantastic" exclaimed an excited Lauren.

"What is going to happen?" asked Claire, who had started to share Lauren's expectations.

"We can return to the facilities half an hour before sunset" explained Lauren, her face lighting up with impish glee "…and our boiled rice will be salted and they will even drop a spoon of honey into our tea. We get that luxury only on Saturday nights."

Claire rolled her eyes and reflected with sadness on how, when one is in deep shit any minimum improvement to one's condition is enough to call for a celebration.

Among the recently arrived, people dreamt of freedom, of fleeing the camp. The senior *trainees*, however, the ones who after many years in the camp had accepted their fate, warned that all these were fantasies, and actually very dangerous fantasies that could undermine the *security*, that's the word they used, that the group as a whole had achieved by *leaving* the West and avoiding the ill fate that the woke parties would have brought on them all. Like most civil servants like to do, they labelled as *secure* the insignificant life that they lived. The only certainty was the slow but inevitable death that awaited them at the end of the tunnel, which in this case was the process referred to as re-training. They preferred this *certainty* to the *risk* of trying to improve their condition, to get free. After all, many of them had been engaged in working for large oil companies and governmental energy institutions, where the staff are indoctrinated to follow the rules and processes, that are usually rigid and so they often lack common sense. As such, living in a re-education camp, where they did not need to proactively take decisions, because all was decided for them, felt for many of them very natural, a simple extension of the type of mental attitude they had when working for their segments of the oil industry. Among the inmates there were several *lowlifes*, as always occurs when a vast number of individuals are obliged to live shoulder to shoulder for a long period of time. In the group labelled by the Chinese with the generic name of *Administrators*, one could find the worst of the worst; many of whom had worked in *Human Resources*. They carried on their culture often by snitching on colleagues, reporting to the Chinese guards any infraction or presumed infraction committed by other inmates. The prize for them was an extra spoon of unsalted porridge or a second glass of bitter tea. And the warm feeling that they had achieved something important with their life.

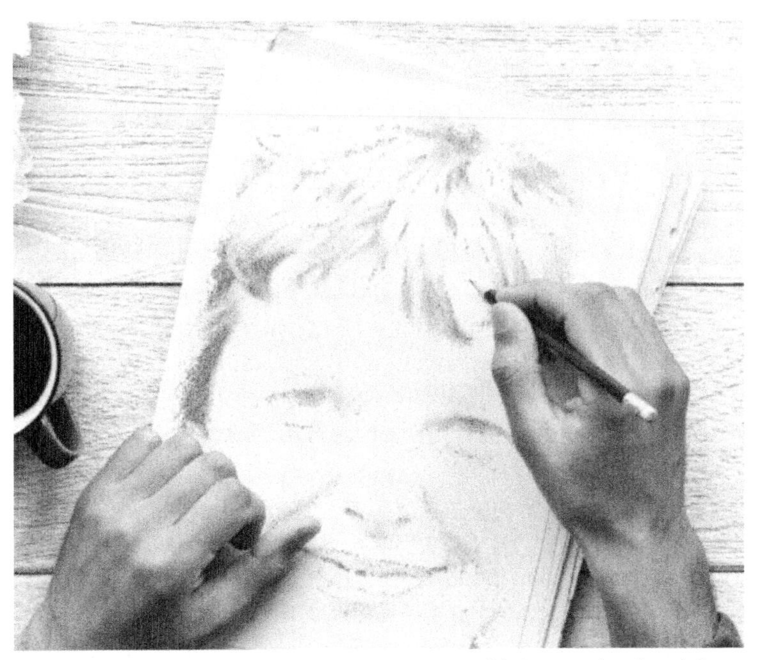

After a few weeks of the camp routine Claire noticed, with apprehension, that she had started looking forward to the regular Saturday food improvements. She realised that if she had stayed in the camp much longer, she would become like most of the other inmates. She would become passive and accepting that their fate was out of their hands. Maybe she would also become happy, like many were, to park her body and spirit in a sort of safe harbour so to speak. A situation where, day in and day out everything was predictable. She decided to try and escape this destiny. But she barely knew where she was in China. Xinjiang was an unknown place to her before reaching the camp and even then, she had no clue where the camp was actually located within the Xinjiang. She had no idea either, what countries bordered that part of China or if any of them was a safe place to hide in the unlikely event she could escape her fate. The thing she knew was that despite the poor alimentation she had to keep fit physically and mentally to be able to find a way out of her predicament.

And then Michelle arrived. Michelle was 40 years old, thin, tall and naturally nervous. One of those people whose body pulsates so to speak. She was often unable to complete a sentence, simply because her mind was already racing on to the next thought. Being mixed race meant for her having two races rather than being a composite, so much was her energy and joy of life before being captured and imprisoned. Her father had been French, her mother a black African from Djibouti. She had graduated in France in petroleum engineering from the prestigious IFP and had worked most of her career with Total, the French major, which had, in the mid 20's renamed itself TotalEnergies to sound more environmentally friendly. But Michelle was more than a simple engineer. She spoke various languages fluently, including Arabic, and had been a sergeant in the *13th Régiment de Dragons Parachutistes*, or simply the *13e RDP*, which was one of the French elite special forces. Among other achievements during her military career, due to her mastering of Arabic, she had been seconded to the French army fighting the Islamists in central Africa, and as a result she had participated in various bloody clashes. She often joked with friends that she had left some of her body parts in Timbuktu, referring to a particularly violent ambush against the local jihadists in which her left little finger had been cut off during hand-to-hand combat by the knife of an insurgent. She had eventually killed him with her own *war knife*, as she liked to call it, finishing the insurgent by cutting his throat. This meant that she was someone who had seen more of life than the normal experience.

Because of her background, it took her only a few days to realise the nature of the environment in which she had landed. And not only the fact that this was a prison, whatever name the inmates and guards liked to call the camp. As was the case with Claire, Michelle's shock was compounded by the fact that most of the inmates appeared resigned to their fate. She was certainly not.

Accustomed to appraising her environment, a skill learned when behind the enemy lines in the Sahel, Michelle quickly identified one of the Uighur ladies who prepared their meagre meals as someone energetic like her and who showed empathy to the other inmates. As a senior figure among the cooks, she projected authority, or whatever authority her position allowed in a concentration camp. They could not communicate properly because Arzu, the Uighur lady, only spoke Turkic. However due to her Muslim religious education Arzu spoke some pidgin Arabic that was enough to communicate a few simple things with Michelle.

In time, Claire and Michelle came to each other's attention amongst their group of prisoners. One could even say that they *recognised* each other, although they had never met before. Michelle and Claire, with their swagger, and the sheer energy that her bodies oozed, stood out from the other inmates and their sad, broken and destitute bearing.

They finally communicated one evening before going to their bunk beds.

"Hi" said Claire smiling "my name is Claire."
"Pleasure Claire" replied Michelle, before continuing "I am Michelle. Like me you have been here for a short time I think…"

"Short…and too long Michelle" confessed Claire.

"I noted your sense of humour when working the tedious, repetitive chores we are forced to do" continued Michelle "which is the sign that you have not yet surrendered."

"They say that irony is the freedom of the prisoner" replied Claire.

"Great sentence, Claire" Michelle replied back "I will try to use your technique. But I have to confess that I am rather short of patience."

"What are your plans?" asked Claire, she could plainly see that Michelle wished to open herself up.

"I will escape at the first opportunity" replied Michelle.

"Gosh!" exclaimed Claire in awe.

"But I need to know where we are" continued Michelle.

"We are in a prison camp…" commented Claire with irony.

"I know that!" shouted Michelle, before regaining her calm and explaining "I mean, that to plan an escape I need to know where our camp is located within the Xinjiang and the surrounding region."

"As a geologist I tend to notice maps" commented Claire "and I am afraid I have not seen one to date, certainly not in the zones we prisoners are allowed to see."

"That's bad news, really bad news" replied Michelle "I need a map, even a sketch of some sort, to plan my escape."

"Our escape, Michelle" commented Claire, smiling "I have no intention to die as a prisoner myself. Much better to die in the open air of a desert, a glacier, anywhere really, if I cannot become a free person again."

"Understood Claire" replied Michelle "it makes sense to plan our escape together. Whatever plan we can come up with…"

They managed to rearrange the occupancy of the bunkbeds so that they could sleep shoulder to shoulder, continuing their conversation on freedom, or rather their dreams of freedom, late in the nights. They had to make sure though that the prisoners that had worked in HR would not notice their planning and their dreams lest they alert the

Chinese guards. Eventually they became lovers, the *assertiveness* of Michelle and the *nurturing* of Claire were the *Ying and Yang* that created every night the *magic circle* that made them free until the next morning call.

The prison boss, the short and fat Colonel Qiang, had always made sure that his team met whatever target the CCP required for the containment of the Uighur's. Among this was the monthly quota of rape of the Uighur women, that they had always exceeded with gusto. This, after all, had been part of the ethnic cleansing driven by the CCP, to demonstrate the Han's superior race. The sexual violence helped to keep the Uighur women in a state of submission, and as a side benefit, often resulted in inter-racial pregnancies. This helped to move the ethnic cleansing in the right direction, at least this was what Colonel Qiang explained to his subordinates, that their brutality was not only supported by the CCP but also that it had a logic, a good objective so to speak.

With the arrival of the European fossil fuel prisoners that situation had changed though, in the sense that the CCP had not enunciated any policy in respect of sexual violence towards the new prisoners and the main concern of the EU (the CCP client) was focused on detention, re-education and veganism (DRV as referred to in the Brussel's offices). Therefore, if the sexual violence and rapes had continued, it was just a proof that colonel Qiang was an entrepreneurial bureaucrat who could act on his own initiative. In a way, Colonel Qiang and his senior staff were actually enjoying the change, the fact that from week to week they could violate women whose skin colour varied from the porcelain white of certain northern European races to the olive green or black from the Mediterranean region or countries that had influx of Africans immigrants at some time in their history.

Therefore, it was not a surprise that the striking figure of Michelle had struck a chord with colonel Qiang. He ordered that Michelle be brought to his office. This was a rather sparse place. A desk, a comfortable leather armchair, obviously *his armchair*, a couple of plastic chairs for visitors, and a sort of medical examination table that he used for his rapes and sexual violence in general against the women prisoners. But when Michelle was brought into the office and forced to sit in one of the plastic chairs, she noticed something, that for her had major significance. A map of the region that showed all the main cotton growing areas of the Xinjiang and, even more importantly, the location of camp 102-R-W, was on the wall behind Colonel Qiang's desk. If visual memory had been for Michelle a natural skill, this had been, through her highly specialized military training, reached a very high level, that allowed her to memorize, after just a short sighting, a huge amount of information that she would then be able to redraw with high accuracy.

After dismissing the guards that had brought Michelle, Colonel Qiang went straight to the business he had in mind.

"Naked" colonel Qiang ordered in a highly accented English.

"What?" asked Michelle, who had not understood the meaning of the abrupt instruction.

Qiang leapt immediately into action. He jumped across the desk separating him from Michelle and started trying to touch her small but well-formed breasts. He didn't get far, because as soon as Michelle realised his intentions she reacted rapidly. She grabbed and squeezed the testicles of the Colonel with her right hand while with the left one snatched one of the pens from the desk and pushed it into Qiang's right eye. Blood spurted across the room. Qiang screamed. The guards outside his office could not intervene immediately because Colonel Qiang, unwisely as he had now discovered the hard way, had locked the office from the inside. They had to break down the door and even as they finally entered the office, Michelle neutralized them with precise karate strikes. Eventually, only the arrival of a guard with a taser, who could hit Michelle from distance, avoiding her violence, was able to bring her down. They beat the shit out of her and eventually put her in one of the cold windowless caves that had been prepared in the basement of the prison to hold mischievous inmates. She spent a month in this dungeon, recovering from the beating; her only daily food a spoon of unsalted, overcooked porridge and a glass of water. However, from time to time, her spartan diet was improved by the occasional dollop of honey that Arzu managed to smuggle into her porridge. During her internment in the cave, Michelle focused her mind on remembering the fine details of the map she had seen in Qiang's office. This gave her the inner strength needed not to succumb to desperation, especially because she did not know beforehand if and when she would have been returned to the main camp.

Eventually Michelle was released from the cave and returned to the normal, so to speak, prisoner's routine. Her body remained frail from the experience but her mind was even more determined to escape the prison camp. During one of the morning trainings sessions, she tore off one of the notebook pages and hid it, together with a pencil, in her underwear. That night, while Claire kept a watch for spies, Michelle spent several hours drafting the map. They finally had a lead, something on which to hang their dream of escaping the camp.

Now that they knew where the camp was relative to China and Xinjiang, Michelle started putting together a plan for their potential flight. She knew that the Silk Road ran approximately East-West along the Kashgar River. Further to the West the road connected with trails that eventually reached Samarkand. While neither Michelle nor Claire had ever been to Samarkand, they knew that it had become a sort of *Central Asian Dubai.* Samarkand, one of the oldest inhabited cities of central Asia, had prospered in ancient times with the advent of the Silk Road, becoming an important trading and cultural centre linking China to Europe. Nowadays the city found itself located in a country like Uzbekistan, that had shrewdly remained outside of the power struggles being fought in central Asia by Russia, China and the Taliban. Indeed, the country had become like a *Central Asian Switzerland*, a formally neutral country surrounded by dictatorships that needed a *free port* so to speak, for their dark trading, which included money laundering on an astronomical scale.

Samarkand had gradually become inhabited by a large number of expatriates from various nations, including Europeans and Americans, attracted by the booming economy that was in stark contrast with the meagre lifestyle in which the West had plunged its citizens as a consequence of the ecologically driven de-growth policies of its governments. Like a *new Dubai*, Samarkand mixed its ancient buildings, the *Bibi-Khanym Mosque* and the *Registan*, which was the heart of the old city, with modern skyscrapers where, what remained of the old western multinationals, from JP Morgan to VISA Inc, from IBM to Allianz and many more had relocated their headquarters.

And so, Samarkand became the target of the escape of Michelle and Claire. Eating a succulent sheesh kebab while downing shot after shot of the local vodka…that was the idea of freedom that permeated their dreams.

Michelle focused on finding the loopholes in the prison security system that would give them the chance to escape unnoticed. They hoped at least for a few critical hours, to put a significant distance between them and the Chinese guards. This, after all, was her professional mind set, both as an operational petroleum engineer and an elite soldier. She knew that sourcing water was a key element of their escape and planned that, once at a decent distance from the camp, they would hide during the day and search for the rivers and streams in the darkness of the night. They might have to make do with little food, but she believed that they could steal some along their path to freedom.

By contrast, Claire, who as a sedimentologist was more used to counting the grains of quartz in rock samples, would always find reasons why Michelle's plan would not work. She would always spot the *imperfect circle* in Michelle's planning, the anomalous shape of a rock fragment that could not be properly cemented to the rest of the stone. Indeed, she often compared Michelle's escape plans to one of these uncemented sandstones, full of holes so to speak, driving Michelle crazy in the process.

The security protocols of the camp were relatively lax because escaping was considered virtually impossible. To start with, outside of the prison the western inmates were easy to spot and apprehend. Most of the remaining Uyghur's would not dare to hide them because of the potentially lethal consequences that the CCP would bring on them. Furthermore, the Han's that had partially replaced them were always on the side of the CCP, their protector. Moreover, the inmates, like castaways marooned in an island surrounded by a vast ocean inhabited by ferocious sharks, had no place where they could return to. Indeed, for many, their *point of origin* was exactly where they had been captured by the woke parties and sent to Xinjiang.

The geography also played an important role in dissuading even the craziest inmate from trying to escape. To the east was the inhospitable Taklamakan desert and further south the Kunlun Shan high mountain range that separated China proper from the Chinese occupied Tibet. To the west there were only a set of relatively narrow valleys, with the exception of the Allay Valley in Kyrgyzstan that was up to 30 Kms wide and dotted with blue water lakes. These had a general east-west orientation insinuated between the rough mountains of the Hindukush and the Central Tian Shan and Alay range. This rough path was what had been referred to since time immemorable as the *Silk Road*, or more precisely as the northern route of the *Silk Road*, because there was another route further to the south that passed through Afghanistan.

After the Great wall of China was completed at the end of the third century BC to keep at bay the nomadic tribes of the steppes, this road had become an important trading route that, from west to east, connected several city states, now located in modern day China, Mongolia, Kyrgyzstan, Tajikistan and Uzbekistan. From Hami to Turfan, Karashahr, Kucha, Aksu, Tumshuk, Kashgar (which was the general area where the camp was located) and eventually to Samarkand. Despite the road's name, the trading of goods involved much more than silk. And with the trade also came the mingling of peoples. Indeed, the *Silk Road* fostered a continuum of changes, not just of landscapes but also of foods, cultures and religions.

Hashog had been raised since a young age by his grandfather. This was because his mother had died following a gang rape by the Chinese guards of the camp where she had been interned. His father had gone missing, probably snatched up or killed during one of the repression initiatives of the CCP against the Uighur's. As a result, Hashog's education had been mixed to say the least. He knew how to write and read in Turkic, but his education did not go much farther than that. On the other hand, he had learned from his granddad a great deal on how to survive in the harsh environment that nature and the Chinese had made of the land of the Uighur's. He was very skilled in hunting. And if at the beginning his hunting had focused on hares and birds, his hatred for the Chinese had eventually led the adult Hashog to form a combat group. This was what the Chinese referred to as Islamic terrorists, groups that took advantage of any possible opportunity to harass the occupiers of their land.

Initially they did not have access to firearms though, so their weapons consisted of bows, long knives and the eagles that, like drones, they had trained to attack soldiers of the Chinese army. Most of their targets were patrols distant from their bases, so that after any attacks, Hashog's group had time to melt away into the silent landscape prior to the arrival of reinforcing Chinese forces. After each successful action, they were able to gather more and better weaponry.

The morning of 17 January 2027 was different though. Their mission that day was to rescue one of Hashog's aunties who had been moved to a prison camp within their zone of operations.

The labour day at camp 102-R-W had started as usual. After the education session, the group containing Claire and Michelle, all dressed too lightly for the frosty winter day, had gone to tend the cotton fields at around 10 am accompanied, as always, by two guards. While Claire harvested the cotton pods with the geologists, Michelle daily chore was to repair the irrigation system that a strong wind had put out of use the previous day.

By lunchtime, however, Michelle, always attentive to any environmental changes, had noted something unusual. This time their meagre snack had been brought not by one of the European prisoners working in the kitchen but rather by Arzu. And even more bizarre was the fact that when Arzu gave Michelle her dumpling she winked and told her in her basic Arabic, which was their only common language:

"Taeal maei (Come with me)."

Michelle, full of curiosity and expectation, followed Arzu to the limit of the cotton field where a solitary lightly armed Chinese guard was lazily paying attention to the work being done by the prisoners. In the space of an instant the pandemonium started. An arrow penetrated the neck of the guard who screamed loudly from the pain and surprise. A second later, another arrow hit the guard's body perforating his heart.

The guard fell dead, while the second guard, who had observed from a distance, rushed over, only to be attacked by an eagle directed by Hashog. The guard's eyes were gouged by the skilled strikes of the eagle's claws before several arrows finished the wretched man.

Following these attacks several horsemen arrived on the scene, including Hashog, who had come to set free Arzu.

Arzu signalled to Michelle to escape with her on one of the men's horses. Michelle had no doubts about what to do, but she needed to convince Claire to follow her. Because she knew that one thing is the *planning,* and another thing is the *opportunity and implementation.* It is one thing having a sketch map to know in which direction freedom was, and another to actually risk all by breaking free from the prison. Her military experience gave her the insight that in any operation involving many unknown elements nothing goes as planned and the *opportunity* is the un-expected wild card that makes things happen.

"We are not ready" said Claire with the typical approach of a non-operational geoscientist, someone more used to doing her analysis of rock samples in an air-conditioned laboratory rather than on the front line.

"We will never be *ready* Claire" replied Michelle before continuing "but this is the catalyst, the opportunity to start our journey towards freedom, towards Samarkand."

They discussed the situation before them for several overlong minutes, while Arzu had to fight her own battle with her liberators who obviously wished to leave the battlefield immediately. Eventually the assertiveness of Michelle won the day. They escaped with Hashog's group.

Six adventurous months later the whiff of the grilled meat filled the informal restaurant where Michelle and Claire sat sipping homemade vodka from large teacups while devouring luscious kebabs during an intimate dinner.

They reached Samarkand, but not on foot,

as originally planned. Something that would have been very difficult to achieve. However, pressured by Arzu, Hashog had agreed to take them there with one of his caravans getting provisions from Uzbekistan.

During their succulent dinner, Michelle and Claire discussed the status of their work assignments.

"I have now registered over 1,000 ancient books" explained Claire smiling, before adding "cleaned them up from all the dust and in some cases sand that the desert winds had brought into the Central Library at the Samarkand Institute of Archaeology. This is the follow up to the fantastic work done in the early 2000's by Professor Maurizio Tosi."

"On my side" replied Michelle "I am almost done with the restructuration of the *Shirdar Madrasa*, the 17th century educational and religious building in Samarkand, located on *Registan Square*."

Far from both their oil industry activities and their countries of origin, out of their comfort zone and skill set, they had embraced a civilization that at one time was alien to them. Their mission now is to preserve ancient manuscripts and buildings. In their own small way, they are the line in the sand to protect humankind from the *deserts*, plural; the one physically encroaching the town and the *cultural desert* brought in by the cancel culture of the woke parties.

Chapter 9
The State of the Nation
Washington – 2035

- ***Attendees:***
- Dr Kamelia Jarris – The *POTUS*
- Mrs Julie Hashard – Democratic Party International Affairs Analyst

They reviewed the state of the nation.

Julie Hashard explained the geopolitical situation, or at least the geopolitical situation as interpreted by a down-to-the-core Democrat.

"Madam President" Julie said after having had the visual confirmation that Kamelia was wearing a pink bracelet, "after all, Biden's rapid withdrawal from Afghanistan was probably the best foreign affairs action ever undertaken by a US administration since the defeat of the Soviet empire engineered by Reagan (with the key support of Thatcher and Pope Wojtyla)."

"Really?" asked Kamelia in disbelief.

"Yes, I know what you think Madam President" resumed Julie "the 2,500 US deaths, the hundreds of thousands of civilians that were the collateral damage during the twenty years of war."

"Also, Julie" Kamelia pointed out "the 500,000 killed by the Taliban in reprisal when they regained power in 2021, the many thousands of cases of rape and forced marriages, millions of refugees in the neighbouring countries and more…"

"Yes, I know Madam President, of your sincere humanitarianism" continued Julie "but all this bad news really only lasted in our media for less than a month, and were quickly forgotten. Less than a *second* in world history, then everybody was happy that Afghanistan had regained a sort of calm. Even some of our infection specialists agreed with the Taliban doctors that the Burqa was more effective than the FFP2 face mask in preventing respiratory diseases."

"I see" commented Kamelia "it is a matter of spinning what otherwise would be just bad news, that's it?"

"Not only that Madam President" explained Julie "the long-term implications of the creation of the Islamic Emirate in Afghanistan have been very good for our foreign policy."

"Explain please" asked Kamelia with a quizzical expression on her face.

"You see Madam President, after the *Disengagement Act* we needed a serious and reliable ally to do the dirty work for us outside our country's borders."

"And?" asked Kamelia.

"The Taliban have proved very effective. To start with, their expansion across Central Asia and North Africa has checked Russian aggressive posturing in Europe and the Mediterranean. The Russians now have serious problems to protect the Caucasus from the Islamic hordes and as such, their Army has stopped its encroachment toward Western Europe. If the Taliban had not taken over, by now the Russians would have also retaken Poland and part of Germany."

"I start understanding Julie" Kamelia commented.

"And also, the Taliban's China policy has been extremely efficient. When we fought them the production of opium was irregular. Now that they have full control of their territory, production has grown year on year. Currently, with 20,000 tons per year, they are able to flood the Chinese market with raw opium but also the best quality heroin" explained Julie.

"What about the US?" asked Kamelia.

"Our de-growth has virtually eliminated the use of drugs in the US. People have hardly enough money to buy food. On the contrary the booming Chinese economy has resulted in a large upper-middle class with plenty of money and time to enjoy narcotics. And the Chinese money goes to finance the Taliban expansionism in Central Asia and North Africa."

"That makes sense" commented Kamelia with a smile.

"Now you understand my analysis. If for a moment we put aside the inhumane conditions in which most of the Afghans live now, the Taliban have done a great service to our country, undermining both Russia and China" explained Julie pointing to a map covering Europe, North Africa and the Middle East on which she had marked the regional geopolitical situation.

"Like the Chinese say, 'a picture is better than 1,000 words' commented Kamelia with pleasure, before asking: "what about the Shia of the Persian Gulf?"

Europe -North Africa - Central Asia Geopolitical situation - 2035

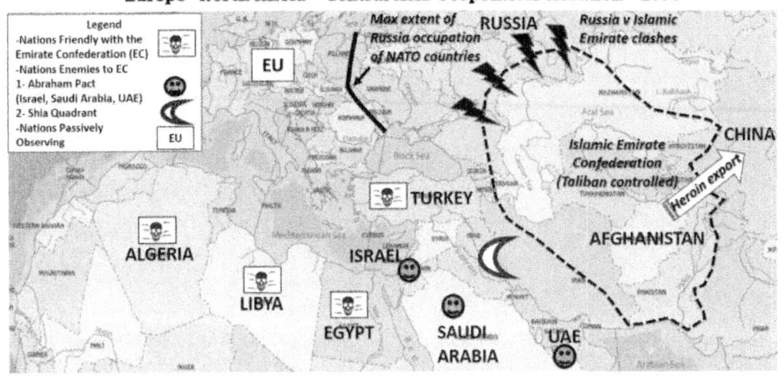

"As you remember, the Shia had always been the enemy of the Taliban. Scores of Shias belonging to the Hazara tribe had been killed by the Taliban in the 90's and they currently still are being killed" explained Julie before continuing "However since we have removed the Iranian nuclear threat, Iran has improved its relationship with the UAE, Saudi Arabia and, believe it or not, even Israel."

"Unbelievable" interjected Kamelia.

"Well Madam President" resumed Julie, "Israel is the only country in the Middle East with atomic weapons and whoever is not on friendly terms with the Islamic Emirate Confederation is almost obliged to seek the protection of Israel, since they possess the only army capable of defending the region from any further expansion of the Islamists."

"I have to confess that makes sense" admitted Kamelia before asking "I noted that Turkey and most of the North African countries are on friendly terms with the Taliban."

"Yes Madam President. You may remember what happened in 2011. What the western press referred to as the 'Arab Spring revolution' that it was hoped would bring democracy to the Arab world. What a joke this turned out to be. The West thought that this was like the fall of the Berlin wall of 1989. It was not, because the Arabs believe more in their tribes rather than abstract concepts like *freedom* and *democracy*" explained Julie.

"Yes I remember those days and the mess, the tribal wars that followed" commented Kamelia.

"Eventually new dictators took command of those nations and, just like Saudi Arabia after the 1979 Makkah terrorist attack by the Islamic extremists, they have accepted an Islamic view of their society more to protect their power than because they really believe in the Sharia etc. They are *Taliban light* so to speak" explained Julie.

"I assume that their economy is still mostly based on what remains of the fossil fuel industry" queried Kamelia.

"Indeed, Madam President" confirmed Julie, "but now that the West does not import fossil fuel anymore, their main markets are China and South-east Asia."

"I also noticed on your map that the EU is referred to as 'passively observing'. What do you mean by that?" asked Kamelia.

"I tried to be polite in the description. Since Brexit the main focus of the EU has been on resolving the problem of importing to Europe the Spiny Spider crabs from Wales. Every year it seems that the EU and the UK are close to reaching an agreement and then either one or the other party finds a reason to reject the deal. I mean that the most the EU has projected for many years into the regional geopolitics has been the smell of rotting crustaceans" explained Julie with a sad smile while concluding her presentation to Madam President.

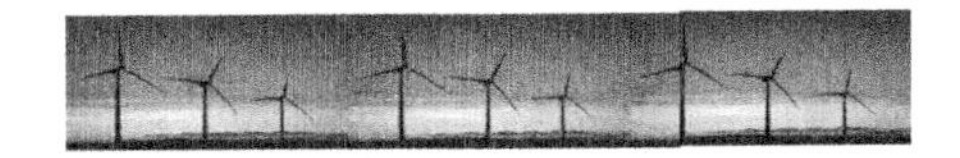

It was time for Kamelia to talk privately to Dr Tearfault. She remembered his facial expressions in their last meeting, a clear indication of how he felt to be an outsider in the Energy Transition team led by Mr. Therry. That team had provided an over-optimistic view of the progress made in the Energy Transition from fossil fuels to renewables which, she knew, Dr Tearfault did not entirely agree with.

- ***Meeting with Dr Tearfault***
- ***Attendees:***
- Dr Kamelia Jarris – The *POTUS*
- Mrs Jane Witchwood – Senior Assistant to the *POTUS*
- Dr Tearfault – Energy Transition Geoscience Advisor
- Mr Kim Jung – Head of US Department of State

"Good morning to you all" Kamelia welcomed the attendees before continuing "I set up this meeting to review where we stand with the Energy Transition program. But…I don't want to hear the self-fulfilling propaganda of Dr Therry. I want to hear your honest opinion on what is going on"

Dr Tearfault, a short and plump man, visibly started sweating. After all he was an office geoscientist, not someone who would criticise his superiors or take a stance that could be construed as non-politically correct. He knew that had he been a different type of person, a more adventurous individual, he would not have worked for the US government but… probably he would now be one more of the prisoners taken care off by the Chinese in Xinjiang. And therefore, he contented himself with being a coward.

"Dr Tearfault" said Kamelia getting straight to the point "I know that you don't like confrontation. But what I am asking today is for you to be honest. I noticed your grimaces during the meeting on Energy Transition led by John Therry and Dr. Snowfall."

"I am sorry about my facial expressions at that meeting, Madame President" Dr. Tearfault tried to excuse himself, "I did not sleep well the night before…"

"Don't worry Dr Tearfault" replied Kamelia "I have no intention to reprimand you. On the contrary, I would like to know what you really think of the situation, whether you slept well or not last night!"

Dr Tearfault realised that, for once, he would have been better off, maybe even getting promoted, by opening his heart and mind to the POTUS.

"If that is ok, Madam President, I will focus my talk on a few key interconnected points, all relevant to the implementation of the Energy Transition, which, to say the least, express opinions that are…not politically correct" said Dr Tearfault.

"Please go ahead" replied Kamelia, her eyes showing the curiosity that had led her to organise such a meeting with Dr Tearfault.

"You see Madam President" explained Dr Tearfault "they say that geology is like the skin of the balls…that you can pull it in any direction you want. This means that even among good geologists certain geological occurrences, like the migration of hydrocarbons or the depositional environment of an unusual type of rock laid down millions of years ago, can be explained with theoretical models, some of dubious scientific relevance, that sometimes are conflicting with each other."

"Very interesting Dr Tearfault" replied Kamelia "but what is the relationship between your statement on Geology and the Energy Transition, which is the subject of this meeting?"

"Because the way in which Energy Transition and indeed Climate Change, are presented reminds me of Geology. Scientific models that are often questionable are passed off as facts by the *Greens*. It is a bizarre situation Madam President, being *Green* is like belonging to an intransigent religious sect. Albeit, theirs is a weak religion that requires scientific proofs rather than just faith. Consequently, they pick and choose what evidence they require to support their science and religion, disregarding in the process anything that does not suit their agenda."

"I've got you Dr Tearfault" replied Kamelia "but I think that certain things, like the effect of CO2 and methane on Global Warming cannot be refuted."

"The problem, Madam President" continued Dr Tearfault "is that the earth is 4.5 billion years old. The glaciations, that are the key to climate changes, last hundreds of thousands of years and yet the *Greens* would like us to believe that what has happened in the last 10 years is representative of the next 100 or even 10,000."

"I see your point now Dr Tearfault" conceded Kamelia.

"It is like a lizard predicting the end of the world because it happens to find himself in an area affected by a large high tide and assumes that the world is all being submerged, not recognising the size and cyclicity of the phenomenon" summarised Mr Jung, who had studied natural science at university.

"People tend to generalise. It is their way to believe that they are, if not in control of their environment, that at least they understand the world they live in" explained Dr Tearfault before adding "a classical example, going back to Geology, is that when in Pennsylvania oil was discovered in 1859, indeed the very first oil discovered in the US, the science of that time predicted that oil existed only in that State."

"This was despite the fact that hydrocarbon seepages had been known about since ancestral times in various parts of the world. In Egypt, for instance, a mountain has even been, very appropriately named, *Gebel Zeit* (the *Mount of the Oil*, and they did not mean Olive oil!); in the Middle East there were even religions that believed that the fires resulting from natural gas seepages were an expression of God. And so on" commented Mr Jung.

"Truly amazing!" commented Kamelia.

"That was the first point of my observations, Madam President" commented Dr Tearfault.

"Ok go to the next please" replied Kamelia.

"The second point I would like to make is that fossil fuels are needed for the industrial scale production of the tools required for what is referred to as Renewable Energies" continued Dr Tearfault.

"What do you mean Dr Tearfault" Kamelia asked.

"Wind turbines require steel, which is an alloy of iron and carbon. The environmentalists will counteract this by saying that the carbon is a small fraction of the total weight of the final product" Explained Dr Tearfault.

"And..." queried Kamelia.

"They omit to say that most if not all of the steel production in the world is done using coal fired plants. It is an incredibly carbon-intensive process actually responsible for 5% of all total CO2 emissions" explained Dr Tearfault.

"Is 5% a lot?" asked Kamelia who was not too good at numbers.

"It is as much as the CO2 that the entire aviation industry used to generate. I said *used* to because by introducing the *Aviation Carbon Tax* for the US and the EU airlines, these now fly many fewer planes than they used to. Unfortunately, a significant portion of their slots have been taken by the Chinese air companies, that until 2100, do not need to implement any additional tax on their aviation" explained Dr Tearfault.

"Madam President" intervened Mr Jung "there is also a geopolitical side to the production of steel."

"Please explain" said Kamelia.

"Already in 2020, 15 years ago, that is well before the most stringent environmental policies were put in place in the West, China accounted for 57% of total steel production worldwide" commented Mr Jung.

"And now?" asked Kamelia.

"The West stopped the use of coal fired plants, except the UK that as you know, following Brexit, has been in an economic downturn and could not afford a full implementation of Renewables. On the contrary, China has increased their steel production capacity. The net result is that nowadays China is responsible for 95% of world steel production. Indeed, most of our Wind Turbines are produced in China with steel fabricated using their coal fired plants."

"In respect of the Solar Panels, the situation is not any better" commented Dr Tearfault.

"In which sense" queried Kamelia.

"The production of Solar Panels requires a very specific mineral called polysilicon, which is a hyper pure form of silicon, produced by heating silicon dioxide with carbon at temperatures approaching 2200C" explained Dr Tearfault.

"The same situation of the Wind Turbines then" commented Kamelia "one needs coal, which is the worst of the air pollutants, to produce what is passed off as an eco-friendly Renewable."

"Indeed, Madam President" commented Mr Jung "but there is more to the story. As with the steel, China has been, since the early 20's, a major producer of silicon. At that time China's production accounted for 67% of total world production. Most of the silicon was mined by forced labour, the Uyghur's, in Xinjiang. Nowadays China produces around 90% of total world silicon."

"The Chinese have us by the balls" reflected Kamelia, her face showing the irritation she felt.

"Indeed, Madam President" agreed Mr Jung.

"Energy Transition worked well, Madam President" explained Dr Tearfault with an inward smile "until we could put fossil fuel on the table. Because aside from the issues previously discussed, Renewables are not reliable. You need the wind blowing and the sun shining. And it is expensive and impractical to store large quantities of Renewable energy, as opposed to the fossil fuels. That's the third point I wished to make."

"Now that the West has virtually stopped producing fossil fuels" commented Mr Jung "we are totally dependent on products fabricated in China, that has no internal political objections to using oil, gas and coal."

"This is serious shit!" Kamelia shouted, "How can we counteract this disaster?"

"Madam President" replied Dr Tearfault "I am just a Geoscience Advisor, not a politician. I am not able to answer your question, I am afraid."

"The reality is, that exposing our discussion of today, these sad facts, to the general public will bring your government to a crisis never seen before" explained Mr Jung.

"I know" said Kamelia "the left of the Democratic Party is in bed with Renewables at any cost."

"They are a small fraction of the party, but very vociferous and supported by the so-called liberal media" admitted Mr Jung, before reflecting that "after all the fact that our party is called *Democratic* is a joke, because the majority of the party members do not see eye-to-eye with the extreme left of the party. Indeed, we are *Democratic*, in the same way as it was the *Democratic Republic of East Germany* or it is the *Democratic Republic of Congo...*"

"But without the support of the left I would not be where I am" commented Kamelia.

"That's the problem" replied Mr Jung "at the end of this year there will be the next Presidential election. If you stir the pot with the truths we have discussed, I bet that the Democratic Party will drop you and select a candidate more aligned with the Renewables fanatics and…the Chinese."

"True. Luckily the Republican party is divided and not a serious contender. Let's wait until I am re-elected and then we will envisage a policy change to gradually take back our energy independence."

With the above fatidic words, the meeting was adjourned.

Chapter 10
Climate Change
Washington – 2036

US Presidential Election 2036

The political agendas of the parties competing in the 2036 Presidential election were all 'for more' and could be summarised as follows:

Democratic Party = More Green
Trump for God = More Trump
Republicans Classic = More Energy

Each party had a key pledge that would dramatically change the course of American history, or so they said, if their presidential candidate was to win the election.

The Democratic Party supported an even stricter approach than had been applied to date to *greening* the world, that would increase food production and the happiness of the population. The East coast would be dotted by a new generation of powerful green windmills swirling in the wind to increase the eco-friendly energy supply; a new wool and metal mix would soon be available to supply more resistant tires for the electric vehicles, produced by *Goodplanet*, as the *Goodyear* company had been renamed following the demise of conventional combustion engines. New strains of carrots and cabbage seeds would be imminently available from which edible food could be obtained in a matter of weeks and in any season of the year. A *green dream world*, that to the sceptics sounded familiar to previous dream worlds that had never materialised.

The promise of the 'Trump for God' party was that if they won the election, they would drive a significant change of the US constitution that would guarantee a more stable democracy. The new political system was to be called *Religious Democracy*. It meant that the Trump family member who was president at any given time would isolate himself in the Nevada desert, the land of the Mormons, one month before his or her 4-year term was due to expire to seek God's advice on whom he or she *should choose* as the next US president. To control the fairness of the process, God would be allowed by the new constitution to re-select the Trump who was president at the time not more than 5 consecutive times. Apparently, the idea had come to the Donald through his frequent conversations with Putin who, with a different protocol, had been doing the same thing in Russia for decades. Putin's slogan stated that *'the important are not the votes but who checks the votes'* which Trump had tried to implement in a cumbersome and non-Russian way (which in this context means *ineffective*) during the 2020 elections. But the final touch to the idea, the *religious component*, had been born through the so-called *Peace talk of Doha* with the Taleban in the early 20's (what future historians would compare to the 'unconditional surrender' of the Japanese that ended

WW2, albeit run in an air-conditioned hotel rather than on the deck of a battleship in Tokyo Bay). Mullah Abdul Ghani Baradar had explained to Zalmay Khalilzad, the senior US envoy, that "once God is on your side elections are unnecessary."

"How the hell is it that we haven't thought of this before" had apparently exclaimed the Donald, when he had heard of this sophisticated political concept.

The *Religious Democracy* concept had been a hit with the many US religious communities and zealots. They could finally reconcile the absolutism of their religion and a new political protocol that, at least in its name, referred to democracy and therefore sounded politically correct.

The pledge of the 'Republican Classics' was, on the contrary, that increased access to energy would be the focus of their re-building of the nation. They did not specify, however, what they actually intended to do. This was to avoid putting off the democrats and republicans who had realised that energy independence was essential to overcome the economic gloom but, after so many years of eco-friendly brain washing, would not have accepted the fact that solar and wind power would never provide enough energy to support a thriving economy.

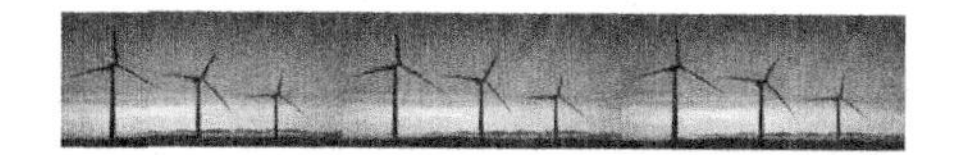

Further to the chronic energy and food shortages the support enjoyed by the Democratic Party for many years had dwindled. They were counting, however, on the Republican split to retain the majority of the electoral vote and extend the Presidency of Kamelia Jarris for one more term.

While the Democratic party had stuck to their traditional symbol, a big donkey, that perfectly represented their stubborn and often stupid policies, the two factions of what originally had been the Republican party had needed to be more imaginative with their new symbols. "Trump for God"*, now headed by the youngest son of the late Donald, had adopted a golden elephant with Donald Trump's face that reminded one of those amulets often found in the tombs of the Pharaohs*. Conversely, "Republican classic" had adopted as their symbol a vintage bottle of Coca-Cola, however ensuring it was *zero calories* to adapt to the times. Their leader was Mary Cheney, the great granddaughter of Liz who had defied the old Trump's order in 2020 and had conceded the victory of the Democratic party in that presidential election.

* *The body of the Donald had been put in a cryogenic liquid to preserve it intact for a future resurrection. The scientific world voiced doubts that the brain could be totally re-activated at the resurrection, but since even when alive that had not been of great use to the Donald, the living leadership of "Trump for God" had not worried too much. And only an injunction from the Supreme Court had stopped them listing the undead Donald as the VP candidate for the 2036 election.*

Mary had started as the underdog in the 2036 presidential election because no foreign power supported her. Conversely "Trump for God" had the support of the hackers set up by the Russians since the 2016 election. The Russians had been blessed by old Trump's withdrawal from large swaths of the Middle East and North Africa in the early 20's which had allowed Russia to fill the resulting power vacuum. For a while, until the complete Islamization of North Africa, Russia had controlled Syria, Lebanon and Libya, which meant they had a solid foothold in the Mediterranean region. In addition, they retained a solid grip in Venezuela.

The Democratic Party had, instead, the strong support of China and its highly sophisticated teams of hackers. China indeed, had a deep appreciation of how ineffective the ruling US party had been at containing their worldwide military and commercial expansionism.

Despite all the above, Mary had managed to turn the situation around. To start with she was *vegetarian*, rather than *vegan*, and *straight lesbian*, with *no gender fluidity*; this had eventually attracted the moderate portions of both Republicans and Democrats. Her real winner, however, was an advertising campaign including a short video full of political innuendo, where she had been pictured in the only Morton's steak house still open in the Red Meat district of Houston, surrounded by half a dozen large, bearded, gun carrying bikers, pretending to eat a rare T-bone steak. This political advertisement had only been streamed in Texas and Oklahoma, the strongholds of "Trump for God" and had won her enough support from the right wing of the Republicans to win the presidential election. It was a close call, but the T bone won it.

Never before had a piece of beef been so momentous and consequential in the history of mankind. From the beginning of her term the focus had been on how to revert the fortunes of the nation and terminate the disastrous *de-growth* policies that for the last fifteen years had been implemented by the Democratic party.

Following her formal inauguration as the new POTUS, Mary organised a meeting with her leadership team to discuss the state of the nation and forward plans.

25 January 2036
White House
Economic Growth Committee

- ***Attendees:***
- Ms Mary Cheney – The POTUS
- Ms Helen Trust – Finance Minister
- Mr Rob Tinderlam – Foreign Affair Minister
- Mr Rod Huff – Energy Expert
- General Harry McCarry – Supreme Commander of the US Army

Mary Cheney looked at attendees and sadly realised how they all were underweight and physically small by the standards the US had pre-Energy Transition. Being all in their late 40s and early 50s they had been directly affected by the food shortage and lack of animal proteins during their period of growth. The only exception was General McCarry that at 1.70 metres, was easily 10 cm taller than the tallest of the rest. He was rumoured to be a *meaterian*, this was how people that included meat in their diet were called in the late 30's. She compared her team's appearance, that reminded her of a group of scavengers, with the pictures she had seen of the Chinese leadership. They were all tall and well built. They were the *Americans of Asia*, so to speak. And in that very moment she realised that she had to put a stop to this situation and reverse it. How to do that she did not fully know at the time and, even more, from where she should start that process.

Mary went straight to the point. That was her way of leading a hard-headed team, the one she had pulled together to restart economic growth:

"Ladies and Gentlemen, our nation is in deep shit" said Ms. Cheney getting straight to the point, before explaining "the last fifteen years have seen our great nation not just losing its standing as a leader of the free world but, even worse, becoming a *soviet style* institution where only one voice could be heard. And that voice, made up of ecological bigotry and unrealistic promises of a better future, has destroyed not just our economy and our way of life. It has also affected the life expectancy of the generations to come."

The meeting's participants knew of Mary's sharp tongue, but they were still surprised at how fast she had got to the main point. Her summary, the 'deep shit', was probably the best characterization of the US state of the nation in 2036.

"What do you propose?" asked the finance minister Helen Trust.

"We need to agree on priorities" explained Madam President "and work to accomplish the required targets asap."

"The economy is certainly one of these priorities" replied Helen "as you know our GDP is ridiculously low compared not just to the one of China but even to the one reported by San Marino."

"Ok" said Madam President "revitalizing the economy is certainly one of the priorities."

"Food" wryly suggested the Foreign Affairs Minister, before adding "I do not think we can revitalize the economy if the workers, at whatever level, are not fed properly."

"A very good point" replied Madam President "and what do you suggest?"

"We should go back to eating a dairy-based diet" replied the Foreign Affairs Minister "I mean meat, both beef and pork, milk, cheese. All the things that are necessary to provide proteins to fuel the energy to the working masses."

"You have a point" conceded Helen "but how can we restore the food chain that propelled the US economy prior to the vegan / eco-friendly disasters?"

"We simply need to produce more meat, milk and cheese" replied Energy Expert Rod Huff.

"Easier said than done" exclaimed Madam President "only a few low-fat cows and pigs are currently available in the US, not enough to boost good quality meat, milk and cheese production."

"The zoos Madam President" explained Mr Huff.

"What do the zoos have to do with meat production?" asked Madam President.

"The old cow and pig species have been preserved in the zoos across our great nation" explained Rod "so that the new generation have a knowledge of the time gone by, when fat cows and pigs were allowed."

"That's a great idea Rod" concurred Madam President "let's get these species out of the zoo's and into the farms. I will sign immediately the *Prime Beef Act*."

"But this won't be enough Madam President" continued Rod "without energy independence we will never be able to achieve any long-term improvement in our economy."

"What do you propose Rod" asked Madam President.

"I have a few ideas, a few leads, but before putting them before you I need to do a few checks, I want to be sure they are feasible" explained Rod.

"Agreed" said Madam President "you have four weeks to come back with your proposals. In the meantime, I will appoint you as *Energy Resuscitation Czar*."

Shortly after, the meeting was adjourned.

1st March 2036
White House
Energy Resuscitation Committee

- ***Start-up meeting.***
- ***Attendees:***
- Ms Mary Cheney – The POTUS
- Mr Rod Huff – Energy Resuscitation Czar
- General Harry McCarry – Supreme Commander of the US Army

After the formal greetings, Rod stood up. Well, as high up as his short and skinny one and half meter frame would allow. He was proud of having been promoted from *Energy Expert* to *Energy Resuscitation Czar*.

"We had very little success with the *Energy Truth and Reconciliation program*. It was designed to try and duplicate the 'success' feigned by the South African post-apartheid *Truth and Reconciliation Commission*. Very few fossil fuel professionals trusted that our governments intentions were genuine and not another way to trap them" explained Rod Huff.

"You bet, after over 20 years of sending them to the Chinese lagers or killing them straight away…" commented Mary.

"Also, most of the trials were not credible. I remember when we had paid one of the *Green Jackets* to plead guilty and the guy went way over the top. He accused himself of having cut in two a reservoir engineer using a light sabre. A weapon out of Star Wars. Even the judge had a hard time not to laugh…" commented General Harry McCarry, before continuing: "The additional problem was and still is that, as you certainly recall, most of the fossil fuel professionals have been imprisoned in China. The Chinese will not give them back to us. Plus, they have become like *farmed salmon*, with a bland taste (and little remaining brains) that even if available they would not be of great use to restart our oil industry."

"What do the Chinese do with them currently?" asked Mary.

"The best is sent to explore and produce hydrocarbons in their territories that, as you know, now include most of Africa and Latin America" explained Rod.

"And the rest?" queried Mary.

"I understand that they have replaced the Uyghurs as forced labour in the cotton farming in Xinjiang" explained Rod.

"You mean that oil industry people are now farming 80% of the worlds cotton crops?" asked Mary while her jaw dropped.

"Indeed, Madam President" continued Rod, "the Chinese have discovered that the petroleum engineers are very good at planting the cotton trees. It is a job that does not require imagination. And, as opposed to the oil fields that lay kilometres under the ground, the cotton tree plantations are in plain sight. For once they can see what they are doing and this new situation makes them feel empowered. The results are perfectly aligned cotton plants, spaced at an equal distance. Apparently, they enjoy the routine and repetition of their work."

"Very interesting" commented Mary "and what about the Geologists?"

"They are good at recognising the anomalous crops, the ones whose manufacture will be marketed in South East Asia.

The best crops on the other hand, are sold to the west at a premium" explained Rod.

"You are telling me, that the previous administration has agreed a deal, which is for the Chinese a win-win? We pay them to detain the oil industry professionals and they use them to generate crops that are worth gold, particularly in the west."

"You could say that Madam President" reflected Rod.

"SO, WHAT'S THE PLAN?" shouted Mary with an angry voice.

Rod hesitated for a moment. He had noticed that Mary Cheney was upset and he was worried to have already put too much meat on her plate in a single session, particularly considering her vegetarianism. But then, he decided to try his luck.

"As you know, the West has closed all the Universities teaching subjects related to the oil industry" Rod commented speaking at a tangent, "aside from the fact that we bloody well need oil professionals now, not in 5 or 10 years."

"I know that" Mary was getting agitated because Rod was not getting to the point.

"You remember *Techfuture Inc.*?" asked Rod.

"You mean the JV between the governments of Israel, UAE, the Saudi's and what was left of Schlumberger and Halliburton after we shut down the oil industry?" asked Mary.

"That's it" confirmed Rod, before adding "they are mostly known for the production of the *Faisal-Cohen* anti COVID pill, used to counter-act the biological wars that the Chinese unleash periodically, Madam President, but they do many more high-tech things."

"Such as…???" queried Mary.

"For instance, they have developed a new satellite system that allows the rapid scanning of large areas of the earth for *brain impulses*" explained Rod.

"*Brain impulses*? You are talking Chinese, pardon my French" exclaimed Mary.

"They can detect the brain activity of agglomerations of individuals" explained Rod.

"And….???" Mary asked with puzzled eyes.

"Apparently, they have discovered that the fossil fuel professionals hiding in the wild have higher brain activity than the average population" clarified Rod.

"Jesus!" exclaimed Mary, "so we have a lead."

"Yes, Madam President. Not only that. They have also discovered that while the wild fossil fuel engineers brain activity is higher than the normal population but rather steady, the wild fossil fuel geologists show a spiky brain activity which is their very unique signature."

"Unbelievable Rod" exclaimed Mary, "this sounds like science fiction."

"It's all real Madam President" intervened General McCarry showing a graph to make the point, "we can use this technology to identify and capture our targets… I meant bring them back home."

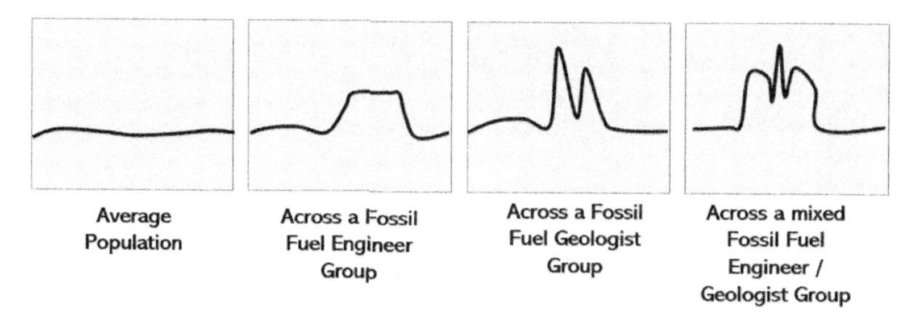

"Have our scientists understood the reasoning behind this signature difference between engineers and geologists?" queried Mary.

"To be honest Madam President" replied Rod "I have heard many theories. However, one that I found plausible is that while the engineer thinks in a linear way, the geologists do not. Strangely, they believe in geological models that are often so different and conflicting, that this generates the brainwave spikes."

"Fascinating" commented Mary, before adding: "go ahead with the plan Rod and General McCarry. You have my blessing. Let's call the plan *Operation Climate Change.*"

Epilogue

Every oil professional would recount a different story of how he or she had been found by the parties sent by the Energy Resurrection Czar.

"Don't worry, we are not going to harm you" explained Major Thomas to Armando "we are here because the US government has finally realised that they need oil professionals."

This was the first time in decades that Armando had been referred to as an *oil professional* rather than the demeaning term *fossil fuel geologist;* he found this bizarrely endearing.

"At 81 I am too old to be of any use to you guys, too late I am afraid" Armando had replied smiling.

"Don't worry, the only thing we need is a small patch of your skin" said Major Thomas.

"And then?" asked Armando.

"We will grow it in a steel tank, absolutely sterile and therefore no antibiotics needed" had explained Major Thomas to reassure Armando of the eco-friendliness of the process.

"Like the fake meat?" had queried Armando with a quizzical face.

"Indeed" Major Thomas had replied, "after 6 months the embryo will be mature enough to be placed into a human-like frame and will be ready to explore for oil and gas."

"Ha ha" laughed Armando, "this is science fiction, a mixture between *The boys from Brazil* and *Blade Runner*."

"You sure got the point quick, but you should also appreciate that each one of us calls *science fiction* whatever our brain does not manage to imagine. The boundary between *reality* and *science fiction* is therefore *subjective* and blurred at best. In this particular case, however, this is what *Techfuture* does for us in their secret laboratories in the Negev desert" Major Thomas explained, before continuing "you see Armando, Mengele, the Nazi doctor, who, in *The boys from Brazil* tried to clone new baby Hitler's, was an amateur compared to the medical staff of *Techfuture*. They don't just duplicate your genome from a small patch of your skin, they are also able to extract your life experiences. And pass them on to each *born again oil professional*; *BOP* is how we refer to them in the Army, a term that I understand resonates with you oil guys. Each *BOP* will carry the professional experience and memories of his or her lineage; that's why no University or training is needed to have them up and running, so to speak."

"Amazing!" exclaimed Armando.

"And as opposed to the *Replicants* of *Blade Runner*, they are not programmed to die" explained Major Thomas.

"Even more amazing!" commented Armando.

"Your memories of adventures, successes and failures *will NOT be lost in time, like tears in the rain*" continued Major Thomas paraphrasing the famous monologue at the end of the *Blade Runner* movie.

"Really incredible" commented Armando who was taken aback by the thought that the *BOP* who would be born from a small piece of his skin would live for ever.

"It is so expensive to produce *BOP's* that we could not possibly afford to have more generation gaps, like the ones we have experienced in the last couple of decades" explained Major Thomas, before continuing "and you will finally be able to go home, a free person who nobody will bother anymore, Armando."

'Home?' thought Armando. He felt like a modern Ulysses. He had been away from home for a decade. And for both his and his family's safety he had never tried to contact them. And now, according to Major Thomas, he should appear from nowhere, just saying 'I am back'. What a load of pathetic nonsense.

Armando closed his eyes while offering his right arm to the nurse carrying out the small incision. The same arm where the woke party had tattooed the ***G*** to signify that he was a fossil fuel geoscientist. It was his small revenge.

And while a morsel of his skin was removed and then dropped into a glass tube containing a cryogenic liquid, he realised that, among other memories, he had also passed along his moments of happiness. Taking refuge from a spring shower with the love of his life under the purple jacaranda trees in *Plaza San Martin* in Buenos Aires; the faces and names of all the ladies who had broken his heart; the languages and expressions he had learned to reach out to their souls: *tenerezza, tenderness, ternura, tendresse, нежности*; the aroma of a *bife de chorizo* sizzling on the grill of *Los Anos Locos* in *Costa Nera Norte* along the *Rio de La Plata;* the complex bouquet of a 10 year old bottle of *Cava de Weinert's* Malbec; the savoury crispness of the *bolinhos de camarao com catupiry* consumed with Brazilian friends at *Bracarense*, a *pe' sujo* off the Leblon beach, while drinking cold beers; the crunchiness of the snow crabs magnificently fried at *Zafferano* on the Swan river in Perth; the fragrance of the orange trees blossoming along *Avenue Bourguiba* in Tunis; the fiery taste of a *shakshuka* cooked to perfection at the *Amphitheatre*, an unpretentious beach restaurant in the outskirts of Tunis; swimming with the crabs in the warm and salty waters of the Persian Gulf off *Palm Jumeirah*; the penetrating scent of the *oud* burned in the mosques of Dubai; the enveloping aroma of the *frankincense* shampoo discovered by chance during a trip to Musandam in Oman; the sweet textured September figs collected from the trees in the hills of the lake of Garda.

Armando realised that, after all, his work had been more than a profession. It had been a life style which had expanded his universe; it had taken him to amazing places across exciting cultures and let him cross paths with a very varied part of humanity that had enriched his life. Despite having been obliged to hide for more than a decade and eat some terrible food in the process, he would not have changed his past for anything.

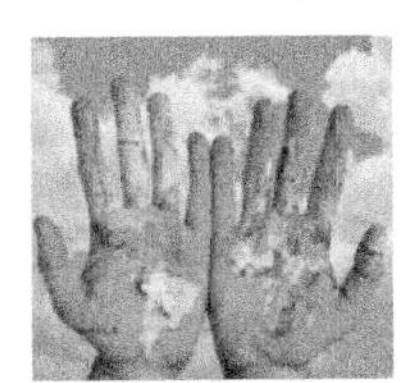 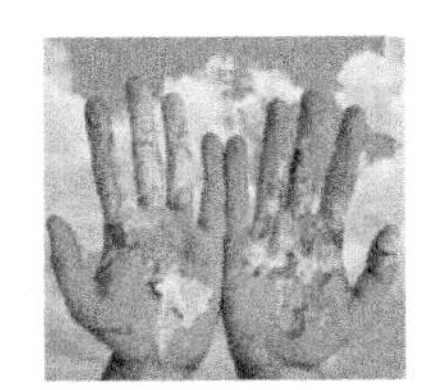 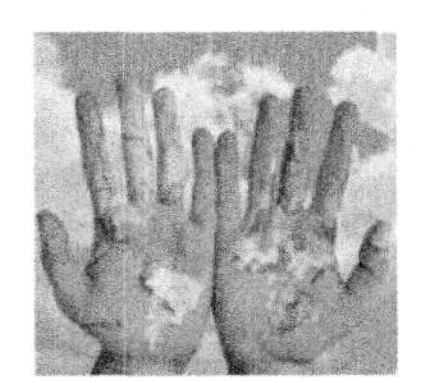

Even in the darkest hours he had found comfort by observing the leathery texture of his palms with the curiosity of an explorer. Each blemish a feature that connected his body to his soul. Like a treasure map designed by a skilled cartographer the palms of his hands contained only essential physiographic features. The *mounts of Venus* and *Jupiter* like the many *mountains* he had been obliged to conquer, the *Line of Life,* one of the many dry rivers he had crossed time and again in the Arabian deserts. The long *Line of Fate* showed as many interruptions as the tragedies that had embittered his life but that had not turned him into a bitter person, because in his cupped hands he had protected from the evil his world made up of adventures, aromas and stars.

THE REALITY WHICH UNDERPINS MY NOVEL

THE 'WEST' AND THE "RENEWABLE ENERGY" TRAP (SET BY CHINA)

The following annexes illustrate with factual information and data how the so called 'Renewables' are neither renewable, because they depend on minerals that are finite, that are as fossil as the hydrocarbons they are meant to replace. Neither are they clean because most of the mining of these minerals damages the environment and/or is based on exploiting the labourers, including forced-labour and child-labour. Additionally, most of the mining, processing and marketing of these minerals is undertaken by China that, in this way, controls the destiny of the West.

ANNEX 1

HOW IMPORTANT ARE "RENEWABLE ENERGIES" FOR WORLD ELECTRICITY GENERATION?

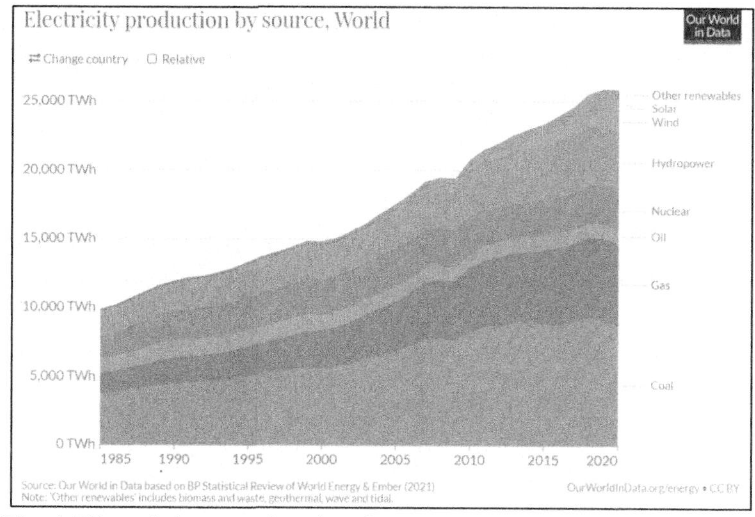

Fig.1 Electricity production by source. Note that "Renewables" account for less than 10% of current total.

My take:

1. *So called "Renewable Energies" (from Solar Panels to Wind Turbines to Hydrogen production, etc.) account for only around 10% of the worlds electricity production.*
2. *Even a steep increase in "Renewable Energies" generation would not suffice to offset in the medium to long term the use of conventional energy (from hydropower, nuclear, oil, gas and coal) to electrify the world.*
3. *Cutting down on the use of conventional energy would consequentially result in an economic downturn (degrowth) and impact negatively the quality of life of people affected*

ANNEX 2

CO2 EMISSIONS

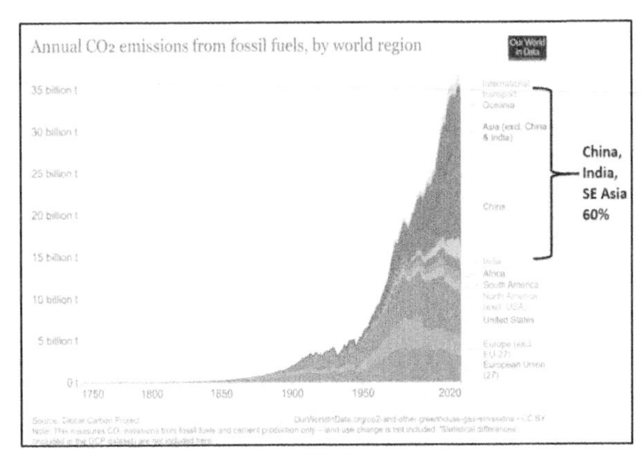

Fig. 1 China, India and other SE Asian countries account for 60% of the total CO2 emissions resulting from the use of fossil fuels (oil, gas, coal)

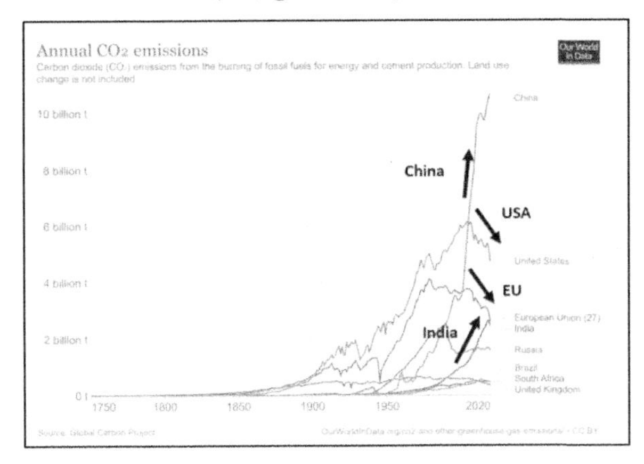

Fig.2 USA and Europe have decreased their CO2 emissions in the last 20 yrs. However, China and India have dramatically increased theirs such that the total CO2 emissions have increased by 30%

My take:

1. *China, India and in general the SE Asian countries rely significantly on fossil fuels (oil, gas and coal) for their continued development.*
2. *The reduction of CO2 emissions of the US and Europe will never address the CO2 issue, unless the CO2 emissions of China, India and the other SE Asian countries are significantly reduced.*
3. *As it will be demonstrated in the following appendices, the sad irony is that the West (US, Canada, Europe, Australia) strives to increase its use of so-called "Renewable Energies", with an increase in cost of energy, using products (Wind turbines, Solar panels, etc.) whose production is mostly performed by China, that uses fossil fuels, mostly the high polluting coal, for their manufacturing!*

ANNEX 3

THE ELECTRIC CAR & THE LITHIUM-ION BATTERY

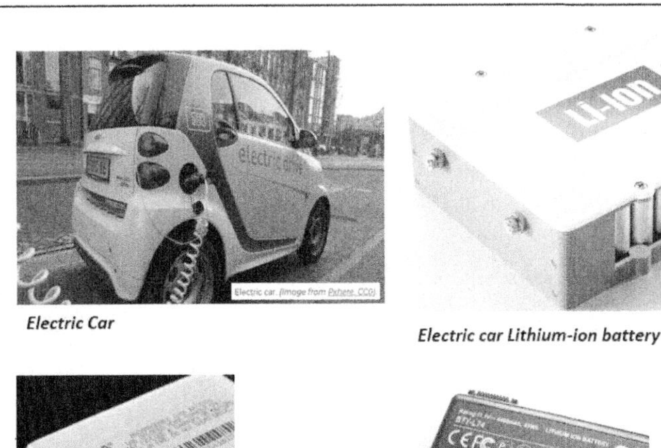

Electric Car

Electric car Lithium-ion battery

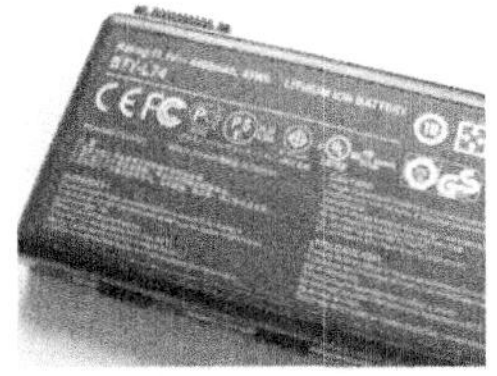

Phone Lithium-ion battery

Laptop Lithium-ion battery

Electric batteries of various shapes and sizes are essential to store electricity produced by so called "Renewable Energies". These batteries are the backbone for the development of Electric cars, that supposedly are the workhorse of clean transportation.

This chapter will review:

- *Cost of EV batteries vs combustion vehicle batteries;*
- *The key minerals needed to produce electric batteries and their availability, environmental impact and geopolitics;*
- *Demand vs. supply to fulfil the projected growth of EV units globally*

<u>*COST OF EV BATTERIES VS COMBUSTION VEHICLE BATTERIES*</u>

The cost of an EV battery ranges between $ 12,000 – 15,000 which is several orders of magnitude higher than the cost of a battery for a comparable combustion engine vehicle, which typically costs only a few hundred $.

While future economies of scale could reduce the cost of the process to produce EV batteries, the raw materials needed to produce an electric battery depends on minerals which are scarce and intrinsically expensive to mine and process, typically Lithium, Cobalt and Nickel. This means that the cost of these minerals is contrarily likely to increase with the projected expansion of EV's.

The following, is a quantitative analysis of the cost of these minerals as of Nov 2022.

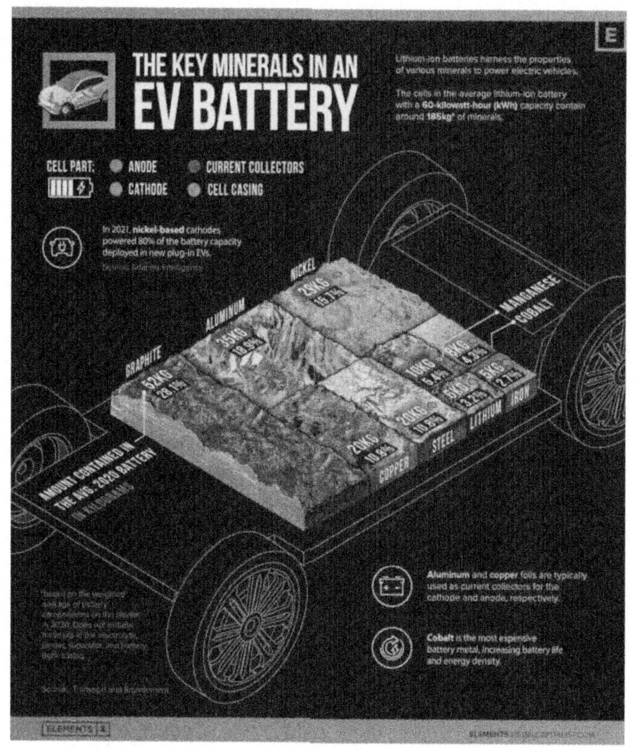

Fig. 1 Minerals needed for a 60kWh batter

Lithium-ion battery capacity is measured in kWh (Kilowatt hours). Battery capacity ranges from 40kWh to a 100kWh capacity. The battery capacity of a typical car will have a direct impact on its range. This is the number of miles that can be driven on a full charge, hence the higher the kWh the better. As an example, Nissan suggest that the 40kWh battery in its Nissan Leaf model will give you a 168-mile range.
Fig. 1 shows the quantity of metals needed for a middle of the range 60-kWh battery.

At the time of writing of this book (Q4 2022) the costs of these minerals can be detailed in the table of fig.2

	$ per ton	Kg needed for 60-kWh battery	$ cost per battery	
lithium	74000	6	444	
cobalt	51500	8	412	
nickel	25000	29	725	
copper	7980	20	160	
aluminium	2300	35	81	
steel	1220	20	24	
graphite	848	52	44	
iron	92	5	0.5	
manganese	4	10	0.5	
			1890	**total cost**

Fig.2 estimated cost (as of Nov 2022) of metals required for a 60-kWh electric battery

---

KEY MINERALS & THEIR OVERALL IMPACT ON GEOPOLITICS AND THE ENVIRONMENT

China accounts for 50% of the production of Electric Batteries as shown by fig.3. This has obvious geopolitical implications, as China is also predominant in the mining, processing and marketing of the key minerals required for electric batteries, which will be shown later.

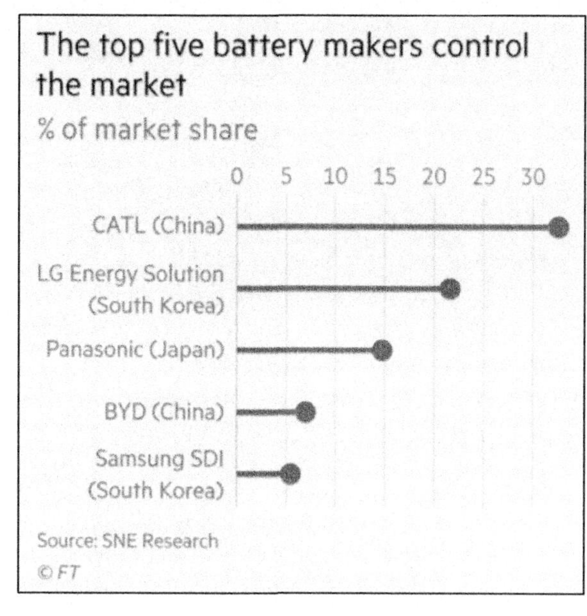

Fig.3 China makes around 50% of all electric batteries

Let's now review the story behind four key minerals used in electric batteries

***Lithium**: This is a soft, silvery-white alkali metal. Lithium-ion batteries are key components for most consumer electronics, from cell phones to laptops to electric vehicles. Much of the world's lithium reserves are contained in fossil lithium-rich brines in the so called "Lithium triangle" located between Chile, Argentina and Bolivia. However, Australia is currently the major producer of Lithium from conventional open pit mines. Lithium-ion batteries have higher energy densities than lead-acid batteries or nickel-metal hydride batteries, so it is possible to make the battery size smaller than others while retaining the same storage capacity.*

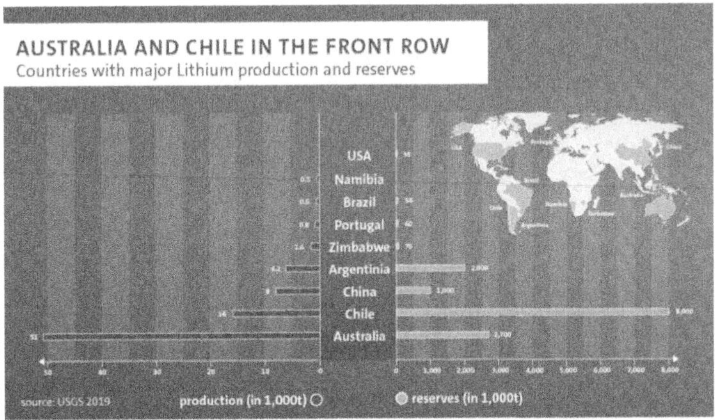

Fig.4 Although Australia is currently the leading Lithium producer from conventional mines, most of the global Lithium reserves discovered to date are located in the fossil waters of the salt flats of Chile and Argentina

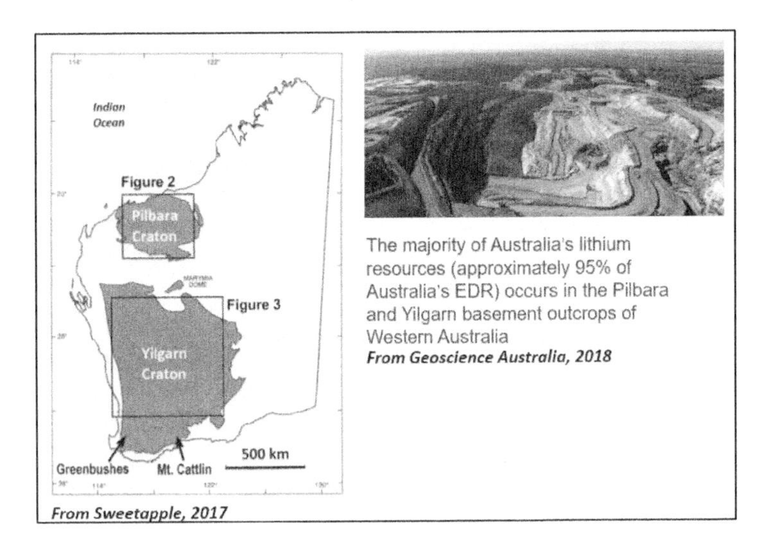

Fig.5 Maps of West Australia and its cratons where Lithium is extracted in open pit mines, like the one of Greenbushes, currently the largest producing Lithium mine in the world

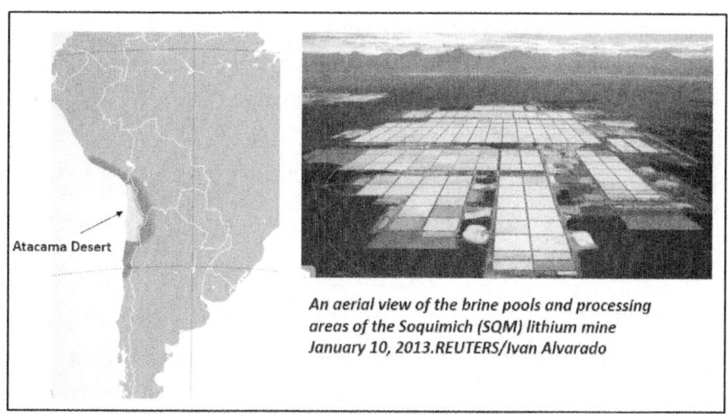

An aerial view of the brine pools and processing areas of the Soquimich (SQM) lithium mine January 10, 2013.REUTERS/Ivan Alvarado

Fig.6 Most of the world's Lithium reserves are in fossil brines in and around the Atacama Desert (Chile, Argentina, Bolivia) that are extracted from the underground aquifers and set to evaporate in man-made ponds to increase the lithium percentage of the ore

Company Ranking	Countries of Projects
Jiangxi Ganfeng Lithium Co. Ltd: Based in China with a market cap of $38.6bn	**China, Australia, Argentina, and Mexico**
Albemarle: Based in Charlotte, North Carolina, with a market cap of $26.8bn	**US, Chile & Australia**
Tianqi Lithium: Headquartered in China with a market cap of $24.39bn	**China, Chile & Australia**
Sociedad Química y Minera de Chile: A Chilean chemical company with a market cap of $14.03bn	**Chile**
Pilbara Minerals: Pilbara Minerals is an Australian lithium mining company with a market cap of $6.8bn	**Australia**

Fig.7 The five largest Lithium producers/manufactures include 2 Chinese companies with a combined market cap of $ 63 bn

By their own nature the Lithium-rich brines are finite, i.e., they are fossil waters that once extracted cannot be replenished. Also, the salt flats in South America where lithium is found are located in arid territories. In these places, access to fresh water is key for the local communities and their livelihoods, as well as the local flora and fauna. The production of lithium through evaporation ponds uses a lot of water - around 21 million liters per day. Approximately 2.2 million liters of water are needed to produce one ton of lithium. As a result, in Chile's Atacama salt flats, mining consumes, contaminates and diverts scarce water resources away from local communities.

Cobalt: *a silver-grey metal produced mainly as a by-product of copper and nickel mining. More than 60% of cobalt is mined in the Democratic Republic of Congo. Cobalt ensures cathodes do not easily overheat or catch fire and it helps extend the life of batteries which automakers usually guarantee for eight to 10 years.*

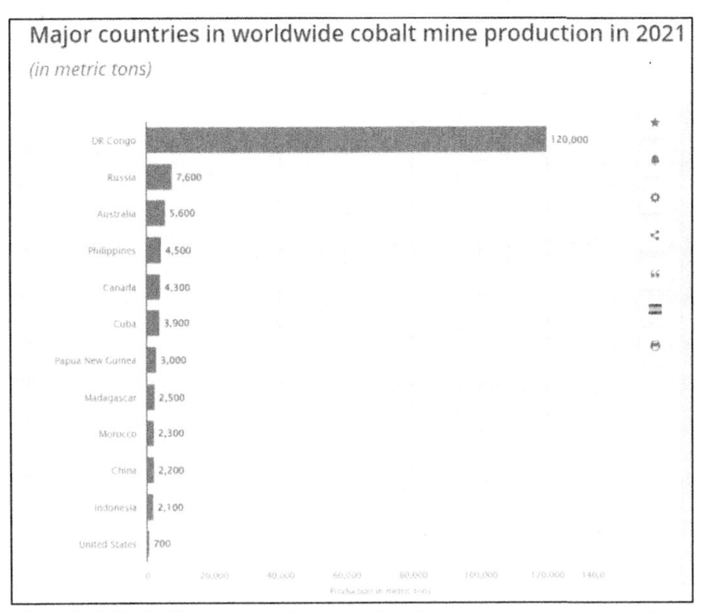

Fig.8 DRC Congo is by far the largest world producer of Cobalt. Out of the 19 DRC Congo's cobalt mines, 15 are owned or controlled by Chinese companies, making China the dominant mining player for this commodity.

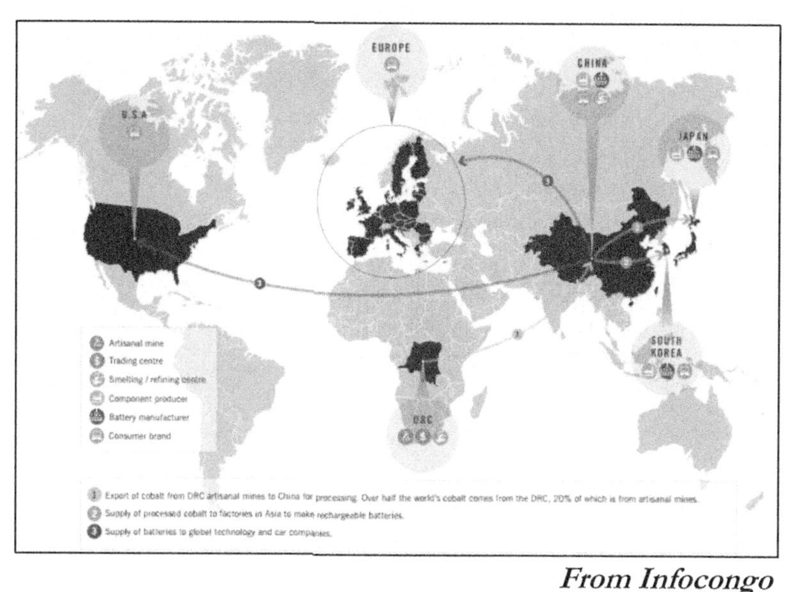

From Infocongo

Fig.9 China also has the total control of processing and manufacturing of the DRC Congo's cobalt, that aside from the portion used in China, is then shipped to the US, Western Europe, South Korea and Japan.

Fig.10 Unregulated child labor in unsafe artisanal mines contributes to 20% of the overall production of Cobalt in DRC Congo

"(…) cobalt mining was associated with increases in violence, substance abuse, food and water insecurity, and physical and mental health challenges. Community members reported losing communal land, farmland and homes, which miners literally dug up in order to extract cobalt. Without farmland, Congolese people were sometimes forced to cross international borders into Zambia just to purchase food.
"You might think of mining as just digging something up," Young said. "But they are not digging on vacant land. Homelands are dug up. People are literally digging holes in their living room floors. The repercussions of mining can touch almost every aspect of life."
Waste generated from mining cobalt and other metals can pollute water, air and soil, leading to decreased crop yields, contaminated food and water, and respiratory and reproductive health issues. Miners reported that working conditions were unsafe, unfair and stressful. Several workers noted that they feared mineshaft collapses." (as reported in a study by Northwestern University, 2021)
All quoted text from "Understanding cobalt's human cost" – authored by Northwestern University, 17 December, 2021

<u>**Nickel:**</u> *is a silvery-white lustrous metal with a slight golden tinge. Nickel resists corrosion and is used to plate other metals to protect them. It is, however, mainly used in making alloys such as stainless steel. The use of nickel in Lithium-ion batteries lends a higher energy density and more storage capacity to*
batteries. This improved energy density and storage capacity means that electric vehicles can get more miles out of a single charge, a concept that has been a key challenge for widespread EV adoption.

Nickel is found in nature within intrusions rich in sulphide ores (fig. 11) and in the form of laterite (fig.12) which is both a soil and a rock type rich in iron and aluminium formed through weathering in hot and wet tropical areas.

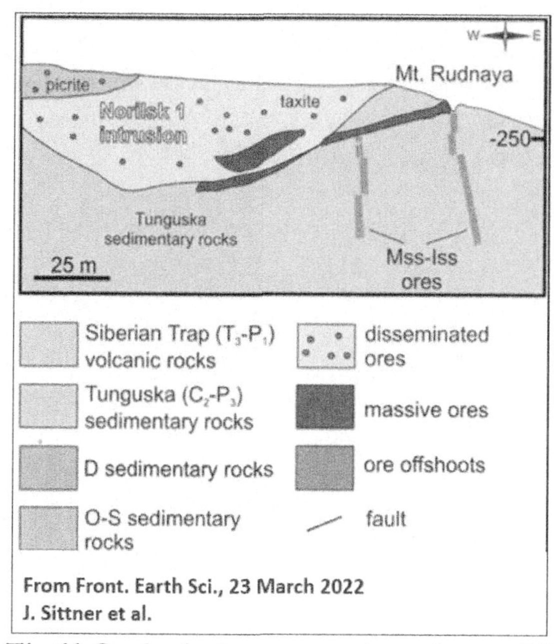

From Front. Earth Sci., 23 March 2022
J. Sittner et al.

Fig.11 Geological cross-section of one of the largest Nickel accumulations in the world at Russia's Norilsk Mine in the Artic.

Laterite deposits in the Zambales Ophiolite Complex is in west Central Luzon, Philippines

Fig.12 Example of laterite deposits from the Philippines

Currently only 5% of mined nickel is used for electric batteries (fig. 13). Of this, only class 1 nickel (the purest), which currently account for 50% of total nickel worldwide production, can be used for EV batteries. This is mostly derived from sulphide deposits occurring in Russia, Canada and Australia.
China accounts for 25% of the refining of class 1 Nickel. The bottom line is that autocratic countries account for a significant portion of the availability of this mineral in general and for EV vehicles in particular.

An additional issue is that to meet the projected demands for EV vehicles Nickel allocated to the EV batteries should increase by 18 times in 2030 relative to the amount used in 2020. This represents a steep change that is unlikely to be met, as illustrated by the graphs of figs. 15 and 16 underneath.

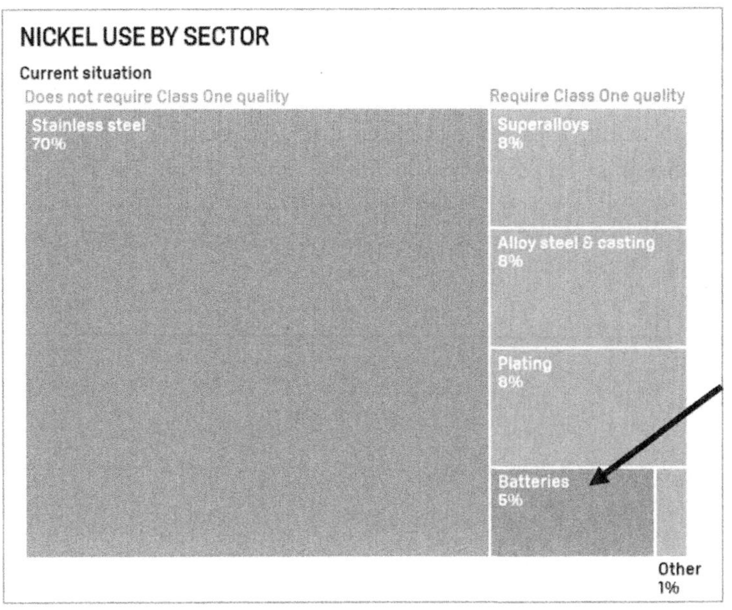

From Henrique Ribeiro et al 2021

Fig.13 Currently only 5% of Nickel is used for batteries, the rest is mostly used for the production of stainless steel and alloys

The majority of the Class 1 mines are located in Russia, Canada and Australia; nickel is being refined in China, Russia and Japan.

Class 1 mining production by country, %[1] of global production, 2019

Russia 21.1, Canada 17.1, Australia 14.4, China 9.6, Indonesia 6.8, Cuba 5.0, Philippines 4.9, South Africa 4.5, Finland 3.7, Madagascar 3.2, Papua New Guinea 3.1, Others

1,042 kilotons

Class 1 refined production by country, %[1] of global production, 2019

China 25.3, Russia 15.1, Japan 13.7, Canada 12.4, Australia 9.8, Norway 8.3, Finland 5.2, Madagascar 3.1, Cuba 1.6, Others

1,108 kilotons

[1]Figures may not sum to 100%, because of rounding.
Source: MineSpans by McKinsey

Fig.14 Class 1 nickel mining mostly depend on mines located in Russia, Canada and Australia. China however refines over 25% of all class 1 Nickel.

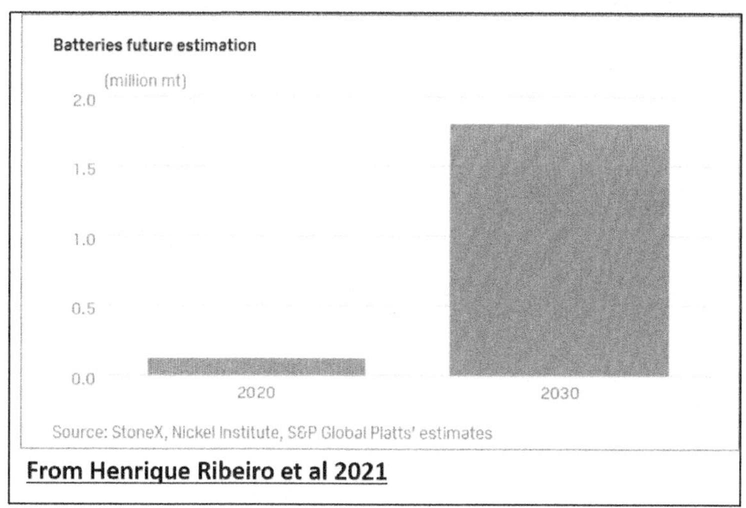

From Henrique Ribeiro et al 2021

Fig.15 Projected growth of Nickel class 1 production to meet EV vehicle requirements by 2030.

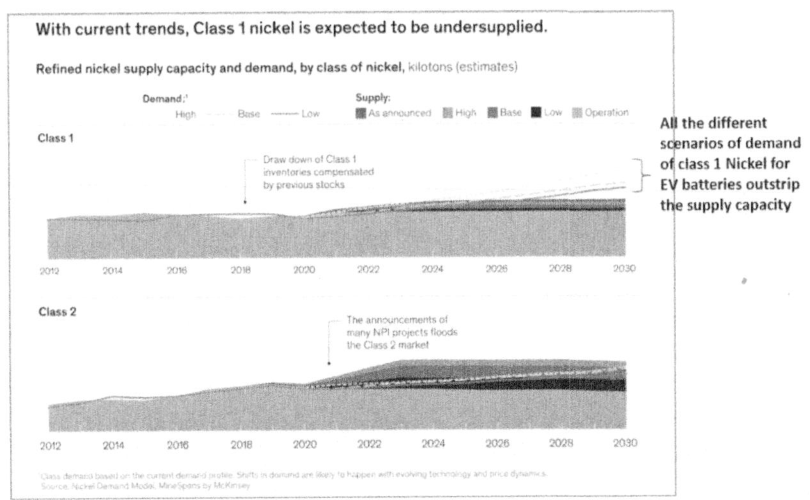

Fig.16 All different demand scenarios for class 1 Nickel outstrips the supply capacity

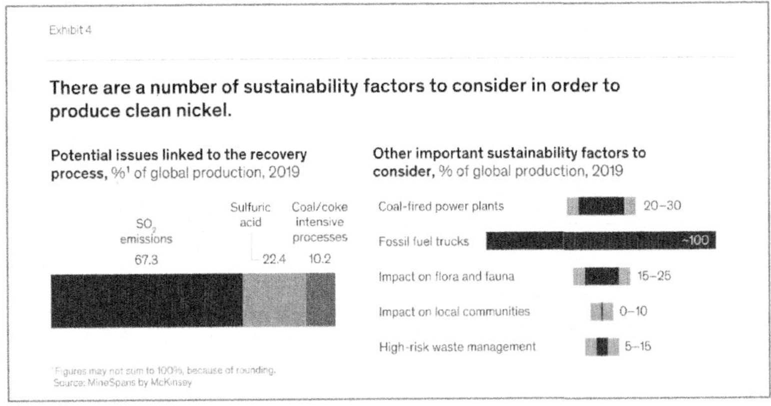

Fig.17 Environmental impact of Nickel mining and refining

Mining and refining of Nickel, either from sulphide or laterite deposits is neither clean nor low energy and result in emissions of SO_2, Sulphur Acid and CO_2, often leaked into the environment as illustrated by fig.15. As an example, the Norilsk Nickel mine is known to be one of Russia's largest industrial polluters (fig.16), releasing approximately 1.9 million tons of *sulfur dioxide into the air annually as of 2020, accounting for 1.9% of global emissions. Ore is smelted on site in Norilsk which is directly responsible for severe pollution, including acid rain and smog.*

Fig.18 Sulphur rich fumes resulting from the smelting at Norilsk mine in Russia

----

Graphite: *is a crystalline form of the element carbon. The main producer of graphite is by far China, as shown in the graph underneath. Graphite is an essential ingredient in EV battery anodes, a terminal inside a rechargeable cell.*

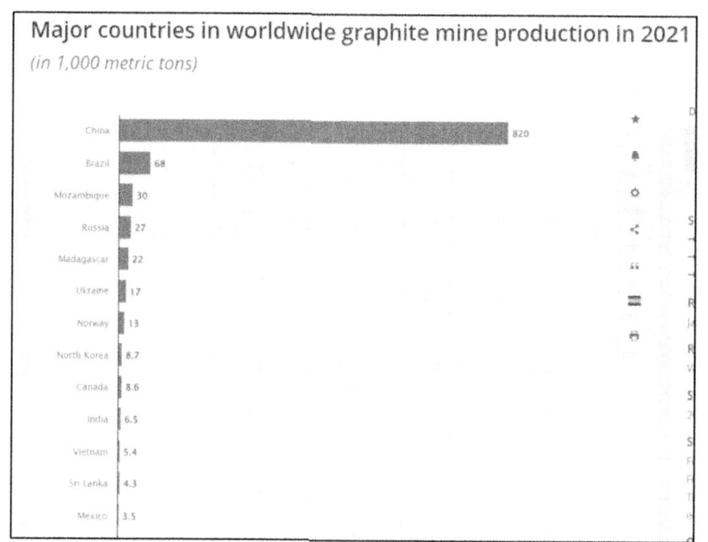

Fig.19 China is by far the largest producer of natural graphite.

Graphite occurs in two ways: Natural Graphite that accounts for around 45% of the Graphite market and Synthetic Graphite that accounts for 55% of the market.
Natural graphite is mined (see graph above) while Synthetic Graphite is produced from calcined petroleum coke, and 20% coal tar pitch is used as a matrix binder, i.e. Synthetic Graphite requires a fossil fuel as a starting product.

Both the <u>purification</u> of Natural Graphite and the <u>production/purification</u> of Synthetic Graphite are energy intensive, requiring very high temperatures (3000+C) for which mostly coal fired plants are used.
China is the dominant player in the mining and processing of graphite using mostly coal-fired power stations, thus significantly contributing to CO2 emissions.
"Natural graphite mining that can cause dust emissions, and the purification of battery-grade anode products requires high quantities of reagents such as sodium hydroxide and hydrofluoric acid, which may be harmful to both human health and the environment"

"Synthetic graphite production, on the other hand, is more energy-intensive, which has led operators to seek the cheapest power sources that tend to be coal dominant, generating a higher overall carbon footprint"

"The (Minvira) firm's experts found that the calculated global warming potential (GWP) values for producing 1 kilogram of anode grade graphite in coal-based grid mixes, like Inner Mongolia (China), are ~800% and ~1,000% higher than the commercial database value for natural and synthetic routes, respectively."

<u>All quoted text from «Climate-change impacts of graphite production higher than reported» – authored by MINING.COM Staff Writer, July 7, 2021</u>

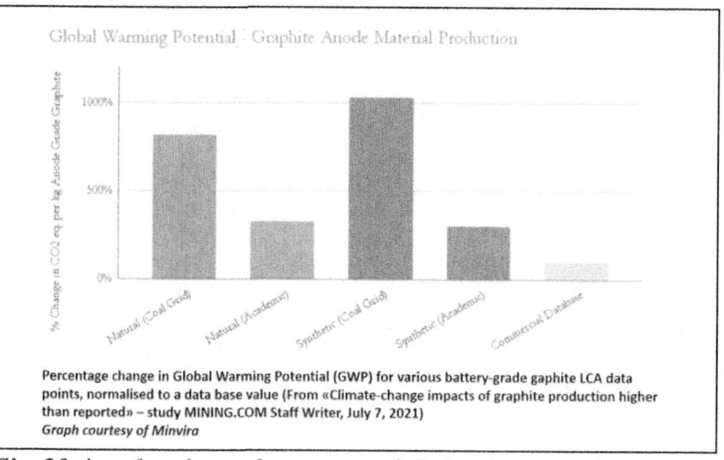

Percentage change in Global Warming Potential (GWP) for various battery-grade gaphite LCA data points, normalised to a data base value (From «Climate-change impacts of graphite production higher than reported» – study MINING.COM Staff Writer, July 7, 2021)
Graph courtesy of Minvira

Fig.20 Academic and commercial database underestimate of the CO_2 emission impact of natural and synthetic graphite obtained using coal.

DEMAND VS SUPPLY OF KEY MINERALS NEEDED FOR RENEWABLES, INCLUDING ELECTRIC BATTERIES

The growth of mining and refining of minerals required for the sustainable development of Renewables is astounding. The EIA (Energy International Agency) has studied in detail the implication of current environmental policies on mineral mining and processing, and the graph of fig.21 shows that relative to 2020 mineral demand is expected to grow by 7 times in 2030.

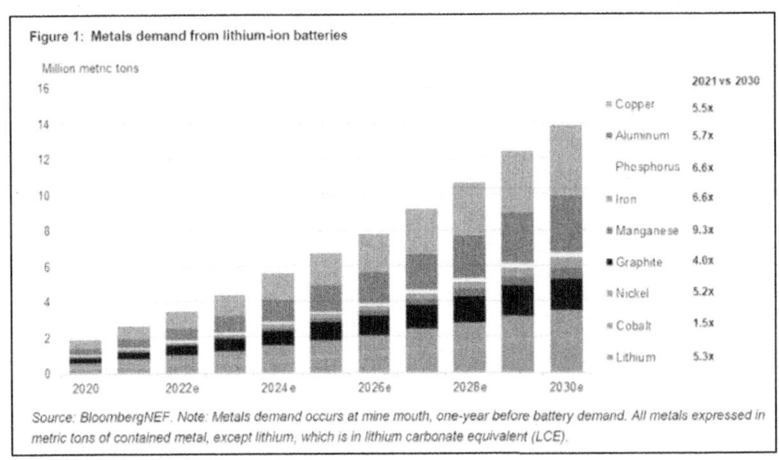

Fig.21 EIA forecast of total mineral demand for so called Renewables to meet the sustainable development scenarios of current environmental policies. Note that by 2030 demand is expected to be 7 times bigger than in 2020.

Is this feasible? ***Probably not****, as illustrated by the graph of fig.22 by Benchmark Mineral Intelligence. This graph compares the production of key minerals in 2022 vs. the one required in 2035 to meet the projected increase of EV vehicles. For each mineral the graph shows the differential between 2022 supply and 2035 demand which would need to increase as per the table underneath:*

Lithium 5.9 times

Cobalt 2.7 times

Nickel 1.9 times

Natural Graphite 7.9 times

Synthetic Graphite 2.5 times

The graph also shows the indicative number of new mines needed to supply the 2035 requirements. Considering that this is not a sausage type production, that is to open a new mine one needs first to find an economic quantity of the mineral to be mined and it takes 5 to 10 years for a mine to be productive, it is unlikely that the demand of 2035, as stated by the current economic policies, could ever be met.

Additionally, the cost of these key minerals, due to the low supply vs high demand situation, has significantly increased after the covid 2020 economic slowdown, as shown in fig.23. This makes it unlikely that the cost of the electric battery would reduce with more EV being implemented.

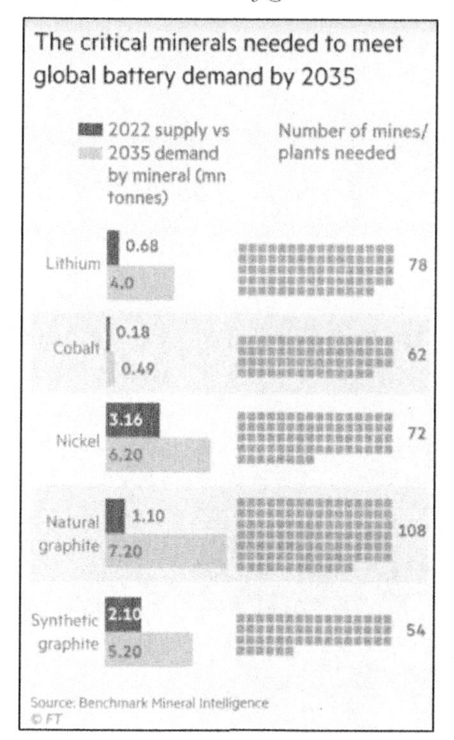

Fig.22 Benchmark Mineral Intelligence: critical minerals needed to meet global electric battery demand by 2035. Note the significant gap between 2022 supply and projected 2035 demand.

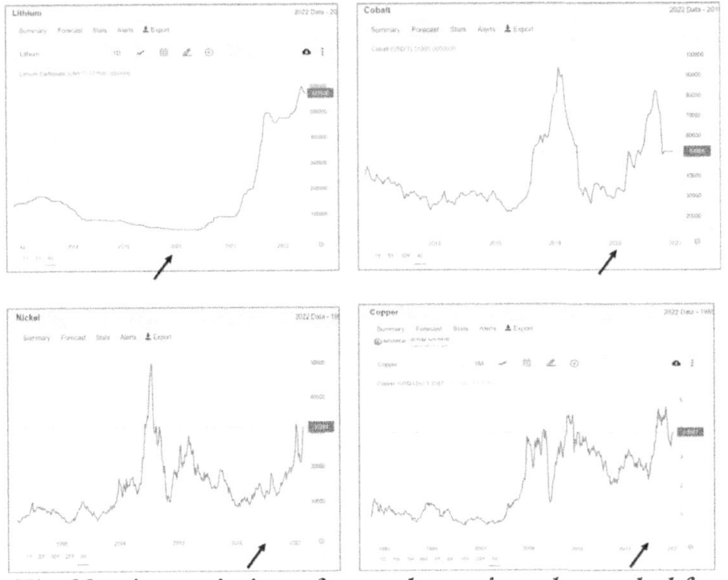

Fig.23 price variation of some key minerals needed for so called Renewables. For timing comparison, the arrows indicate year 2020

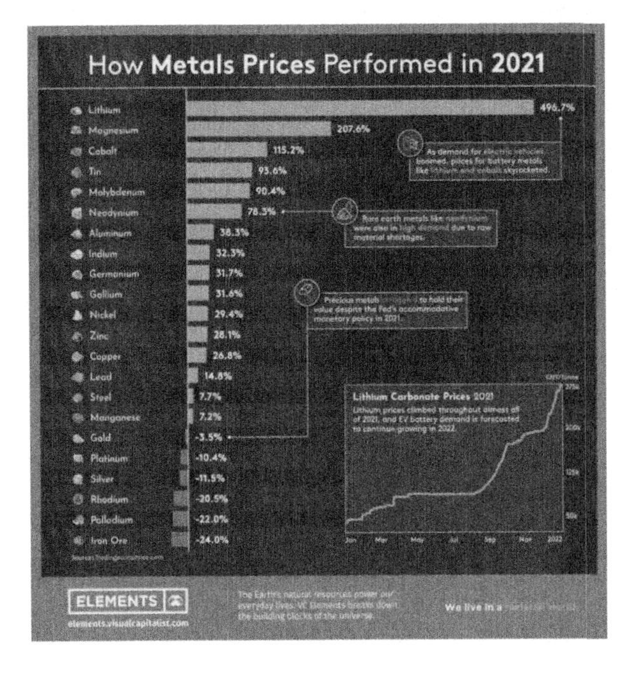

Fig.24 price variation of metals in 2021. Note varying degree of increase for metals required for Renewables

ANNEX 4
COPPER

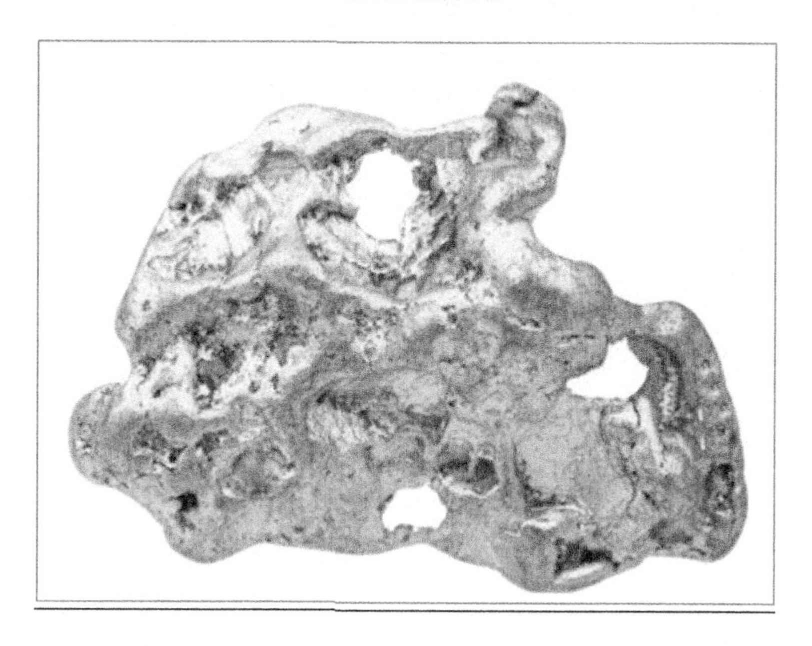

Copper *is a soft, malleable, and ductile metal with very high thermal and electrical conductivity. As such it is the backbone of most "Renewables", from Wind Turbines to Solar Panels, from Electric vehicles and their battery storage to electric networks.*
Not only, but also Copper usage averages up to five times more in renewable energy systems than in traditional power generation, such as fossil fuel and nuclear power plants.

Chile accounts for 27% of worldwide copper production. Other major producers are Peru' (20%), China (8%) and the DRC (8%).

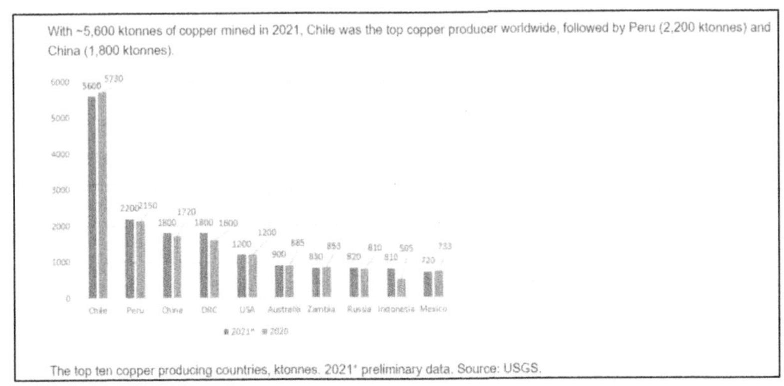

Fig.1 top ten copper producing countries, 2021 vs 2022 production.

Almost the *<u>totality of Chilean copper production is exported to China</u>* *which it uses to make technological devices, electric cables, cars, motorcycles, refrigerators, plumbing lines and much more.*
Chinese state companies are also the main producers of copper in Perù, which means that *<u>China directly or indirectly controls 55% of worldwide copper production</u>*, *which obviously represents a significant geopolitical risk*

Fig.2 Copper is mined through large and deep open pits which result in major environmental footprints. associated to the implementation of "Renewables" in the Western world.

Copper ore is smelted using temperatures of 200 degrees Celsius to separate copper from the sulphide and oxides it contains, leaving just the metal behind. The refined product is then put into a mold and turned into concentrated black powder, or shipped off to China in block form.
This process emits large quantities of trace elements, particulate matter and Sulphur oxides, which can have adverse environmental and health effects.
In the particular case of Chile, the winds of the Atacama Desert further act to lift particles from the soil and circulate toxic gases generated by copper extraction.
Additionally, the copper refining process is water intensive, which requires a significant amount of fresh water from the already limited resources of the Chilean (and Peruvian) deserts. An example of the adverse effect of the above is the $93 M penalty that BHP had to pay in 2021 for its indiscriminate use of fossil water (that is not replaceable) from the salt flats around its Escondida mine, the largest copper mine in the world.
This pollution is compounded by the need to remove almost 500,000 tons of waste a day, which is done using ultra-heavy trucks that consume three liters of diesel per minute.

Fig.3 Heavy equipment used to dispose of the waste from the mining of copper

The Chilean mine of Chuquicamata is the largest open pit copper mine in the world and produces around 5% of total world copper production. It is also an example of the <u>extreme</u> <u>adverse impact</u> that copper mining can have on both <u>environment and population</u>.

The original Chuquicamata town, which housed all mine workers and their families (over 10,000 inhabitants in the nineties) from early in the mine's development, was finally abandoned in 2007. Health and safety concerns over the high levels of dust from the mine and gasses from the smelting plant caused Codelco to relocate all the families. Today, the entire town stands abandoned with boarded up buildings, fading signs, and wind blowing through the empty streets. As the town was only relatively recently abandoned, and because it is still on mining company property, it has suffered very little decay and vandalism. Although it is not possible to enter any of the buildings, even wandering the streets offers an evocative insight into the harsh realities of life here.

Fig.4 Abandoned children's playground next to the former school in Chuquicamata ghost town, that was abandoned in 2007 due to high level of pollution linked to the nearby copper mine.

ANNEX 5
WIND TURBINES

WHAT IT TAKES TO MAKE ONE & HOW FRIENDLY THEY ARE TO THE ENVIRONMENT AND HUMANS

My take:

1- *Wind turbines are the work horse of wind generated energy.*
2- *The size of Wind turbines is highly variable but generally growing with time and technological advances (fig 1)*
3- *A significant amount of steel, copper, cement, aluminium, rare earth elements and other minerals are required to build any Wind turbine (fig 2)*
4- *Depending on the make and model 11-16% of a Wind turbine is made up of fiberglass, resin or plastic (USGS) (these are all by-products of the hydrocarbon industry).*
5- *The Wind energy industry is copper intensive. In conventional power it takes 1 tonne of copper per installed megawatt while Wind technology requires four to six times more (Wikipedia on Copper in renewable energy).*

6- *The Wind industry is also iron intensive. "Material requirements per unit generation for low-carbon technologies can be higher than for conventional fossil fuel generation: 6-14 times more iron for wind power plants" (E.G. Hertwich et al, 2014).*
7- *All minerals used to produce Wind turbines are fossil, i.e. cannot be replaced in nature. In particular steel is an alloy of iron and carbon mostly produced through coal fuelled power plants which are the most polluting of all fossil fuels.*
8- *China is the largest producer of steel in the world (fig.3), accounting for almost 60% of total world steel production in May 2021. In 2015 the energy consumption of China's Iron and Steel industry consisted of 69.9% coal, 26.4% electricity, 3.2% fuel and 0.5% natural gas (YCISI, 2015)*
9- *According to the U.S. Energy Information Administration, steel production is one of the world's most energy-intensive and carbon-rich industry. In 2020 the production of steel alone was responsible for 7% of all global carbon dioxide emission.*
10- *Most of the copper production comes from Chile and Perú, from open pit mines often associated with production practises that are both human and environmental unfriendly (fig.5)*
11- *Bottom line: every time you see a Wind turbine remember that it could not be made without hydrocarbons by-products. That is very likely that its steel has been produced in China using coal (the most polluting of fossil fuels) and that it is also likely that its copper comes from one of South America's mines plagued by production standards that are unfriendly both to the humans and the environment. So much for a green energy!*

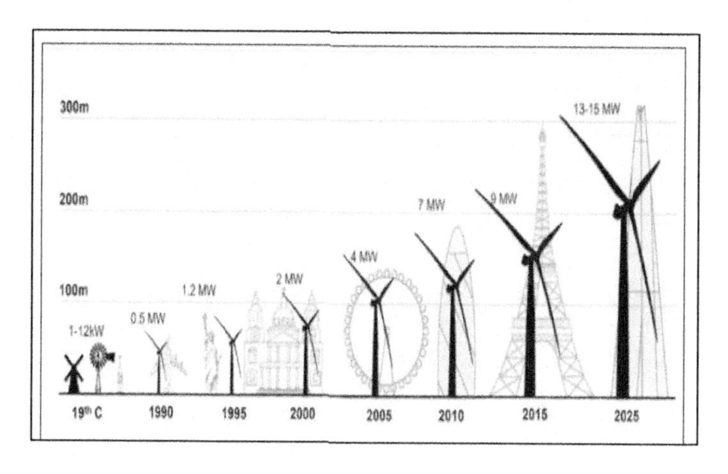

Fig1 Evolution of the size of wind turbines.

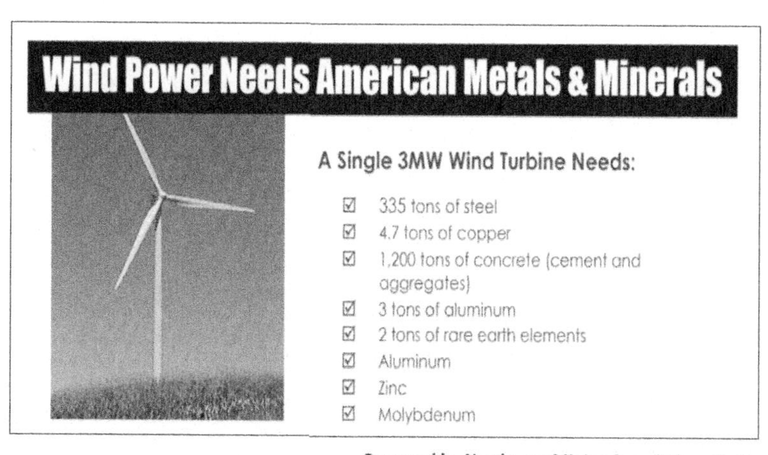

Fig.2 What it takes to build a 3MW Wind Turbine, which by current standard is a small size

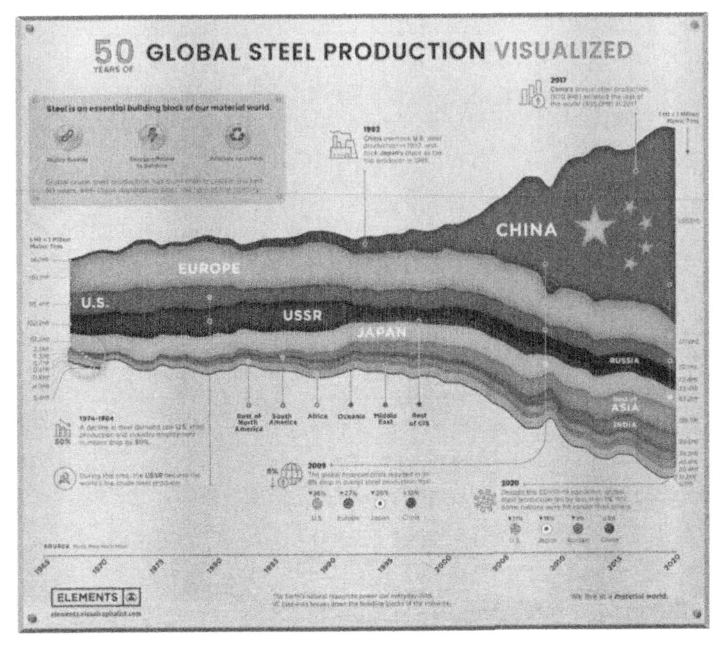

Nicolo Conte (2021) Fig.3

Fig.3 Evolution of the production of Steel. Note dramatic increase from early 2000 onwards and that the majority of steel is produced by China using coal -fired power plants like the ones shown in Fig.4.

A coal-fired power plant in China's Jiangsu province – Xu Congjun – IMAGE CHINA fig.4

Fig.4 High polluting coal-fired power plants are Chinese workhorse to generate cheap electricity used for the full spectrum of "Renewable" manufacturing.

Fig. 5 China imports almost the totality of the copper mined in Chile, that is the largest world producer of this metal, with significant environmental and human impact as in the town of Chuquicamata, abandoned in 2007 due to the toxic air caused by the smelting of copper ore.

ANNEX 6

SOLAR PANELS

WHAT IT TAKES TO MAKE ONE & HOW FRIENDY THEY ARE TO ENVIRONMENT AND HUMANS

My take:

1. *Solar panels are the work horse of sun generated energy.*
2. *Figure 1 illustrates how solar panels are made.*

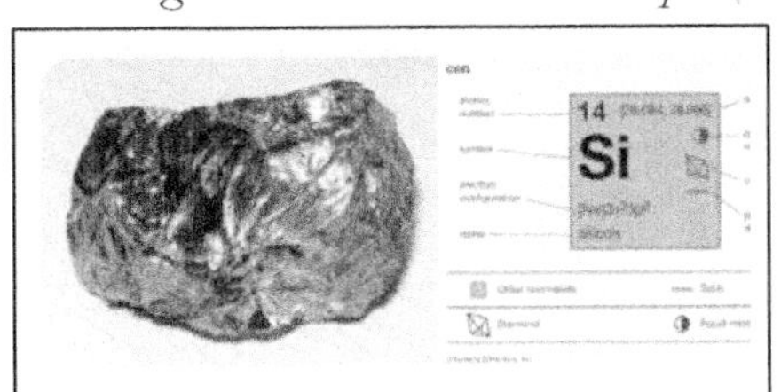

Silicon is **a chemical element (its symbol in chemical formula expressions is "Si") that is present in sand and glass and which is the best known semiconductor material in electronic components**. Its atomic number is 14. The most common isotope has atomic weight 28.

Solar panels are manufactured using polycrystalline silicon (usually referred to as polysilicon, a high-purity form of silicon), glass, and metals. Solar cells are the building blocks of any solar panel (fig.2).

3. *China is the leader in manufacturing of polysilicon, currently producing over 75% of world polysilicon in the solar-grade sector (fig.4), with 7 Chinese companies being within the first 10 producers of polysilicon worldwide (fig.3).*
4. *China is also the predominant player in wafers, cells and modules (fig.5).*
5. *About 45% of worldwide polysilicon production occurs in the Xinjiang province of west of China (fig.4). This is because the Siemens process to produce polysilicon requires, aside from high corrosive acids, also heat above 1,000 degrees Celsius, that is obtained through power plants which use coals, very abundant in Xinjiang, to generate electricity (and heat).*
6. *"Xinjiang is also where China has detained and arrested hundreds of thousands of Uyghurs, a Turkic minority. Government documents suggest some are then forced into government work programs, as well. In June (2021) the U.S. banned Xinjiang polysilicon from five Chinese companies. So if the rules are it has to be third-party verified from the source but the Chinese company that is the source won't report that, then nobody is going to get a clean bill of health. Which means there's no way to guarantee where that polysilicon is from, a huge headache and raising the question, can solar panel companies even buy it legally from some of the world's biggest polysilicon makers?" (Excerpt from the podcast of Emily Feng, NPR News, Shanghai, July 2021, for the full podcast see link attached)*

https://www.npr.org/2021/07/06/1013266774/how-did-china-become-the-worlds-dominant-polysilicon-producer?t=1654076819488

7. *Metals required to build solar cells are the by-product of primary commodities whose mining practises are often neither human nor environmentally friendly (see for instance chapter on copper mining in South America):*

By-product commodity	Primary commodity
Cadmium	Zinc
Gallium	Aluminium, Zinc
Germanium	Zinc, coal
Indium	Zinc
Selenium	Copper
Tellurium	Copper

The bottom line is that every time you see a solar panel it is likely to have been manufactured in China with polysilicon produced in Xinjiang using forced labour and high polluting coal and containing metals coming from mining practises that are neither human nor environmentally friendly. So much for green energy!

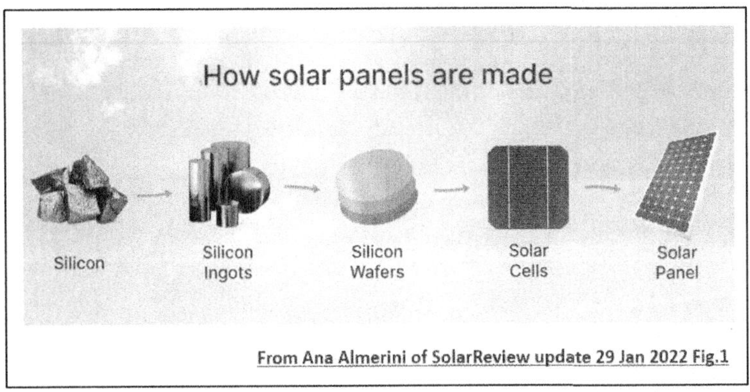

Fig.1 Scheme illustrating the components of a solar panel.

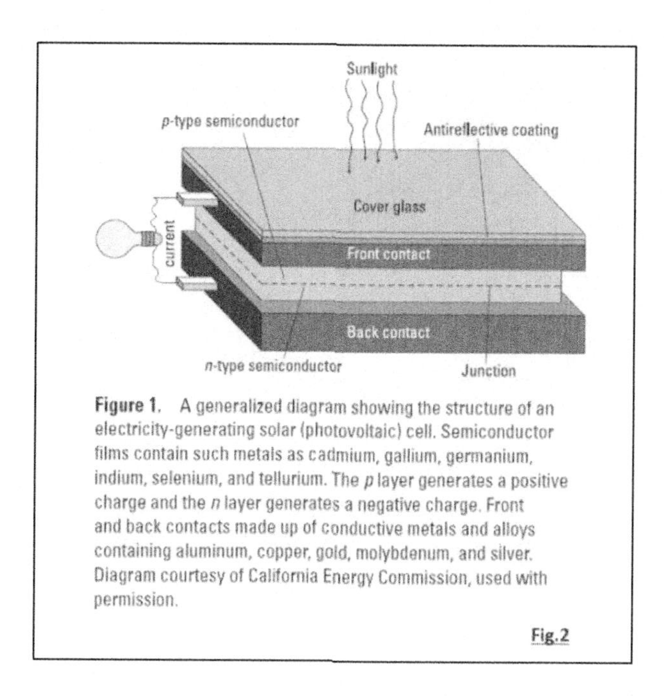

Figure 1. A generalized diagram showing the structure of an electricity-generating solar (photovoltaic) cell. Semiconductor films contain such metals as cadmium, gallium, germanium, indium, selenium, and tellurium. The *p* layer generates a positive charge and the *n* layer generates a negative charge. Front and back contacts made up of conductive metals and alloys containing aluminum, copper, gold, molybdenum, and silver. Diagram courtesy of California Energy Commission, used with permission.

Fig.2

Fig.2 Generalized diagram illustrating the photovoltaic cell

The top 10 polysilicon manufacturers for 2021 include:

1.Tongwei (China)
2.GCL (China)
3.Daqo New Energy (China)
4.Wacker (Germany/United States)
5.Xinte Energy (China)
6.Xingjiang East Hope New Energy (China)
7.OCI (South Korea/Malaysia)
8.Asia Silicon (China)
9.Hemlock (United States)
10.TianREC – joint venture of Shaanxi Non-Ferrous Tianhong New Energy and REC Silicon (China)

Fig.3

Fig.3 Among the top 10 polysilicon manufacturers of 2021, 7 are Chinese

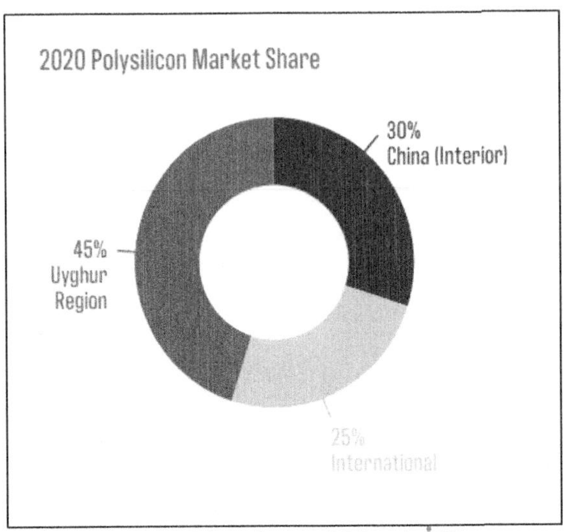

Fig.4 China has a 75% market share in the production of polysilicon, out of which 45% is produced in the Xinjiang, the province where the Uyghur population is discriminated against, incarcerated and often used for slave labor, including in the polysilicon industry

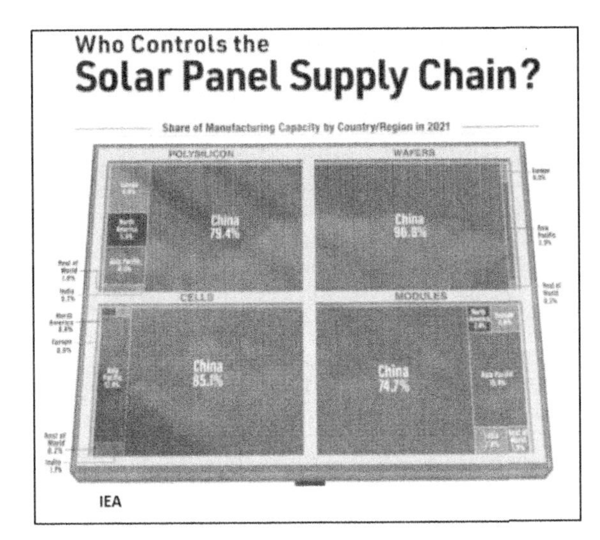

Fig.5 Therefore it should not be a surprise than China has virtually the full control of the solar panel supply chai

ANNEX 7
HYDROGEN

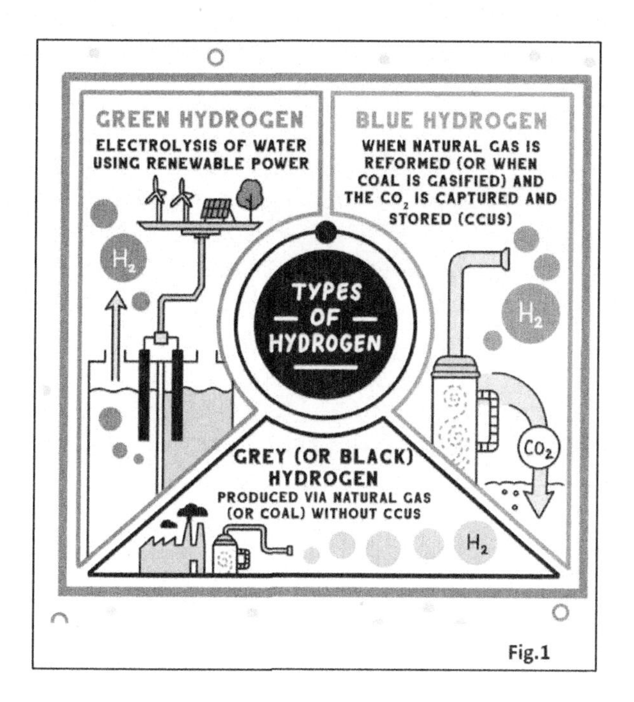

Fig.1

My take:

1. *Hydrogen is an energy carrier that, technically, can be used to replace fossil fuels in many applications.*
2. *Hydrogen can be used in fuel cells to generate power using a chemical reaction rather than combustion, producing only water and heat as by products. It can be used in cars, in houses, for portable power, and in many more applications.*
3. *There are four main sources for the commercial production of hydrogen: natural gas, oil, coal, and electrolysis; which account for 48%, 30%, 18% and 4% of the world's hydrogen production respectively. Fossil fuels are the dominant source of industrial hydrogen.*
4. *Figure 1 illustrates how hydrogen is made industrially:*

- *GREY or BLACK HYDROGEN is produced using natural gas or coal without the capture of the resulting CO2.*
- *BLUE HYDROGEN is produced with natural gas or gasified coal with the capture of the resulting CO2.*
- *GREEN HYDROGEN is produced through the electrolysis of water using either Solar or Wind power.*

5 *There are several practical issues that make unrealistic the mass use of Hydrogen, including: current and foreseeable lack of scale of commercial Hydrogen production, safe storage of Hydrogen, required modification of vehicle's engines, etc.*

6 *However, the consideration often omitted by environmentalists is that every type of Hydrogen production requires FOSSIL FUELS on a massive scale. While it is obvious for the GREY/BLACK or BLUE HYDROGEN, many miss the point that even GREEN HYDROGEN requires Wind Turbines and Solar Panels that are produced mostly using electricity produced through COAL FIRED POWER STATIONS (see Annexes 4 & 5)*

ANNEX 8

RARE EARTHS

WHAT THEY ARE FOR & CHINESE DOMINANCE

My take:

1. *"Rare Earths" are a unique group of 17 metal elements on the periodic table that exhibit a range of special properties, such as magnetism, luminescence, and strength. Rare earths are important to a number of high technology industries, including renewable energy and various defence systems.*
2. *China processes 97% of all "Rare Earths", i.e. it has a super-dominant position.*
3. *"Rare Earths" have a lot of application in modern technology as shown by the underneath figure.*

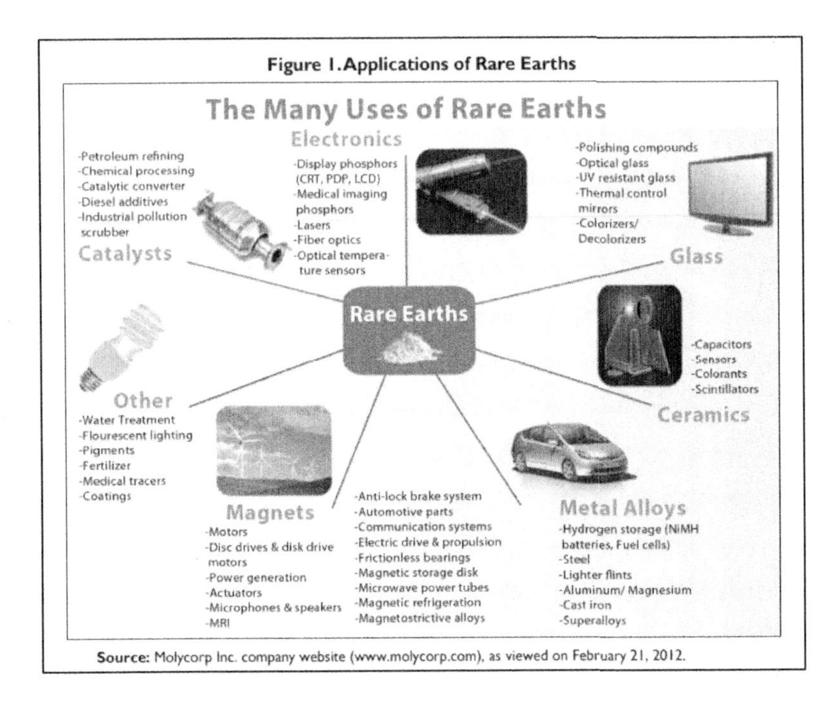

Figure 1. Applications of Rare Earths

Source: Molycorp Inc. company website (www.molycorp.com), as viewed on February 21, 2012.

4. *Since 2002 China has implemented a number of trade restrictions to keep its predominance and maximise its profit from the market of "Rare Earths" which include:*
    - *Foreign companies are prohibited from any rare earth mining business;*
    - *Foreign companies are not permitted to participate in rare earth smelting and separation projects by themselves. Exceptions will be made when they form joint ventures with Chinese partners.*
    - *Foreign companies are encouraged to invest in downstream rare earth processing in China and development of new rare earth applications and products.*

Attached is a link to a relevant report prepared by the Congressional Research Centre in 2012 https://sgp.fas.org/crs/row/R42510.pdf

ANNEX 9

CHINA, CHINA & MORE CHINA

Where Clean Energy Metals Are Produced

Production of key resources is highly concentrated today. Charts show the top three producers.

0% 20% 40% 60% 80% 100%

Copper: Chile, Peru, China

Nickel: Indonesia, Philippines, Russia

Note 1 — Cobalt: Democratic Republic of Congo, Russia, Australia

Rare earths: China, U.S., Myanmar

Lithium: Australia, Chile, China

And Where They Are Processed

China dominates the refining and processing of key metals.

0% 20% 40% 60% 80% 100%

Copper: China, Chile, Jpn.

Nickel: China, Indonesia, Japan

Cobalt: China, Finland, Belgium

Rare earths: China, Malaysia, Estonia

Lithium: China, Chile, Arg.

Source: International Energy Agency   By The New York Times

Note 1 – 15 out of the 19 mines extracting cobalt in DRC belong to Chinese companies

Source: IEA as published by The New York Times (Note 1 by the author)

My take:

1. *China controls either the source (mines), the processing, or both of the majority of metals used for what are referred to as "Renewables Energies" (from Solar Panels to Wind Turbines to Hydrogen generation).*
2. *Defining "clean energy metals" the ones used for the so-called "Renewable Energies" as per the attached graph produced by IEA) is an oxymoron, considering the adverse impact on the environment and humans that their mining and processing has. Obviously, unless "clean" is used in a West-centric sense, recognising that the West has outsourced the pollution and human cost of its environmentalism.*

ANNEX 10

<u>MINERALS, SUPPLY RISKS AND THEIR USES</u>

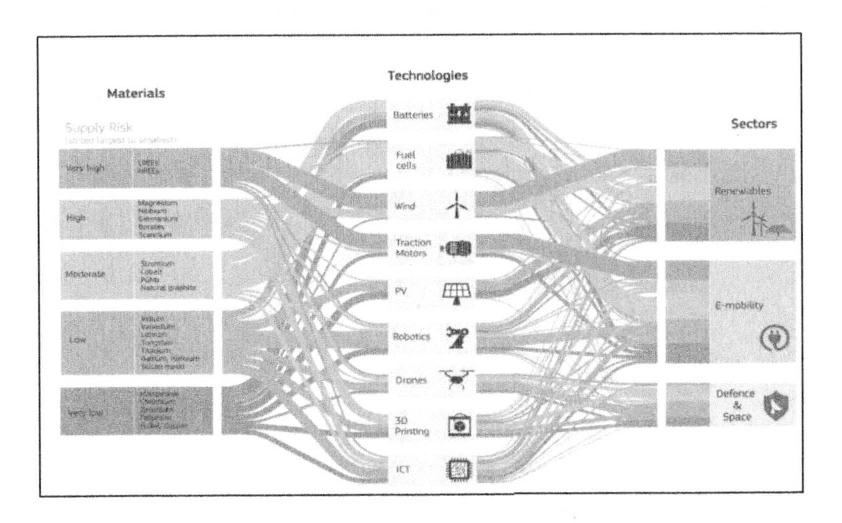

by David Thorpe, September 2020

My take:

1. *so called Renewables Energies (from Solar Panels to Wind Turbines to Hydrogen production) rely on fossil minerals whose supply (and geopolitical) risk ranges from very high (like the Rare Earths = LREE & HREE) to high / moderate (like Magnesium and Cobalt) to low (like Lithium and Manganese)*

ANNEX 11

GEOPOLITICAL RISK OF "RENEWABLES"

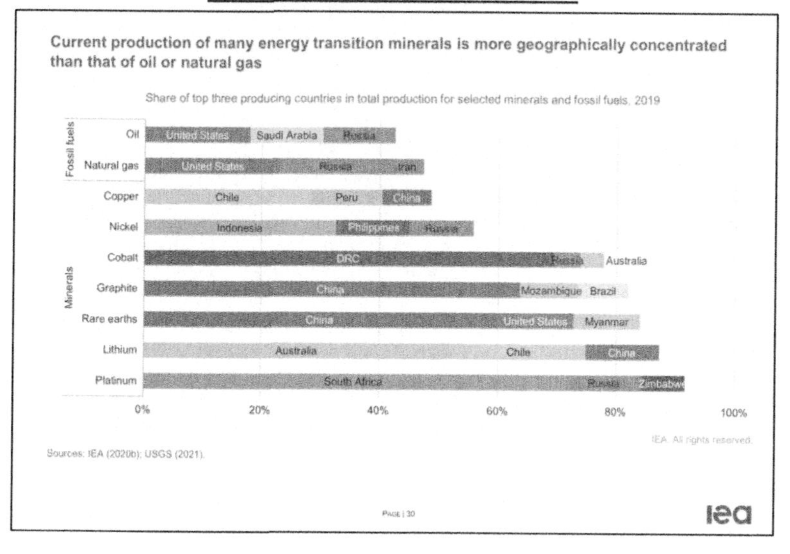

Fig.1 - Geographical distribution of key natural resources. Note that the majority of reserves of each mineral needed for "Renewables" is located within only 3 countries (high geopolitical risk) as opposed to fossil fuels where 80% of production is spread across 19 countries (see Fig.2)

1. *The 3 nations with largest oil and gas production contribute to less than 50% of total fossil fuels world production of each segment. Indeed 80% of fossil fuel production is shared by 19 countries, as shown in the graph of fig.2, making fossil fuel significantly less geographically and politically focussed, i.e. with less geopolitical risk than so called 'Renewables'.*
2. *On the contrary up to 80% of each (fossil) mineral world production required for so called 'Renewables' is located in only up to 3 countries making it a resource that is geographically and politically focussed and hence with higher geopolitical risks than hydrocarbons.*

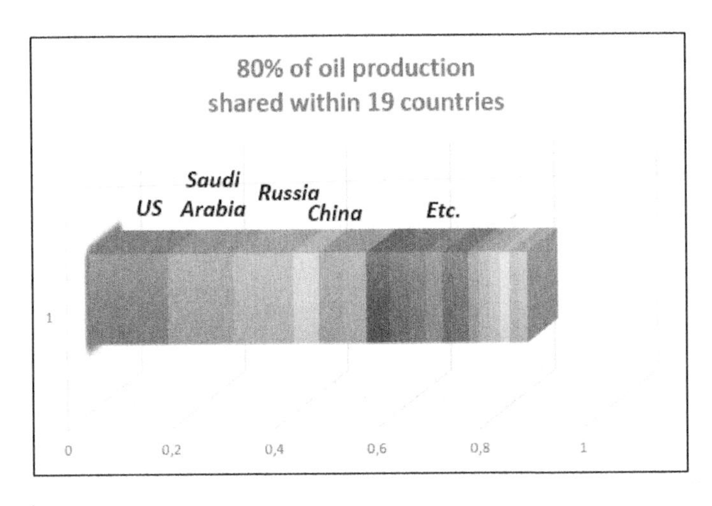

Fig.2 - 80% of fossil fuel production is shared across 19 different countries (much reduced geopolitical risk than access to minerals for "Renewables").

ANNEX 12

XINJIANG, THE LOST PARADISE OF CHINA

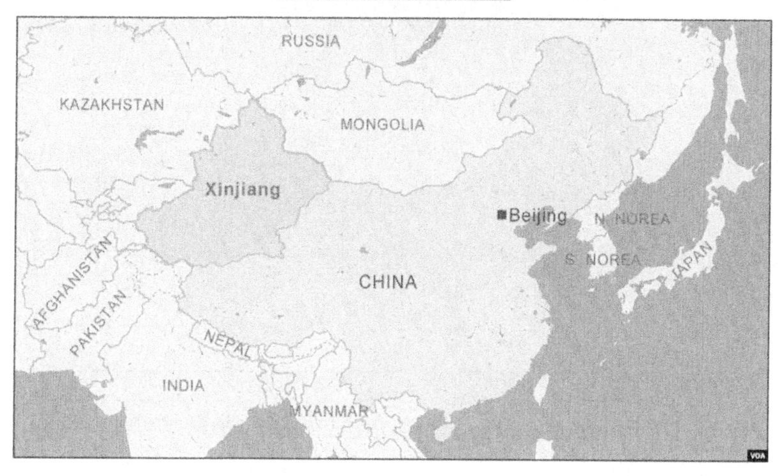

Fig.1. The Xinjiang province of China is located in the extreme NW of the country and extends over 1.6 million km2, that is more than 3 times the size of France.

Xinjian means "New Borders". It was annexed by the Qing (Manchu) dynasty in the 18th century. It is is a very large province of China which has many and extensive natural resources.

Plenty of Resources

Xinjiang is China's largest growing base for production of cotton, lavender and hop. Cotton production accounted for 89.5% of the nation's total in 2021 and 20% of cotton produced in the world. Besides, with the second largest pastureland, Xinjiang is one of the major sheep farming areas and fine-wool production base in China.

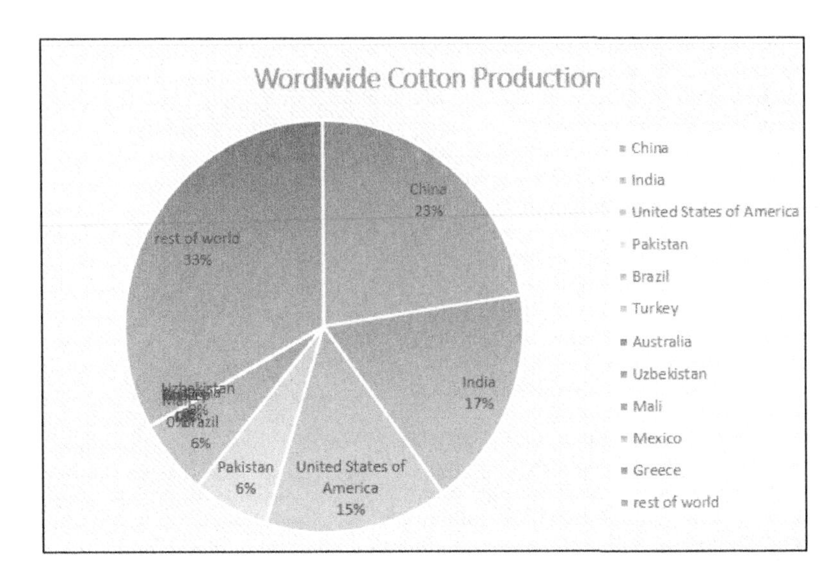

Fig.2. China is the largest producer of cotton (23%). Around 90% of Chinese cotton is produced in Xinjiang, that is 20% of world cotton is produced in Xinjiang.

Xinjiang is rich in energy resources. It has the largest reserves of oil, natural gas and coal in the country. Its coal reserves account for 40% of the country's total. The oil and gas reserves found in Tarim, Junggar and Turpan-Hami basins in the region account for around 30% and 34% of the country's total.

Xinjiang's reserves of mineral resources are great as well. There are more than 150 kinds of mineral deposits, among these is the silicon, a mineral critical for the production of solar panels that after its processing, requiring intensive heat (mostly achieved through coal fired power stations), is transformed into polysilicon, of which Xinjian contributes 45% of worldwide production.

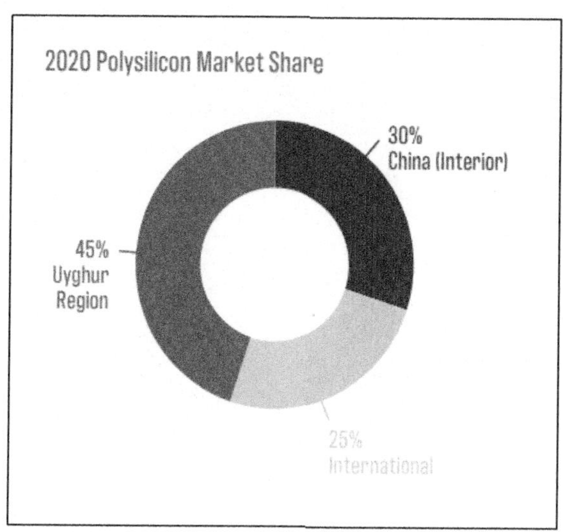

Fig.3 China produces 75% of worldwide polysilicon, out of which 45% is produced in the Xinjiang.

The region's reserves of beryllium and mica are also the highest in China. Some of the region's granite products such as "Xinjiang Red", "Tianshan White" and "Snowflower Black" are famous brands in the country.

Ethnic cleansing of the Uighurs

Technically, the Xinjiang is the autonomous region of the Uighurs, a Turkic Muslim ethnic group originating from and culturally affiliated with the general region of Central and East Asia rather than China. They number around 10 m but originally they were the majority of the inhabitants of the province. Currently, they only represent 50% of the population of the region due to the Chinese government's attempt to replace the Uigurs, which by nature are quite independent, with the Han population, the mainstream race of China (all Chinese leaders are Han). In 2009, Uigur demonstrators rioted in Xingang's capital, Urumqi, against state-incentivized Han Chinese migration to the region. It resulted in the death of nearly 200 people. Islamic extremist organizations, claimed responsibility.

The ethnic cleansing carried out by China includes the construction of prisons (referred to as Vocational Schools by the Chinese leadership) where up to 1 million Uighurs have been detained and a significant number used for slave labour. The camps are reportedly operated outside the Chinese legal system; many Uighurs have been interned without trial and no charges have been levied against them (held in administrative detention). Local authorities are reportedly holding hundreds of thousands of Uighurs in these camps at any given time as well as members of other ethnic minority groups in China, for the stated purpose of countering extremism and terrorism and promoting social integration. Among the atrocities documented by several independent networks, including the BBC, are forced abortions, rape, the marketing overseas of Uighur's ladies' hair.

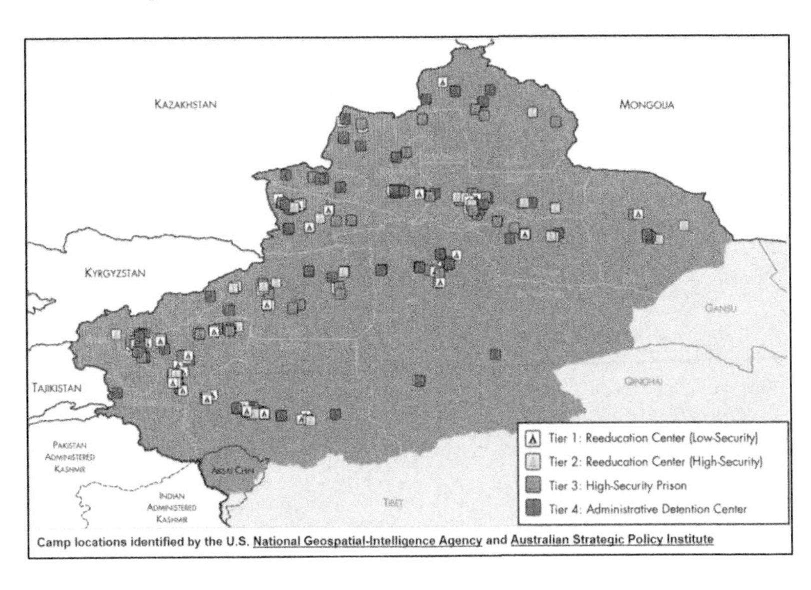

Fig.4 Prison camps where the Uighurs are detained. The camps started being operational in 2017.

Fig.5 One of the Prisons pictured by the investigation done by the BBC

Fig.6 Detainees in a Xinjiang Re-education Camp located in Lop County listening to "de-radicalization" talks.

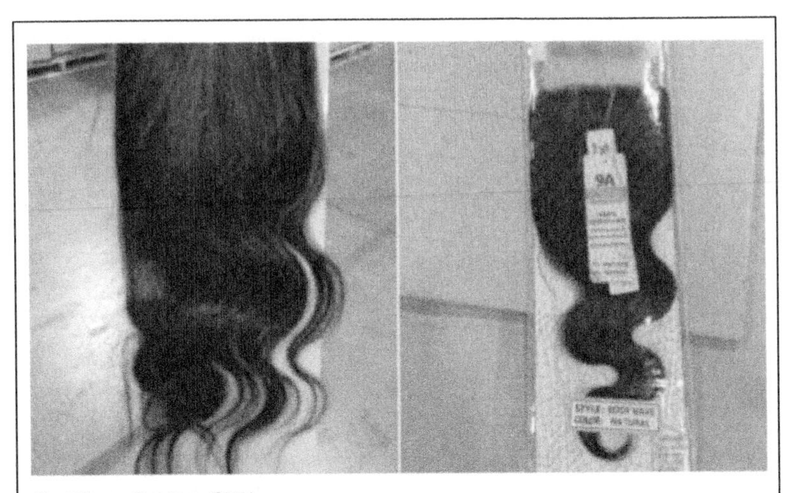

Fig.7 Part of a 13-ton shipment of beauty products such as weaves suspected to have been made out of human hair was seized on in 2020 by US Customs and Border Protection (CBP) officers at the Port of New York/Newark. According to the CPB, the shipment originated in Xinjiang, China, signaling potential human rights abuses of forced labor and imprisonment. The products were worth over $800,000.

Several initiatives have been taken to stem the use of forced labour by China. However, these have limited effect because of the difficulty to trace Chinese export product to specific sources (and particularly the Xinjiang).

For instance in March 2020, the Australian Strategic Policy Institute (ASPI) published a report 'Uighurs for sale': 'Re-education', forced labour and surveillance beyond Xinjiang, which identified 83 foreign and Chinese companies as allegedly directly or indirectly benefiting from the use of Uighur workers outside Xinjiang through potentially abusive labour transfer programs. This is done to try and circumvent the West's attempt to reign in Xinjian forced labour. Indeed, ASPI estimates at least 80,000

Uighurs were transferred out of Xinjiang and assigned to factories in a range of supply chains including electronics, textiles, and automotives under a central government policy known as 'Xinjiang Aid'. The report identified 27 factories in nine Chinese provinces that are using Uyghur labour transferred by force from Xinjiang since 2017.

President Biden also signed in December 2021 the Uighur Forced Labour Prevention Act. It establishes a rebuttable presumption that the importation of any goods, wares, articles, and merchandise mined, produced, or manufactured wholly or in part in the Xinjiang Uighur Autonomous Region of the People's Republic of China, or produced by certain entities, is prohibited by Section 307 of the Tariff Act of 1930 and that such goods, wares, articles, and merchandise are not entitled to entry to the United States. The presumption applies unless the Commissioner of U.S. Customs and Border Protection (CBP) determines that the importer of record has complied with specified conditions and, by clear and convincing evidence, that the goods, wares, articles, or merchandise were not produced using forced labor.

Despite the above, Xinjiang's exports to the United States in September 2022 were still nearly three times as high as the same month the previous year (September 2021, i.e. prior to the implementation of the Uygur Forced Labour Prevention Act , according to the latest Chinese customs data.)

According to Chinese customs data, the top individual product Xinjiang exported to the US in that month was 8 million pairs of synthetic socks worth US$1.56 million, followed by Christmas products valued at US$1.51 million. Machinery and mechanical equipment remained the top category of products from Xinjiang shipped to the US last month, accounting for 28.9 per cent, according to calculations by the Post based on trade data. That was followed by apparel and clothing, accounting for 11.6 per cent and worth US$2.4 million, compared with over US$9 million in August. Both have been flagged by US officials as high-risk sectors subject to the most scrutiny under the Uighur Forced Labor Prevention Act.

Acknowledgement

I would like to recognise the skilful and patient editing done by my dear friend John Luchford, who has not just improved my writing but suggested additions that have greatly benefitted my book.

About the author: Stefano Santoni is an Italian oil geologist who, during his professional career of 40 years, has lived in many different regions of the world, from North Africa, to Latin America, to the US, the UK and the Middle East. In the process he has crossed with pleasure many cultural boundaries, built a multicultural family and learned to speak several languages.

Stefano has previously published a trilogy that describes his professional and family adventures.

'No Safe Harbour' (1st edition published in 2020) is the first book of a trilogy that includes:

'A Picture Imperfect Family' (2021)

'Living the dream' (2021)

All books available through Amazon

NO SAFE HARBOUR (2020)
by Stefano Santoni

The real-life adventures of an Italian geologist across Africa and South America while exploring for oil and building a very unconventional family. When Stefano met and fall in love with a free-spirited young Somali woman in Cairo, he had no idea in the ways it would change his life. Stefano writes vividly and unsparingly about growing up in a small Sicilian town in the 1960's with his sisters and pessimistic, chain-smoking parents who raised him to live period in Italy known as the 'Years of Lead'. He details his struggles as a politicised college student in Florence caught up in the near-civil-war violence between the right and left, surviving bloodied street battles, beatings and prison. Through it all, he longs to see far-off deserts, the wilderness, the world. At 23, on the day the murdered former Prime Minister Aldo Moro's body was found in the boot of a car after 55 days of captivity, Stefano struck out on his first foreign assignment to Libya working with a small Italian mineral prospecting company in the unforgiving heat and terrain of the Sahara Desert. Years later, alone in Cairo with only his black cat Otello for company, he falls in love with Fatima, who lived with her extended family in a crowded apartment in the far reaches of the city. When her strict Muslim relatives find out about their secret relationship, she tells him: "I'm in trouble. They've confiscated my passport and are sending me back to Somalia." Two months passed and she'd vanished. Stefano sets off blindly to look for her in Djibouti, the battered French outpost, and Somalia, one of the most dangerous places on earth, where he finds himself stuck in

a remote backwater in the midst of a cholera outbreak and has to find a way out of the country. Back in Cairo, unexpectedly reunited with Fatima, he converts to Islam to marry her. Together they blaze their way across the Middle East, North and South America, trying to build a happy life while living under sanctions and isolation in Gaddafi's Libya and the socio-economic meltdown in Argentina, as he carves out a career after making some of the world's most fearlessly and coming of age during the significant oil discoveries. In Argentina, they watch from afar as civil war broke out in Somalia, forcing Fatima's family to flee. Stefano sets off to help them, risking prison for smuggling large sums of cash, as well as his own life. On a whim, the couple decide to rescue a baby girl born and raised in a refugee camp, dodging surly officials and bluffing their way across borders. Once they adopted her brother too, they thought their family was complete, but there were always more waifs and strays with unimaginably difficult lives who needed a home. His story, a meditation on kinship, home and freedom, weaves together history, politics and personal narrative into the author's search for meaning and a place to process the losses that came after.

A PICTURE IMPERFECT FAMILY (2021)
by Stefano Santoni

When a series of tragedies struck his household, the almost picture-perfect image that Luciano, a dynamic and entrepreneurial middle-aged geologist, had of his family suddenly evaporates. He finds solace in his workaholic lifestyle, trying to build an exploration portfolio for a small start-up British oil company runs by a set of dysfunctional individuals, as Luciano will discover the hard way. His adventures take him to faraway places where he crosses paths with the most varied humanity and characters: from a charming and mysterious lady in Brazil to an evangelical pastor in the slums of Kinshasa who will connect him to the inner circle of Kabila, the dictator of DRC, to an arm dealer-cum-bon vivant in Tehran linked to the power circle of Ayatollah Khamenei and, in Russia, along the shores of the Caspian sea, an ex-KBG colonel surrounded by his clan that includes some beautiful young ladies. In the process Luciano re-discover his most profound self and that there is always a silver lining.
A novel of grief, adventure therapy, and self-discovery with a vibrant narrative and an ironic view of life.

LIVING THE DREAM (2021)
by Stefano Santoni

The forensic investigation of a business deal gone wrong unravels the intrigues and deceptions at Falcon Oil, a middle eastern oil company in Dubai, and its out-of-worldly set of personnel. In the process, the leading investigator, an old geologist that has experienced more than his due share of personal tragedies, unsparingly reflects on his existence but also on subjects he confronts on his daily life at Falcon Oil, like cultural intelligence, leadership, religious hypocrisy, micromanagement and more, not leaving any stone unturned.
A modern-day parable exploring the contradictions of a society that aspires to be modern and efficient but cannot get loose from a culture based on tribalism and nepotism.
A vibrant and bittersweet story narrated with irony.
The author, a geologist by profession, has lived five years in the UAE.